P9-CBC-604

*Confessions
of Cherubino*

Also by Bertha Harris

CATCHING SARADOVE

Confessions
of Cherubino

Bertha Harris

HARCOURT BRACE JOVANOVICH, INC.
NEW YORK

Copyright © 1972 by Bertha Harris
All rights reserved.
No part of this publication may be reproduced
or transmitted in any form or by any means,
electronic or mechanical, including photocopy, recording,
or any information storage and retrieval system,
without permission in writing from the publisher.
First edition
ISBN 0-15-121855-2
Library of Congress Catalog Card Number: 73-174509
Printed in the United States of America
A B C D E

The excerpts from Euripides' *The Women of Troy* (referred to herein
as *The Trojan Women*) are from the translation by Phillip Vellacott
in the anthology *The Bacchae and Other Plays*, edited by E. V. Rieu,
published in 1953 by Penguin Books.

This book is for Catherine Nicholson

Voi che sapete che cosa e amor,
Donne, vedete s'io l'ho nel cor.
Quello ch'io provo vi ridiro,
E per me nuovo, capir nol so.

Sento un affetto pien di desir,
Ch'ora e diletto, ch'ora e martir.
Gelo, e poi sento l'alma avvampar

E in un momento torno a gelar;
Ricerco un bene fuori di me,
Non so ch'il tiene, non so cos'e,
Sospiro e gemo senza voler,
Palpito e tremo senza saper.
Non trovo pace notte ne di,
Ma pur mi piace languir cosi.

—Cherubino, from Mozart's
Le Nozze di Figaro

Confessions
of Cherubino

I am Ellen, describing the self I have become. I am also Ellen who is describing Margaret. I have her now, as I have myself now, the way we are now; and I am holding us up and together, pushing us through hot sun to my house where my family, my lovers, my son, friends are clustered in their various sounds, sounds that Margaret and I are rejoining, will add to, will modify and make our own: song, piano notes, the glider's metal screech, sucking, the paintbrush's slap, screaming, a gasp for breath, more screaming. I have her now, taking her home the way she is now; but this is the way I was, and she was:

She lay on the beach and felt the sun take her apart, cautiously, slipping first through the snaps of the bathing suit, itself the sun's color; then withdrawing the halter and the pants into its glaring body.

"And now . . ." she whispered through her heat-cracked lips.

And then, pausing just for breath, or to resist a cloud, the sun licked at the tanned pores, sipping on each of them, and leaned on the rough nipples and went to sleep.

She opened her eyes. "Margaret," she said, polishing the

sun's back with the sound of her own name, and holding him hard against her belly. Because it was a young one, only a nine o'clock sun, it was finished quickly and her face ran with sweat. She sat up, pulling the straps back on her shoulders. Her breasts resisted, and she smiled down at them and pulled until they pressed again against the yellow cotton.

Her elbows had gone off the towel and were jabbing, two sensitive bones, into the hard-packed, pebble-studded sand. She was as dizzy as a drunk from too much sun and could not move her elbows away from their pain. Her toes pointed toward the water; her eyes followed their direction.

The bay before her was a sparkling blue blanket of salt. The soul beneath it moved occasionally in its sleep and kicked glimpses of flashing mirrors in her eyes, throwing whole areas of dream from the water to the shore and to Margaret.

The sun rode the water, spurring the waves closer every moment to the shore and to Margaret, for whom the sun would dismount. She moved her fingers and then bent her knees. She was a tired old woman stumbling from heat to water, a tired old woman inside the hot shape of a girl.

She had been there on the beach every day for a long time, two years or three—a long time—and finally knew enough to be bold with water. She shut her eyes and plunged, nearly fainting, from the hot to the cold. When she surfaced, away from a vision of thumb-sized minnows swimming into her face, up from the brown, cloudy stones, she could see that she was alone in the water; all this blue bay of water was hers alone, she was the swimmer for the world, she was the first to swim and bite and gulp the water while the sun stood by overhead to shake occasional light against her fins and scales, while she stroked the water and the water entered her, while she swam for yards or miles on either side without touching human, fleshly legs, without seeing a fur-trimmed intelligent eye gape into her

4

dumb fish one through the towers of seaweed that shot green and yellow into her face and wrapped her shoulders in long-dead female hair.

She dove and came up for breath again and breathed the air again, her face pointing out of the water like a dolphin's snout, her long alive yellow hair like the seaweed rising live again, by mistake, for sun at her every breath. Stroking and breathing, cupping her hands into fins, she drew toward the middle of the bay and toward danger where it was easy to drown in the deepest part of that sleep tossing beneath the surface. But she continued, fear and cold making her swim all the more steadily and tirelessly, the hair on her head plastering her face at each gaping suck for air, her legs churning until at last she was still and face down, watching the bubbles of the last breath escape and then letting herself be moved into the current, floating like bleached driftwood, floating the dead man's float.

She flipped to her back with her last strength. She could not see the shore; or perhaps her eyes had gone fish-blind for sights above the water. What fish can see out of water? She floated; the sun sat on her eyelids, wanting the eyes to open, too, to take her there, too, through the sex of her sight. Her lungs roared for air like old engines that wished only rust and a scrap heap for eternity, not abuse any longer from a female who turned old and young by turns, a female who imagined herself as she lay in the sand something chosen by some god for love; she imagined herself a fish that sneered at poor lungs until, of course, it was hooked and it discovered, as it thrashed in the toe of a rubber boot, some use for air, some use for the motions of in and out.

Her trailing fingers rubbed bottom, and some sand and loose rock dashed into her bathing suit. She lay back in the shallows and let her hair fan out into nothing but another seaweed jungle where those throngs of kindergarten minnows, all black and bunched together (as though this hand-sized pool were all that existed of the ocean), could swim, in and out. But she turned her head, opened her eyes, and snapped her fingers through the water to deceive the fish, who believed in feasts on dead bodies, into believing her alive. She wondered how the thousands of tiny mouths would feel as they pulled and nursed the skin away from her throat and fingertips; and she let the idea sink like a net over the hungry fish, and she hobbled out of the water, hunting for bed and medicine.

Her towel and sunglasses were closer to the water, or the water closer to them. She shook the mud from her pants and composed herself behind the contraption of white-rimmed, high-arched sunglasses to become the masked stranger queen left behind in the hot, fizzled-out ballroom, emptied of nighttime and her court.

For a while, she sat still and listened to the soft snores of the relaxed water. There was no one at all coming, she thought, to wonder about her.

Then, the shrill voices of children, soaking, like her own skin, in the salted, heated air, cried: "A swan! A swan! A swan!"

Six feet, the sixth jerking and wobbling against the spinning progressions of the other five, kicked sand against her body, missed her face only because her chin came up to take the blow. She felt as a blow a few grains of sand against her pointed chin; she felt them as a blow.

What swan? *Ellen,* she thought, *what swan?* Ellen had come rushing—not rushing—stumbling, she explained, the way her heart stumbled, her guts stumbled, as she looked, from the first class to the last dark bite of dinner, all day long for a glimpse of the one who loved her; Ellen had come stumbling into Margaret's gray dormitory room and had said, I have to tell you this! I have to tell you all about how much I am loved!

"Get out of the way!" Margaret screamed at the children. They moved aside, absorbing their first order of the day, the two little girls shuffling in the sand and pulling prissily at the tops of their bathing suits to cover their faint rose dots. They moved aside so that Margaret could see; and the crippled girl's left hip jutted out farther and farther, as though she meant to throw the whole beach off balance and send the four of them falling off the edge of the world. The youngest child, a boy, moved slowest, insolent in his tight trunks, and as he moved bobbed his shaved head at Margaret and stuck out his tongue. The crippled girl threw her arms around him and pulled his face against the weird bone of her hip, punishing him; but Margaret could see the swan coming. It came through the water so close to shore, so negligently streaming, that she could have moved to it easily if she had not feared its size, and its beak, and the heaviness of its green wings; she could have tried to lift the swan and let its neck coil around her own. Green wings. She pulled off her sunglasses; and the swan, in a complete turn of dazzling white throat, looked at her, gave her one sudden white look through the little corridor of children and sand before it turned again and stared only at the water it swam. How did it get there? A swan was swimming through salt water, practically on top of a bathing beach put together by the WPA, a place where policemen took their families, where carloads of Italians set up tables and chairs and stoves and blankets and umbrellas and playpens and radios and portable televisions as far from the water, as close to their cars, as possible; and where their adolescents broke away from them and ate their meals at the hamburger stand behind the lifeguards and sat as far as possible from their shouting, fat relations. How did the swan get there? But how did Margaret, such a girl, such a sleek, easy swimmer who sought out danger points in water, how did she get there? Margaret and the swan, away from everything that wanted to love them and call them their dear sleek-and-white own, back in the places of the world where the water was fresh and drinkable: what were they doing in this salt water?

"Who loves you?" Margaret had asked, and looked up from her book in its lamplight; and, on second thought, had closed her book. She looked through the dark of her room at Ellen, and Ellen (although she was not one for dramatic gestures, although she loved the drama) stood hanging on the doorknob, one long slim hand hanging on the doorknob, one long slim hand hanging on to the green cotton above the place she thought her heart might be. Her hands: Ellen called them *my vanities of vanities*. More than anything, Margaret wanted to know the name of the one who loved Ellen; but even then, in that anxiety to know, she could not help marveling at how they looked, the two of them, the two beauties of them: Ellen in the dark by the door, Margaret in the half-shadow of the lighted desk: Ellen with her white skin and black hair that went down and down her back, and even farther down when she bent to stroke it with her two gleaming vanities of vanities; and Margaret with skin like gold apple peel even in the dead of winter, and golden hair that fell down as far as Ellen's, especially when she stroked it, thinking of all the people who longed to rub the gold if only they could. The perfect friends, perfect together and apart; no beauty and beast about it, said the other schoolgirls. God help them, said the other, bitter schoolgirls, when some morning they wake up and find themselves feeling want, desire for someone not there, incomplete lust . . . "I hope it will be for each other," said their friends. "They deserve to stink like the rest of the world."

"Who loves you? Ellen, come here and tell me." Margaret was waiting for her to begin that long glide, that pale, un-ruffled sweep across the floor. But she was sorry when Ellen came. "What's happened to you?" she said.

Ellen was beside her, reaching out her shaking hand; and Margaret was drawing back: there was a sickness covering Ellen, and she could catch it. Had Ellen said *love?*

She reached behind her for the towel that was as white

and as long as a bed sheet; but was thin as gauze in places, and ragged. She crouched cross-legged with the towel spread from her head to her waist, with her face hidden in its drape; and the air she breathed immediately became private and heavy, ponderous with heat and the smell of towel. I am a worn-out Arab sheik, she whispered, abandoned by my warriors, my harem, my dancing girls, my pretty boys; no more meals of sheep's eyes and grapes for me; nothing but the desert sand and mirages of water for me from now on. . . . I am the Virgin Mary, abandoned by my silly son who loves his father more than his mother. I don't remember any more *about that!*

The children were playing a zigzagging game, running from the sand to the water and back again, and screaming when the tadpoles brushed their feet. The cripple was always late in the race: in the water when the others were out, wet when the others were in the sand, frightening Margaret with her leaning, crumpled hip that was going to tilt them all off the face of the beach and the world.

"Fool, mule, school . . ." she chanted. Memory was happening to her. "School," she said. "Mule," she said. The swan had gone. She heard the brass bowl clank once against her floor and the whispering roll of the apples as they disappeared into the dark corners of her room. Ellen had reached out to touch her and she had drawn back, fearing infection, and had knocked the bowl over . . . the voice was coming louder, hard as hoof against rock.

"Listen to me," Ellen was saying. "This morning I got up, still the same as you. I was singing, you know . . . *Odi et amo* . . . senselessly, the way babies sing 'Here We Go Round the Mulberry Bush,' but with a bright idea: I was going to ask the Sanctissima about setting the poems to music. . . . Catullus is nothing but singing anyway, or so I thought when I got up this morning. I threw on my clothes, happy with my bright idea, and because it was spring, school nearly over forever . . ."

9

"It's still spring this evening," Margaret was answering.

"It was spring this morning. I got to breakfast, and out, before you. . . . When I saw you after the first class, what was I wearing?"

"What you're wearing now? I don't remember. Why would you change?"

"No. No, not what I'm wearing now. I had to change. You'll see."

"Why?"

"You'll see." The mule was stumbling, panicked, excited with the smell of something, food or water, the end of its climbing work. One hoof was thudding hard on her brain, the other three slipping, scraping. "I was thinking," Ellen was saying, faster and faster, "that after lunch we would both be free and we would go in the woods and slosh in the mud and watch the earthworms ooze up and bring home Japanese irises and their smell would drive us wild while we studied tonight, because we did that last year, remember. . . . The flowers would go up in our heads through our noses and mouths, smells you could taste on your tongue, the taste of blue, of periwinkle, the taste of pollen yellow, of white, the furry taste of green . . . until we knew we would never get the translation right until we got rid of those flowers, those tastes. And we did. Both of us pushed the screen out and threw the flowers outside. I thought we would do the same this year; but being a whole year older, I thought we could have the flowers along with the work . . . pleasure and labor together, in one gulp. But we'll never know about that now. . . ."

"Why not? There's tomorrow . . . there was today, but I couldn't find you all afternoon. I had the same idea. You're so odd tonight . . . never in my life . . . look at yourself."

Ellen was stumbling, Margaret gliding to the mirror. They were watching Ellen's hands move in the glass through her hair, down her face, the fingers touching the eyes and mouth: the mouth seemed swollen, as though it had wept for a long time; and the beautiful hands were going farther down their body, exploring, grasping at flesh through cloth, squeezing breasts, clenching waist, until the fingers were at last finding nothing but each other. Ellen twined all ten together and held them up, hiding her face from the mirror and from Margaret. Ellen's straight shoulders were slumping, her loose hair was slipping forward to hide her face, as though it were a sheik's striped burnoose or the blue mantle of the Virgin. Her voice went on.

"At ten o'clock I was knocking on the Sanctissima's studio door, hearing my sopranos repeating over and over *Odi et amo* while the contralto sang the rest of the words louder and louder until the listeners could be sure of what the song meant. Then, I didn't know what it meant. Sanctissima opened the door, not wearing one of those three teaching dresses she owns. She had on an old blue shirt and black pants. She told me later she'd worn her 'true colors'—as she called it—to give herself courage. But her courage was all liquid and all inside. You'll see what I mean. God knows, even the piano keys stank of bourbon; and she could hardly focus her eyes. Ice-blue eyes jabbing out of that crazy Indian chief face: then she went for me. At first, it was like being smothered in those stories that Pathways loves to tell—about monocles and pin stripes and discreet neckties and afternoon tea-and-dancing in Paris at Natalie Clifford Barney's house with Gertrude Stein and Colette and Djuna Barnes. . . ."

"What the hell are you talking about?"

"You never paid attention to Mr. Pathways' stories."

Margaret was beginning to scout the room, bending and brushing her hands over the dark floor; when she returned to the mirror, she had retrieved two dusty apples and her nails were scoring their skins, pressing the sticky juice into her palms. Ellen took one and ate it in four starving bites; but still talked, with juice and pulp hanging from her lips.

"When I opened my eyes, my head was buried in dust and

11

music books. My dress was strangling me around the neck; and she had made me shout her name."

Margaret suddenly squeezed the apple hard; three of her fingers met its seeded core. The seeds slipped against her skin.

"It had taken no time. I've never been so happy in my life, but she wouldn't be quiet so I could tell her that—she was too busy buttoning her shirt up wrong, pulling at her hair, and lecturing on and on about ruined innocence and how the signs in the museums—hands off the sculpture, don't touch the oil paintings—were good and right and that by God, they should hang them on people like me, she said, on good and beautiful people like me to keep people like her from breaking and smudging the happy line. The happy line, she called it. Then I got scared, because suddenly she stopped all that high-speed talk and began banging her head against the wall. I thought that even with those soundproof rooms, the next-door clarinet would be walking in any minute, and I was scared to death."

"Why didn't you leave?" Margaret asked, and walked away, back to the light of her desk; and she did not watch her hand when it picked up a sharp yellow pencil and began gouging shit, shit, shit in heavy letters across the blank page of her notebook. She kept her eyes and mind on Ellen.

"Leave? Are you crazy? I've never been so happy in my life. I kept her quiet. I slipped under her arm, between her body and the wall. And between one bang of her head and the next, I kissed her. It was much quieter the second time—for such a wild old savage, she makes such serious love."

Love, Margaret printed on the page. Music, she wrote. "You look like an old savage yourself. You look old and different, and ugly."

Ellen stretched in front of the mirror. Her expression was like a gelded cat's, who had nothing to dream of but the huge satisfactions of food and sleep. "But I don't feel that way at all," she smiled.

Shit, Margaret wrote carefully, Spencerian style.

Through the halls the sounds of bedtime were coming. Doors were slamming, water was running in the tubs and showers. Bedroom slippers clopped up and down on the floors. Girls coming back from the library were shuffling up the last flight of stairs.

Margaret moved, feeling every muscle and bone slide with the suppleness of always. If it were Ellen moving, her flesh would sound out with aches and creaking joints. Margaret pushed her window up and leaned out. Above, resting its tail of cloud on the chimney of the dormitory across the street, a silver moon hung, transparent as the spring air. The trees in the little wood close by rustled infant leaves. Lights were going out. A car turned a corner, making the soft sounds of going home. Down in the woods, the Japanese irises they hadn't picked were still growing through the dark. The mud was drying. The new grass was blanketing the air with scents that bore the imprint of neither Margaret nor Ellen.

This is still all mine, thought Margaret. I can walk through the woods tomorrow and still see nothing but a tree that is a tree. If Ellen came, she would see a face described in the branches of the tree; a clump of flowers would become someone's hands. When she hears that music again, she will hear nothing but the ways of a drunken old woman in it. She looked back into the room: Ellen was lurching to the door, dragging her hand like a hurt wing against the wall behind her.

"You didn't tell me. Is she the one who loves you?"

Ellen, back in the dark, leaned against the wall as though someone had hung her by a nail.

"Yes," she answered. "She's half of it. But you've only heard the half of it." Her voice was beginning to squeak and pipe, as though it were being throttled; as though it belonged to an aging midget. Margaret remembered it: they were little girls walking down the hometown street through twilight on a Christmas eve warm as fur; but they wore their new rabbit fur mittens anyway and let their hands sweat. They were in the wrong part of town, pretending to be prostitutes like the dictionary said. The bus station glittered and clanked beside them, and a soldier was pressing his buddy against its glass door, saying, "C'mon, c'mon, you know I got to!" The midgets, exactly as tall as ten-year-old girls, got deliberately in front of them. Their faces were paunched, creased blurs in the bus-station electric light, but Margaret could see perfectly how neatly, properly, their heavy double-breasted suits held to their shortness, as though it were the suits that kept the little men from good growth. And they wore silky pale-red neckties that hung down like tongues. The midgets squeaked, "God bless you, little bitches!" and "Merry Christmas, little bitches!" then walked past. Their thick buttocks bobbed up and down in identical motion beneath their identical jackets as they paced away into the darkening sidewalk. The girls saw then that the midgets were dragging a Christmas tree, triple their height, between them on the pavement.

Ellen cleared her throat. "That's enough for tonight. Go to bed. If you care, I'll say the rest tomorrow."

The sharp smell of spruce pine shunted through the room and into Margaret's nose; she could hear boughs drag against the gritty cement. There was an edge of Ellen still left in the door; then she was gone. Panic shot up in Margaret like weeds, choking a lifetime of sane cheer. Cheer went rolling down the hall at Ellen's heels: and now that it was outside, and now that she could see it instead of feel it, what was it but a used-up infant's ball, a silly thing painted with teddy bears and mother's kisses and hearts and posies that looked huge only in a baby's mitts? It could fit neatly under Ellen's high-arched instep, and she could still go walking where she was going. Margaret's lips hung loose in a stupid, unlovely way. Her eyes felt hot and red.

Margaret shut her door and leaned against it. Ellen had

gone in the dark where love was. So that was where love was. At the top of the cragged mountains, hung with mist and spider webs and thick forests, a traveler was riding through the dark looking for a bed and a roof. At last, sick with weariness and dread of the hideous shapes he imagined he saw behind each tree, he came to a castle, ugly in all its aspects. He was welcomed in and given fire and food and a bed. Late in the night, as the traveler slept, his host, a white-faced count with long sharp teeth and burning eyes, appeared in the traveler's sleep disguised first as smoke, then in the wings of a bat. The vampire bent, bared his teeth, searched out the particular vein filled with the richest blood. The traveler's scream was stifled, and he fainted into his pillow. The vampire stretched out his length against the victim and sucked until he was filled. A fly on the wall, knowing nothing of the facts, saw nothing but an ordinary act of love. In the morning, the traveler was as much a vampire as if he had been born to it.

Margaret could see, even then, the long teeth at Ellen's throat. She tore off her clothes, ripping the pink skirt, scuffing the black leather. The silver cross was tangled at the bottom of an empty powder box. She slung it around her neck and felt the cold knock of silver on her chest, felt the pink dust and perfume scatter on her breasts. Even better, she would weave a garlic wreath to put on Ellen's head. No vampire could crash through two charms of good. She looked for signs in the sky. Shreds of cloud were running a race through light nearly as strong as morning's. The black spot enlarging among them was beginning to flap its wings as it came in a slow, circling descent to the room at the other end of the hall. She hurried; she wrapped herself in a white blanket. At any moment, the shape would be larger and blacker than dark, blacker than the blind that covered Ellen's window. With a clapping of wings, it would bend over the sleeping body of her friend. She sped down the hall, the blanket trailing in her wind like a cape. A bat out of hell; he will screech at the sight of me like a bat out of hell. Her thoughts chattered through her teeth. He will leak back to hell through the dark's cracks because of me, because I am purer than driven snow, what is snow? Something else I've never seen; I know it's cold and shines on hard ground like the silver on my freezing chest. I'll make the warm monster's bones rattle, because I am cold and shining and hard like frozen ground. I'm there.

The doorknob fits her hand like a kneecap; she finds the room just as she knew it would be. Ellen sprawls on the bed like a doll abandoned by three grown children. The painted eyes are thumb-rubbed from brown to coffee stain; its mouth, which was new and red and round, is nearly a white blister. The stuffing is falling out of her head. Her dress is a rumpled rag; too much dressing and undressing on rainy days. Yet she sleeps like a child, flat on her stomach, her palms flat on the pillow on either side of her head. The window is closed, the blinds pulled shut, but Margaret says, "It's better with the window open and the blind all the way up. I don't want it sneaking through like smoke or gas. It's better when it comes direct and enormous through a wide-open space so I can know it immediately."

"What in hell are you doing here?" Ellen wakes suddenly from the glare of the moon and finds Margaret crouched in white wool at the end of her bed. Her voice is cracked from hard sleeping and bent by some dream.

"Be quiet, Ellen," Margaret whispers. "Let it think you're asleep and then it will come sooner and then I'll get rid of it sooner and then we won't have to sit and be scared all night long."

Ellen turns over, but her hair is across her face, and Margaret can't see what she really looks like, only that she looks dark.

"It's the vampires and Count Dracula again, isn't it? Go back to bed—promised you last year it wasn't true—just a story—some slobbering village idiot—all dreamed up to scare the poor bastards out of their socks winter nights—back to bed—cut it out."

The overload of sweetness from the blooming horse chestnut beneath the window is coming inside the room now, creeping inside Margaret's blanket and making sticky handprints of smell up and down her body. It is making sweaty paste of the powder that the cross has drifted over her chest. Something overturns, rolls, falls, breaks in the room next to them.

Ellen's voice has dribbled back toward sleep, but Margaret's eyes are even wider than before. The tree's scent is blinding her to the black thing thickening and widening in the sky outside. It is like the patch on a blind eye in a graying wrinkling face, a face leaning closer to Margaret's every minute.

"You used to believe," she says. "You used to take the precautions. Remember the Tolstoi story about the whole family that was infected one by one until they all were vampires, even the little child." She might as well be talking to the dead. To the dozing Ellen, the voice is as silent as a snowfall; the fear in the voice sounds like long, peaceful sleep to her.

"Tolstoi just a fool for village idiots," Ellen mutters.

Margaret lifts a cold, limp foot and shakes it, but the foot fights back. "Where's the garlic, at least? Where is it? You were the keeper of the garlic."

"Threw it out." The good dream is coming back to Ellen, her body is giving up to heat, to hot water. Her whole life rushes past her eyes: she is drowning. On the water's surface, above her, there is an inverted reflection of the old dry world—a big clapboard house slippery with waves, trees with leaves like sand dollars, faces glimmering with fins. But, deeper, the softer water near the bottom is canceling the last sight of land. A fresh face is lifting its lips, inhaling her

17

like air. Shake, shake. The hand is like a hook. She shoots up. The friend at the foot of my bed is built like the House of the Lord. The Virgin, in stale blue, peeks out of her. In the doorway, God stands, his mouth agape: on his tongue, the sizzling orange-purple of a coal fire makes hell. Ellen's warmed there; Ellen's broiled there like pig's crackling skin, pitchforked, spooned over, basted in her own sweat. The face at the bottom of the water is almost upon her. She won't wake up.

Margaret can't wake her up; she leans back on the cold iron foot on the bed and points the perfumed cross at Ellen. How would it be if he came, not bat, not fog, but human-shaped, up the stairs a heavy footstep at a time, boots rapping on the treads, the silver coins of every realm jingling in his pockets—and all the while almost yawning, his mind half on new curtains for the castle's bedrooms or planting boxwood at the front gate or that silly redhead piece he'd had last night—coming casually to the first real meal of the evening in Ellen's throat? With Margaret here watching them—obscene, embarrassing. Different if Ellen were scream-ing, her eyes popping, struggling terrified in his arms; and Margaret jumping around them, waving her cross, shouting, *Begone, Begone, In the Name of the Father, Son and Holy Ghost, Begone*. She can see it: He's opening the door, shrug-ging his bat-cape off, shrugging his shoulders at the sight of Margaret: Well, she's here, so she might as well stay. And stretching his arms, flexing his lips, bending down to Ellen. And Ellen, throwing off her cover, unbuttoning her dress, thinking, glancing at Margaret: Well, she's here, so she might as well stay. And then they get on with it. It is so lonely to be awake at night.

Margaret is so lonely she sees evil everywhere. It waggles its shiny hips at her, bats its eyes at her, shimmys a belly dance, contracting and loosening a hundred suggestions. All around her, the crowd roars to touch it, snatching for one gauzy veil to remember it by. Tear them off: let the mold of you reshape my liquefaction. The barker's cane whistles across the air, pointing the way inside: One small diyum! The tenth pawt of a dollah! All the great big world to see and hold! *Well, me too!* Margaret lets her blanket go: *Touch me, arouse me, change me! I want to be with the sleepwalkers, going inside, opening my arms when dark shapes come off the moon.*

Nothing happens to change the moonlight. The smell of the horse chestnut melts through it, fat in the fire, strengthening the brightness, glossing the sheen. Margaret turns colder in the stream.

Somehow the night passed. At one time, just before dawn, Margaret's mind marched up and down, in and out of a single thought of death. Her guts fought back, clubbed her into stumbling for Ellen's cupboard of food. She became a dog drooling over the plate, a cat formed of bones and dirty fur squalling until the first bite was on its tongue, an animal fighting off the dark by chewing and swallowing. She sat naked on the floor, ripping the top from a biscuit tin, distantly sensing her nails tear. She stuffed two, three at a time in her mouth, barely chewed, forced the hard chunks down her throat not fast enough.

She wanted to throw the food on the floor, bury her face in it, absorb the sweet cake and bitter dirt as water, mud. At the end, she held in each hand a chunk of old Christmas fruitcake and longed to collapse on the floor, curl, groan, fall sleeping like an old dog.

When it was over, she was strung with crumbs and her own saliva; her legs and buttocks were smeared with dust. A red sky pressed into the room and shook the place with birdsong. Ellen's lover had not come, and his last chance had gone with the first light. Margaret stood watching her for a moment, folding the blanket against her shoulders again, listening to the harsh deep breathing, as though she were waiting for it to stop. Slowly, exhaustion numbing every motion, Margaret leaned and kissed Ellen at the bend of her neck, then on the mouth. The cake crumbs came between their lips and stuck with Ellen, fluttering with all the breaths she took.

I t's noon. You're still in bed, and it's soaked. Can't you even pull a window down?"

"I'm so sick."

"You should be. The floor of my room looks like the bottom of the monkey cage. Don't cry."

Margaret shook her tears in all directions. The rain slung bucketfuls through her window and spread a wind that sounded like the return of winter. It had outlined her legs beneath the drenched sheet; they looked like wet plaster.

"Wait, *Ellen!*"

"I'm only going to pull the window down."

"What I want is the rest of the story."

"What story? I think you'll get pneumonia and heave for weeks in an oxygen tent. Miss Nina did that last year and when she got well she said that all the while she was under the tent she'd been having intercourse with the Devil."

"Last night you said that was only the half of it. And I don't want stories about your crazy grandmother." Margaret pulled her legs into the dry upper half of the bed. She turned her face into the wet pillow.

"I can't hear you. What? Sit up."

Margaret bent her tongue against the wet muslin, straining to turn the cry into a frivolous laugh. She tightened one foot against the other. "It's . . . morbid curiosity . . . you know, but I'll die if I don't know what it was she played—on the piano, after . . ."

Ellen laughed at the fresh face in the mirror. "You'll die? Maybe die the sweet death!" She drew one long stroke after another down her hair with Margaret's brush. The swish of bristle through hair made Margaret peek. She could see the palm of Ellen's hand flatten from pink to white through the transparent brush handle every time she raised her arm. Beneath the plastic handle the hand flesh seemed like some monstrosity squeezed inside a paperweight, a calamitous lifeline preserved for the ages. The sound of the brushing was growing ferocious. Margaret curled tighter under the sheets and drove her pointed nails into her thighs. She spoke as fiercely as the electricity that bounded from Ellen's head. "Tell me," she said. "I asked you, *what was it!*"

The night before Ellen's voice had been resonant with fact. Now she looked in the mirror and giggled: *"Für Elise."*

Margaret's legs shot out of the warm ball they had made. She rammed them back into the cold wet. She let the knot of nausea loose and felt it soak her throat as if it were some new rain with a bitter, greenish taste to it. She knew all about *"Für Elise."* It was the first thing Ellen's mother played on her piano every day of her life; her warm-up piece before she crashed into the overture to *Marriage of Figaro,* then into the whole opera from start to finish, even the recitatives, speaking most of the foreign words, but often bursting into croaking song. Ellen's mother was like a gift from the gods at the piano, but when she sang she sounded like a limb rubbing paint off a house through a windstorm: screech and scratch. The opera would roll off the white and black keys, hurrying, on and on, as if there were no time to lose, with the bunches of notes inside the broken-spined

book becoming—as the opera went by year after year—
shinier and yellower beneath the Scotch tape.

Year after year, Ellen's mother hurried the music, but she
never skipped a note. And the little girls, in the back bedroom with the dolls or out in the sun teasing the dog
into a sunbonnet, learned to know in their bones when the
hurrying would stop and the vibrating pause would come
over the house; then the voice, shamelessly loud, would begin *"Voi che sapete."* And then all the other words of
Cherubino's silly song of passion would follow, the words
striking at the tune like the pinched lead shot from rifles
to make food of doves. The tempo, during the song, would
slow, become slower, the awful voice doing its seductive best
—an ugly old thing courting a kiss from the prettiest girl
in town.

And it was during the pause before the song, while Ellen's
mother was catching her breath, closing her eyes, preparing,
that members of her household would come alive: America,
her black cook, would slam kitchen doors shut, leaving a
chime of crystal behind; and sometimes her voice would
follow the noise, slinging out, beautifully, accurately, the
first line of "What a Friend We Have in Jesus." And sometimes, in that moment, Hortense, the family bull terrier,
might find escape from the doll clothes and shunt off
through the shrubbery like a black rat; or maybe the real
gold Crayola in Ellen's hand might snap, or Margaret's heel
might come down hard on the body of a celluloid baby.
And May-Ellen would hear, sometimes, her mother, Miss
Nina, howl from an upstairs corner mysterious prayers: *Oh,
sweet Jesus, let her have it sure and hard and as much as
she wants and give us peace in this life, Amen!* And America's little daughter, Venusberg, might, for that instant,
stop her game of jacks on the sidewalk, close her eyes, and
squeeze her red rubber ball hard. And, just before her
mouth opened wide, May-Ellen might feel her husband,
Roger, pausing somewhere in the town and then lowering

23

his mailbag to a porch and then thinking twice before he made his next Special Delivery. If they were at home, May-Ellen's brother, Welch, and his lover, Darwin Waters, would stop their conversation or lay down their books and stare questioningly into each other's eyes just as the music began.

Even in the quick, hard winter of January and February, when Margaret would spend much of her time in bed, down with ailments Ellen never caught, the music broke through the two layers of glass and clapboard and brick; and Margaret never missed a thing by staying home in bed next door.

The spring when they were sixteen, Ellen's mother had chased them out of the back bedroom and had started carrying in crackling brown bags of pink, blue, white, yellow satin; and for a week the sewing machine back there had hummed and stopped and bounced behind the closed door. And on the last day of sewing, Ellen's mother had run up the stairs barefoot, snapping huge pinking shears in her hand, catching her breath and saying, "Ohhhh! Ohhhh!" while Ellen and Margaret watched her every move and couldn't concentrate on another single thing. When May-Ellen ran back down the stairs, the scissors were clasped between her teeth and her hands were full of real French lace, two inches wide and champagne-colored; and, from above, Miss Nina was shouting, "Oh daughter! May-Ellen! Curse you—that was my trousseau."

Then, after that, every afternoon, for so many afternoons, Ellen would, then Margaret would, then May-Ellen would (saying, "Oh, I can wear anything my sixteen-year-old can wear!") get inside the Cherubino costume and the other two would become the Countess and Susanna and all the other roles; and, while the music spun and scratched off the thick old 78's, they would play the sly scenes over and over while America, back in the closed-off kitchen, broke things and Miss Nina crouched at the top of the stairs and said ugly words.

When Roger got home at five o'clock, he would find his wife and daughter and the girl friend lined up on the piano bench, all in their ordinary clothes, while May-Ellen taught them to play *"Für Elise"*: and they would seem to be nothing more than themselves. Roger would look, then wink and unbutton his sticky shirt and call out the door, "Hortense! Hooooor-*tense!* Come on let your sugar relax you!" And while he laughed at his same old joke, the little black dog would squirm at his feet and May-Ellen would go and kiss him; her bare feet would straddle the quivering Hortense.

Now, Ellen's black hair leaped electrically up to the brush, and she smiled at herself in the mirror; then, powdered to wig-white, it had been tight inside a ribbon and the smile beaming above the crush of trousseau lace had pantomimed passion, on her mother's orders, for Countess Margaret. Ellen in the bass, Margaret in the treble, with two slow fingers had played the opening notes of *"Für Elise"* waiting for Roger to come home.

Deep down in the dormitory, doors slammed and umbrellas shoved up into the rain that still fell so thick it might have been absorbing all the air that was left to breathe in the world. Margaret's own body, drenched with sweat, might have hung in it all night long and been brought in to warm but not to dry.

"I want to hear the rest of the story. Now, Ellen." She was croaking, as though she had inherited May-Ellen's voice; but there wasn't a drop of blood between them, and May-Ellen's real daughter could sing like a lark. Ellen was sitting beside her on the bed. Her eyes weren't looking at anything, but her fingers were combing clumsily through Margaret's hair that had turned greenish brass-colored in the damp air, the color of her apple bowl; and she picked crumbs of cake and red-and-green candied fruit from the ends of the matted strands until she made the beginnings of a little feast in the palm of her hand.

"I said go on and tell me!"

25

Ellen started talking; and piece by piece, while she talked, she nibbled away the bits of fruitcake from Margaret's hair until they were all gone.

She said, "I said I wanted to go home now; as nicely as I could, I said I wanted to go home, but she wouldn't stand for that and followed me outside patting my hand and whispering in my ear until I had to run from her. I ran inside the giant cherry willow that's planted on the corner; a big room inside the branches, a dark green circle of room inside the branches, well, and I ran around and around inside the tree and she ran around and around outside the tree, and she would poke an arm through to snatch me and drag aside the branches, but I was too quick and they were too heavy. Three times around I went, and I couldn't see a thing but that thick round mash of green broth inside and outside my eyes until then there was another thing I saw: there was a kid inside there with me hunched down by the trunk. He was little and wearing a red shirt, but his feet were bare and his shorts were down and he was peeing into a circle of stones he'd made on the ground. I let her run on. I went straight to the boy and touched him on his head; I could hardly breathe I was so tired. But he hit out at me. He cried, 'Go on, old woman, I'm waiting for my mama!' So I went on and held my hands outside the leaves and caught her when she came around again and pulled her in with me. She fell on me, but I stopped her. I was so scared he was going to hurt his feet on the broken glass and the beer cans inside the tree. It's a ruin inside that old tree; that's where they've gone and made love for years and years after the leaves are thick. I said, Stop it—look at him there. But she said, 'Oh, that's just the baby who's been raised on Bartók; I play trios once a week with his mother and father and he's destined for the flute.' And the boy paid us no attention either; just pulled his pants together again and then undid his circle of stones and made a triangle of them. '*Wo bist du?'* called a voice through the leaves; and the little boy threw his head back, burst into tears, howled into my face, 'Mama: *Hier bin Ich!'* German words crying out in that cracker voice! He ran out to his mama. Sanctissima grinned and held her hands out again and rubbed her feet over the boy's wet stones. I stopped her. I said, *Wo bist du?* And when she didn't say the answer, I ran away."

Ellen took her fingers out of Margaret's hair and looked into the space of the room. "Listen," she whispered. "Listen, Margaret. Lust is cold; you wouldn't expect it to be, but it is, like the blade of a sharp knife, cold even after it's sliced through hot meat, and just as sharp. The finest blade on anything is on lust." With her fingernail, she speared the final piece of green candy on her palm and then put it between her teeth. Margaret shut her eyes.

Ellen whispered, hoarsely, as though she were talking half in her sleep, "This room. It's like the bottom of a polluted pond today, stagnant; with bunches of scum and dead leaves floating on top. No one ever comes here to fish or swim. How do you like being a sea monster down here with me?"

Margaret untightened the blanket beneath her chin and ran her tongue along its satin edge. "Move," she said. "I want to get up now."

"Stop a minute. That's still only half the story."

"How can there be more?" Her voice could drag itself up so high that it could float free and clear of the water. What dirty pond? This was her room; nothing more. Ellen's arm held her down.

"Pretend you still love me so you'll listen."

"Take your arm away."

"All right. It's gone. Listen. I ran on down the street. I slapped my sandals down hard so that my feet would ring clear up to my knees, so that I'd be sure I was really running away. I passed the German mother and kid pulling a grocery cart together. They were singing loud, together,

'Smoke Gets in Your Eyes'—that's true; I didn't dream that! My skin felt like a million hands were rubbing over it. I felt blank; I felt hectic . . ."

"Christ, you make me sick." The blanket satin was between Margaret's teeth; the wet from her mouth was spreading around it.

"All right. I felt pure, washed out clean down to the bone. What I was hunting for was the rub of dirt around again; a wallowing among the public until all the average sensations climbed over me again. I wanted strangers to touch me."

"Touch . . . feel . . . hectic . . . pure!" Margaret spat the blanket out. "You sound like some damned pervert! I don't know you anymore. Get out of my bed, get away from me!" She was screaming to get the words out, as though she were giving birth to her first words. Her voice shot up and up, the one live fish in the pond, surfacing, hunting for the hook, if it really was a pond they were in. Her hand, cold with damp, spun as high up as her voice and rang like a heavy splash against Ellen's cheek.

The floor might just as well be hot wax, thought Ellen, because as I'm going away I'm leaving my going-away footprints imbedded there forever, pointed away from her forever, from Margaret in the Cherubino satin, from Margaret in the Countess's pink net, from Margaret in the low-down cut of Susanna's little apron. She could not remember a single note of any of that music.

She turned the doorknob. She said, "Thank you, anyway, for sitting up all the night to protect me. Maybe you're right, that there is a vampire to be afraid of. But you were just too late; it came before you knew it. That's what's wrong now." Anger grabbed her by the shoulders and shook her hard; Margaret looked drenched in redness. She chattered out the rest of the story in a furious whine.

"You want to be the beauty and me the beast? Then just listen: the rest of the story. Being the tale of how Ellen, our wandering adventuress, pleasantly distracted in her mind and body from a sweet afternoon closeted with a lady of high degree, arrives in a low part of the town and quickly joins with a coarse young soldier lad who plies our heroine with drink and pretty blandishments, complimenting her on the turn of her ankle, on the sparkle in her eye; and who duly hastens the befuddled maiden into a house of ill repute and proceeds there, without further aid, to fuck her. Do you see what I mean? You won't lift your face. Suppose I never see it again?"

Her breath caught up with her with a deep gasp and held her tight until she was outside and the door was shut behind her. She exhaled in little spasms. They were croaking her name through the intercom box in the middle of the hall to come to the telephone. The voice croaked, then snapped shut.

Ellen took her time. She stopped still in the quiet, damp hall, tired, dragged out, thinking: More exhausting telling it than doing it. And then, always conscious through my sleep, all night long, of her gleaming down at the foot of the bed, saving me from the terrors with her little cross. Looking something like the vampire herself hovering there, but all gold and white instead of red-eyed and black. Why did I have to tell it to her? Because I thought she'd say, Oh darling! and promptly weave a bridal wreath for my perspiring brow, kiss the bruised lips of the bride? But impossible not to tell her. She would have noticed the change sooner, not later: Two little baby girls both born on Christmas day twenty-one years ago. Two pretty mamas lying in twin hospital beds waiting for the embarrassed daddies to bring bunches of cold florist flowers and holly; celebrate the nativity. Little girl-christs. Children of God, raised up right in sunny, adjoining gardens that grew every leaf and bloom the climate could support.

No one seemed to be at home in the hall. The rain was making a twilight of the afternoon. It was as chill as November, as a tunnel dug deep beneath the earth. At each end of the hall, the rain poured and wasted itself against the high, narrow windows. Wasting myself, Ellen thought, pouring and dripping against the glass and the wall until I rest encased in a single drop on some bush leaf below; until the sun comes tomorrow and sucks me up. Her hands trembled; to make them stop, she remembered what they could do: deep in the sun of the garden, her fat baby fist closed tight on a dandelion, crushed hard until the flower went to sap, until the power and system of its color ran inside her skin. That first flower, she thought, drew the lines on my palms, making love and fate and death swoop and lean hard on my flesh. Up and down in her mother's arms, and she had sung with the marvel of levitation back in the yellow day while the baby Margaret had lain flat in her own grass, screaming for her.

The rain flowed faster. A wind whirled and scattered her.

On the trip down the three flights of stairs, the mirrors at each landing flashed out the moving white of her face, the electrical flash of her black hair. Her mind sped signals to her images: I am hungry, what are you going to do about it? I want to crouch in the corner and be Margaret, want to pry open boxes and cans and grovel in food until it hangs from my chin, then sleep and forget how easily, how promiscuously I give myself away. Are you tired, she asked. Yes, her body answered.

She panted hello into the telephone.

"Baby girl! It's Mama!"

"Mama? Why are you calling now? Why aren't you on your way? You're supposed to be here tonight."

"Oh how can I tell you! That's the awful . . . that's the terrible . . . it's just . . . I won't be there at all."

And what does that matter, thought Ellen. She felt sleep pressing close from the hotbox of the telephone closet. It was hot and dark, like the deep firelit cave of Sunday afternoon when even the papers had stopped rattling, when even the piano was dead to the world, and upstairs the bedroom doors were shutting soft and tight. She cracked the telephone receiver against her ear to get her eyes to open. This woman, she heard herself think, as though someone were whispering the information into her ear, was a crazy woman, calling a strange girl long-distance to say odd, personal things to an imaginary daughter. It's best to humor such women, fake a childish love for them until the men can come in their wagon and carry her off to some padded room that's safe for such fantasy. It was only yesterday, Ellen realized, that she had stopped having a mother.

"I'm only in the chorus of the play. It's Margaret who's acting Cassandra. . . . From the audience you'd hardly be able to see me anyway. But tomorrow's graduation. . . . You'll have to come take me home, won't you?"

The telephone crackled. Faint, ringing bleeps announced the distance between them. Ellen leaned against the wall and slid down until her chin lay on her knees. The poor woman . . . dialing at random and finding a random girl willing to play daughter.

"Oh. . . . Well, can't you just speak some of your piece to me anyway? (*The crazy woman was ignoring every word her daughter spoke.*) I can't stand to miss a single thing you do; can't stand it! Oh, you're the one to stop me from feeling terrible. . . . Do it!"

Ellen was melting, was going out with the intensity of the heat that consumed the last of the coal in the grate. She leaned over and propped open the closet door, and there were girls running past, girls in blue gym suits running with basketballs, each face peering in at Ellen as it bounced by. She peered straight back at them, counting the amazing motions of all the knobby, scarred knees. The front door was banging against the wall for the last time; the last white sneaker was kicking at the heel ahead of it before it shot out into the diminishing drizzle.

The hall door stayed closed for a moment. When it

opened again, Janet Sanctissima was coming inside and leaning against the wall and looking at Ellen. Sanctissima was wearing sneakers, too; but they were dirty red, and the nail of a big toe had jabbed up through one of them, bright, hard and jagged.

Ellen swallowed and closed her eyes. The telephone receiver slipped with sweat against her ear.

"Well, go ahead, honey! Please say your piece for Mama so this evening I can pretend I'm there hearing you say it."

Keeping her eyes closed, Ellen made scissors of two fingers and put her nose between them, pretended to chop off her nose exactly at the point where it overhung her lips.

She began reciting. Her voice, at first, sounded scarred; its healing had a hoarse sound:

> "We heard your voice, Hecabe; why did you call?
>   What did you say? As we sat there indoors
>   Thinking of slavery with bitter tears,
>   Your cry of agony came to us, and we all
>   Shuddered with nameless fears."

Even the hoarseness gave out. Her mother's breathing, huge and hard, replaced Ellen's on the line. Her words seemed to inhale and exhale.

"How sad and wrong. . . . Who is Hecabe?" The last words had stopped breathing and were dripping with tears. Ellen, amazed, held the phone from her ear and looked at it, as though it could show her what she imagined: a huge audience of mothers being stunned to tears by Euripides!

"What's wrong with you, Mama? Stop crying! You better tell me what's wrong with you?" Hulking sobs jumped into Ellen's ear, nothing resembling the sounds May-Ellen knew how to make, that she had always made: May-Ellen's legs moved, she sounded like a taffeta petticoat; her fingers dug the dirt around the irises, and, if it were absolutely quiet, the papery petals whispered back against the yellowy down on her bare arms; her mouth smiled, her lips slipped as they went up over her teeth. The Mason & Hamlin, every day of her life, made her sound like Mozart. She was sounding now like a howling dog.

To stop the noise inside her head, Ellen opened her eyes. There was Margaret, her hair flat and gold again; her body upright and neat in cotton. She was standing in front of Janet Sanctissima, handing her something, something like two small white cards; and Janet Sanctissima was bending over it. Everything was very still and serious.

"Daddy's dead!" the wrong voice in the telephone yelled.

Ellen closed her eyes again, waiting to hear more; but there was nothing but the drizzle from her mother's nose, nothing but the suck of a wet mouth as it breathed in. *Dad-dy:* a word of two soft syllables; a father of a child. Ellen had never seen her mother have one of these, alive or dead. She meant, of course, a husband. Faint bleepings popped on the wire, like signals from a distant planet. Ellen was waiting to hear more.

"I tell you, he's dead!"

"What do you mean!"

Margaret was standing in front of Janet Sanctissima; Sanctissima was still holding the small white thing. Her mother's voice was rising, with each statement, into a question mark, as though she were asking verification of the facts from the make-believe daughter, the girl crouched in the sweat she was making for herself miles and miles from the scene of the crime, the scene of the tragedy, the scene of the accident. . . . *Kinderscenen: that* was the music her mother had played early in the mornings for Ellen before Ellen could walk. Now she remembered.

"He was . . . you know? . . . out in his new mail cart this morning? He said, right after breakfast, he said, Well, got to go get in the newfangled putt-putt, old feet aren't good enough anymore to carry the letters with? And I said, Roger, Why, those little motorized carts are good for you? No more lugging that big leather bag from door to door through all the cold and heat and someday dropping dead of a heart attack on some strange lady's doorstep? I said? I said, You just stay put in that little putt-putt with the nice zip-up plastic and keep yourself warm in winter and sheltered from summer sun, and then he said, Well, anything you say, May-Ellen, just have to save up all that energy for you, honey-bunch, at night! Though, he said, I look a pure fool fooling around on three wheels like that. But fool or no, I said, I've still got myself a husband?"

The questions snapped. The howling dog returned over the wire, howling at Ellen, "Honeybunch! Honeybunch!" A husband . . . that's what she'd meant. And, after all, she was meant to sound like a hurting beast: no sound like Mozart, no sound like the shuffling of flowers against her fingers, no silky sounds could make a difference when the harsh shatter of Greek syllables began to storm the sweet wall this mother had built around her easy life. She was, after all, an easy mark for those wild-haired, tough-limbed Trojan women who were going to coil around her and teach her how to wail.

Her mother gasped, growled; gasped, growled; and the whine of the telephone wire keened through her noise. I have to get rid of her, I have to get rid of her, Ellen thought, before twilight, because I have to lead the chorus and see Margaret be Cassandra. For an instant, grief, like a pitted little pebble, appeared on her tongue. It was tasteless and hard and could do injury to the guts, but it was simple to swallow. She swallowed it easily, and it did not choke her.

It was like listening to a hungry zoo over the telephone, a thousand animals wild for food from her, prepared to chew her body up if she could offer them nothing else. "What happened?" she screamed, and waited for the roaring to stop.

Somewhere between Margaret and Janet Sanctissima, the small white things had vanished. Ellen could see nothing, from the telephone closet, of the girl and the woman but the tops of their heads that were bent close together above the parlor's nubby green sofa back. And the tops of the heads appeared to be agreeing about something important: first the grizzled gray of Sanctissima's hair would nod slowly, forward and back; then it would be still while the golden crown of Margaret's head would sweep up and down, quite as slowly; solemnly. A pitchfork of annoyance stuck through Ellen: out there the two of them were doing something drastic toward the ruination of her while she hid in a closetful of death with a woman gone wild because her life's sweet wall had lost a single brick and because, through the gap, nasty things were slithering in to be kissed, embraced and welcomed to a new home. Everything that Ellen wanted to tell this woman was involved in a long scream that meant *let me out of here!*

"Please. Stop crying. Tell me what happened!" But, at least, Margaret and Sanctissima seemed no longer to be plotting her disgrace. Their heads now were motionless, facing forward, staring toward the long French windows at the other end of the parlor; and there could be nothing there to see but the drenched grass of the quadrangle and more rain hurtling to it. She needed to go and push them apart; neither could move without her hand on them.

"Around about an hour ago? The P.O. men came over here and said some big white Caddy with that sixteen-year-old McGehee boy who just yesterday got his license just slung itself around the corner and mowed him down in his little putt-putt just like that Chihuahua Sport that got all smashed last week right under my own eyes out the beauty parlor window. Oh dear God! Roger!" The shriek rose, climbing a scale until a pitch was reached that the throat could not support. Then it broke, and the growling returned, hungrier than ever. From such a sound, there should come a visible sign; and Ellen could see nothing from her closet but the still heads of Margaret and Sanctissima.

"They said from the post office? They said, Mrs. Fairbanks, Roger just couldn't have felt a thing, it was over just that quick, and I said to them, Oh, where was it, where was it? And they said, Don't worry about a thing, they'd take care of everything, but Roger was being fixed up just as nice as they could do it over at the funeral home. And, oh Honeybunch! How I screamed at them! They thought I meant that Roger was *it* when I said *Where was it!* He is an it! They think my husband is the *it!* I wanted to die, them talking like that to me. But then they said, Oh, we're sorry, sorry—it was Greenway Avenue over there in the gold coast section where sixteen-year-old boys can drive around in white Cadillacs and Miss Nina, my own mama, she shamed me, she stood there and spit at them and said bad words one after another and said *nouveau*-this and *nouveau*-that about Greenway Avenue until I thought I would kill her. . . ."

Through hate's magic, the pebble in Ellen's stomach turned to a rising mass of dough, full of explosive yeast; and then it burst and she was strung with sticky fury from her throat to her bowels: it was herself she saw spread across some terraced lawn in the red, white and blue tangle of government-owned metal. And there was a little bastard leaning over her, his tongue hanging out ready to lap her blood off the grass.

"Oh say something! Say something, Honeybunch . . . it was my husband!"

"I'll come home right now."

Instantly, the growl shut down. The voice hummed with strength; it flexed with determination. "No," she said. "I won't have it like this for you. I want you in that play tonight. I want you in that graduation tomorrow."

"I better come home!" I better! I *better* bleed red, white and blue and green on the grass and turn people's stomachs sick like a mashed Chihuahua!

"No, you heard me," the calm voice continued. "I've

never missed a one of your things and I don't intend you missing them now. You hear? You hear? You want to kill your daddy all over again?"

"When is the funeral?" She pulled herself up from the floor; in a minute, she could disconnect the voice that was full of mashed Chihuahua and run like hell to the window at the end of the hall and be cooled. The sweat stuck like glue to her thighs.

"It's going to be Gieseking playing Liszt, I promise you that, and no damn Hammond for my Roger!" The voice was sobbing, bubbling, again. *Gieseking playing Liszt?* "I made Darwin Waters hunt all day and tear up the whole house till he found those records and then he went and broke one but there's three left, and there won't be no damn Hammond for my Roger!"

"Mama! When is the funeral?"

"Day after tomorrow. You come then. But first don't you miss a single thing you're due there. Don't come till it's all over. Is the white dress all right?"

"Yes."

"It better be. Went clear to Raleigh for it, I'm glad to say."

White dresses; death at the door. "Mama? Who's there?"

"You know who . . . who's always here. Except for Hortense. . . . His dog's run away."

Ellen listened, through her mother's voice, to the murmur of who was always there: Welch, Darwin Waters, Miss Nina, America, surrounding themselves with clinks, knocks, rattlings, the noise of a name said over and over, *Roger, Roger, Roger.* The play was at home; Ellen wished to be there and have Margaret with her; she would need Cassandra. To hell with the Greek play. The rain would never stop anyway.

"Are you sure?"

"Goodbye, Sugar!"

She ran down the hall, away from the parlor, to the little window. It grew brighter as she came closer. It was caked with dust and fresh-washed sunlight. She pushed the glass up and leaned out, her hair falling down her arms. The sun, instead of heating, cooled her skin dry again.

Some basketball players were coming home, wandering in arcs and angles through the sodden, greenish breeze, flapping the brief, pale blue skirts of their gym suits and giving Ellen a name for the solid feeling inside her. The name was pleasure; and it was as though the girls were spelling it out, pale blue, with their bodies. Ellen lifted an arm and waved at them. Some even threw her back a kiss.

Pleasure had waved at her, had thrown her a kiss. Pleasure had confirmed Ellen as a fit dwelling place for itself: in a subterranean room, Roger was being pumped dry; up in the sun, Ellen was being filled. The blue girls got on their mark, ran hard, jumped some hedges and rolled away, disappearing, down a hill.

Ellen went in the parlor without a sound and stopped behind the two heads. They were exactly as she had left them. She stuck the fingers of her left hand through the stiff gray of Sanctissima's hair, grasped it, pulled. She curved her right hand over Margaret's head. It was like punching the button of a jack-in-the-box: they sprang upright and wobbled in front of her.

Ellen would not look at Sanctissima; instead, she squinted her eyes, curled her lips over her teeth at Margaret. She quoted, in the Greekiest possible way: " 'You pass off with a pleasant laugh things that should wring your inmost soul;— not that you will have much to show for all your prophesying.' " She dreamed, for a split instant, of heaping ashes over the fresh pink hair ribbon on Margaret's head. Sanctissima and Margaret looked blankly at Ellen.

"Go to hell," said Margaret. She turned and left them, marching into the outdoors as though to the beat of some polonaise that only she could hear. She left the French doors gaping open behind her; her feet met the brick porch without a stumble although her eyes were set on the sky. It was not until she was nearly clear across the soaked quadrangle that she had shaken off the two stares that were clinging to her back.

As soon as there was nothing left for them to look at, Sanctissima went to a chair and sat. She hung her head; her heavy, wrinkled eyelids drooped. She put on a pathetic zoological display: a wild eagle, captured, tamed, taught to mimic shyness. Ellen sat in the chair nearest her; a chair not very near. With the sun pouring rivers of light and shadow over their feet, basking the pale carpet, Ellen was becoming conscious of time again.

"Soon," she said, "I will have to get ready for the Greek play." Janet Sanctissima looked up: the eagle looked out from behind the rusty, bent bars of his cage. "I hope it doesn't embarrass you for me to be here." Her left hand was shaking, so her right hand clasped it. "A student of mine wrote the music for the play. I'll be there. A flute, a drum, a cymbal. That's all, but very effective. But you must know that, from rehearsal."

"Yes." Ellen could feel nothing, but she was being called upon to feel embarrassment. "What were the white things, the little white things Margaret gave you? You'd better tell me." She meant to sound threatening; in fact, she sounded like a father confessor.

Sanctissima's eyes drooped again. She undid her left hand, and its rough skin made a scratching cry as it slid against the silky lining of her skirt pocket. The little thing that emerged was white only on its back; its front was a yellow old snapshot with scalloped edges. Ellen pressed her fingertips into the ridges and looked down at herself, aged sixteen; at Margaret, aged sixteen; and at May-Ellen, always a mother's age. They were wearing the *Figaro* costumes, and that day Ellen had been Cherubino. They were posed in operatic expressions of shock, seductiveness and outrage. Ellen curled the picture between her fingers until she had made a scroll of it.

"Your mother's a pretty thing," said Sanctissima.

"My God!" Ellen looked hard at her, but Sanctissima had not lifted her eyes again, and her left hand was back tightly inside her right. Ellen put the picture in her own pocket, and felt it unwind there against her hip. She did not ask to see the other. Her father's cheek and hands were pressing against her own. The embalming fluid was straining from his limbs into hers, replacing her blood or making it senseless. She rubbed her wrist against the chair's rough tapestry, and there were tears, not blood drops or embalming fluid, starting in her eyes.

Sanctissima closed her eyes. Tears were not worth seeing. "Listen to this," she said. "When I was your age I was already a failure. My father, who was a saint—I martyred him —denied himself every pleasure, every comfort, even necessities—sacrificed his youth—to prepare me for the concert stage. Five major recitals that he spent his blood and guts to get for me, and I was drunk for all of them. What do you think of a pianist who sounds terrific to herself only when she's drunk? That's the trouble—I feel like I have wooden hands when I'm sober at a piano, and how could I go on big stages in San Francisco and New York and play pianos with wooden hands? No matter how Papa guarded me from the booze, I got it somehow. Before the last concert, I kept a full pint taped inside my thigh for three days and nights, hidden from him; and I got every drop of it inside me in no more than thirty minutes before I played. Then Papa got a load on himself and then he shot himself—not right off, you know, but soon, you know, soon enough for me to know why he did it." Sanctissima's right hand held her left hand ever harder. "Somebody got me this job at Redwing. Redwing College for Women. Years and years of this. Every year the girls know less music and are prettier than the year before."

Sanctissima crossed her knees, making a lap to hide the shaking hand in. Two cigarette burns had put two holes through the black and white tweed of her skirt; and it seemed to Ellen that the holes were eyes and that Sanctissima's knee was peering out at her, like a little woolly animal that could bite hard and poisonously if she tried to hold it.

Now what do I say? thought Ellen. Get down on that knee and recite forty million Hail Marys and sixty million Our Fathers and then play, woodenly but sincerely, "Rock of Ages" for some good Baptists, for free, for the rest of your life? Huh? What do I say? screamed Ellen in her head.

Sanctissima stood; the eyes in her knee closed. "You have some time," she said. "If you're going to talk to me at all, let's walk while you do it."

Ellen followed her through the French doors, through the fragrance that Margaret had left there. Almost, thought Ellen, I can almost rub my hand against her, very pink and fresh, here; then, in the sun, they were walking to the woods, with air becoming, as they neared the thick green and shadow, as sweet as flowers in their mouths. Their arms brushed together as they walked, their feet squeaked and went raw against the wet leather of their shoes.

The woods, despite the brambles, the mud, are a country of silky leisure, like a curtained, waxed, drawing-room world, after the open-spaced glare outside them. Occasionally the wind hisses, inhaling the damp, and the leaves on some trees turn up their undersides and look like moonlit bellies. Occasionally, as they hold hands and walk down the narrow path beneath the trees, Ellen and Janet Sanctissima have their eyes closed at the same time, though neither is aware that the other is also blind. When this happens, beneath the four eyelids, spectacles of color and light occur: orange, representing spurts of sunlight, flashes in oval streaks; red, representing some intense bare patch of sky, soaks the eyelids for a split second and then is transformed into purple. When green happens, it is because they have passed out of all light and sun and are walking in deep

41

shadow; trees meet overhead. Continuous bird shrieks and leaf rustles do not disturb their blind pacing deeper, steeply downhill toward the center of the little wood. Only when one of them stumbles and pulls downward with her hand do they both open their eyes. Oddly, it is only the younger woman, it is Ellen, who pulls and stumbles. Janet Sanctissima knows how to walk through the dark or through a den of lions or thieves and come out alive: she has practiced it many times with both her feet and brain pickled in bourbon.

They come to the wood's center, which is like the bottom of a deep green and gold hole. It smells of earth and water. The trees shut out all the sky. With their eyes open, Ellen and Sanctissima draw apart and look down into the deep, narrow stream that makes its first and last appearance here in the wood. It rolls over brown and moss rocks, slides beneath a little footbridge, disappears a few feet beyond into a concrete tunnel to feed a secret, thirsty race at the center of the earth. The water is knee-deep; it is flanked by banks of mud, almost obscene in their slipperiness. Sanctissima, creaking, jackknifes herself down on a flat rock above the bank and pulls Ellen down beside her.

Sanctissima said, "What do you want most, Ellen?"

"All my life," Ellen answered, "I have wanted only one thing most; and that thing for a very short time. Then, I have wanted another thing most. But I have always remained faithful to my wants. They make a long procession, all those dear things, behind me. I could reach out now and touch any one of them—even one that is ten years old—and tell it, I still want you. When I was only two years old I noticed, one summer night, the moon through my window. And they had to walk me up and down all that night, everybody went without sleep, because I wanted the moon more than anything. I remember it was enormous and orange. I have never seen it that way since. They were desperate but, they thought, she will forget it because the moon will change soon to a plain old silver thing and won't be gorgeous. And they hung up dark curtains at my windows to make sure I never noticed it again. But even so, they say, I cried for weeks, even though they took me outside in the dark to show me that the big orange was gone away, because I knew it was still there behind the curtains at my windows and that the hopeless little paper smile they'd pasted on the sky was just a grownup trick to distract me, not my moon.

"Then," she continued (a sharp leaf rattle came from above them. They looked, but it was only two squirrels coming nearer. When the squirrels turned their heads away, Sanctissima and Ellen could see that, below their dark film, the squirrels' eyes were a deep and thick red and seemed dangerous), "when I was six, I wanted, more than anything else, a ghost. I'd learned to read out of a ghost-goblin-witch storybook my grandmother'd had since she was a baby. All the ghosts in that book were of ladies that were beautiful and had died young for love, and all wore precious stones and wept the whole night through in deserted bedchambers. God, I wanted one of those ghosts! Lots of times, I put on a sheet and hid down in the shrubbery outside Margaret's window. I'd go HOOOOO-hoo! and Margaret would finally put down her coloring book and look out at me. Then I would scream. I'd scream at her, *I've come to eat you alive and spit out your bones!* Margaret screamed back for a while, but then she wouldn't come to the window anymore. But one time I got her to come out. I was hiding in azalea bushes with big purplish flowers that looked like horns. I got her deep inside them with me, snuggled down deep; then I held her tight in my arms and made her eat one of the flowers. I thought she would die of it while I held her, and then her ghost would be mine. I held my eyes closed tight while she swallowed. I saw her dead and flying and passing through the walls of rooms. But she could eat all the flowers she wanted and never die of it.

"When I was twelve, it was this boy I wanted. He was

seventeen, and had black curly hair that always looked wet or greasy as pig meat: you know, dammit, that it's not always the pretty things we die to run our fingers through! I saw him only one time and then never again. He was playing Oberon in the senior class play that I got to go to only because I had a fat cousin bumping around as a fool of a fairy in it. But don't think I went home and got erotic over imagining myself Titania! No sir, there he was in purple tights good enough to eat, like sweet damson plum jelly, and a loose blue satin shirt that made me want to stick my head up inside it, and I dreamed (every afternoon) for months, with my ear against the cook's kitchen radio, of being forever and a day Mary Noble, Backstage Wife, and beating starlets off his ass while I handed him the grease paint. He yammered like a Yankee all through the play, and that homemade whine fell like good, cold snow on these hot southern ears. Where is he now?

"I see you, lady. Getting bored, picking in your ear, trying not to yawn. All you want out of a girl is open legs and shut mouth—except when you're trying to kiss them. So what do I care. I'll stop telling you a damn thing and you won't kiss me another damn time either. But just you hear this one thing. If I could get me a ghost—I mean, if I could get somebody to will me her ghost the same way some people will their brains and gizzards to medical schools—then I wouldn't need you or anything like you for the rest of my days. I'd have my ghost—it would be all around me forever, and I'd eat for it and sleep for it and fornicate and pray for it; and I'd work and support it, like a wife or a child. And even when I died I'd never be alone. And we would live in absolute silence: no music, no talk, no singing. . . .

"And if that Yankee actor just, right now, jumped up in front of that pecan across the water there, don't think I wouldn't just wade across and eat him alive in a minute. And how do you think I feel every time the moon turns so big it's going to fall on the world and crush us? And *bright!*

Oh, I feel all the time like somebody, the minute I was born, promised me everything, every heart's desire, then didn't give me a thing. There's something I *want*—and I'll never get old because people don't until they've got what they wanted. And I never will."

Sanctissima drew up her knees and pressed them against her forehead, eyes squeezed shut. Her strong arms and hands met around her legs and cuffed them to her body. The fifty-two-year-old eagle embryo in holey tweed.

Ellen looked away. Musicians, she had once been told, like dancers and actors, were mostly illiterates. And not only, she saw, could they not read: neither could they grasp the sense of a story when it was told to them.

Time was passing, and Ellen wasn't feeling any older. The afternoon was growing rich and fat with gold in its old age, and the bent enclosure of trees around them was becoming the brass pot in which Black Jumbo had carried home the tiger-butter. Black Mumbo should polish the pot: it was much too green and moldy. Now the tiger-butter would poison the entire family, and Little Black Sambo would be buried in his fine new clothes. I will inherit, thought Ellen, the purple umbrella to wind upright in my tail and be the grandest. . . .

"Excuse me for a moment. Please do not go away." Sanctissima was on her feet, her knees wobbling before Ellen's nose from the sudden shock of standing. A scampering rattled through the leaves behind them: her sudden move had disturbed something four-legged.

When she had gone, shuffling heavy in the tracks of the squirrel, Ellen swept at her mind and made it bare. She concentrated on infinity: infinity was a perfectly delivered high C bellowed by lungs as huge as the universe, maintained until the end of all. She undressed, feeling the perspiration dry in patches as each stitch, from cotton down to nylon, came off. When she was naked, she sat at the top of the slippery bank of mud and pushed off. In the stream up to her neck, she gasped from the cold, from the pointed rocks that fought back against her. It was deep enough to float in; she floated, waving her hands like wings or fins to balance herself, staring straight up into the green miles overhead. It was like having insomnia in some giant George Washington's green-canopied bed. She wished to be deep and swimming, like someone awake for the night wishing for sleep; to follow the stream for the hundreds of miles it would take to taste salt in her mouth. She rocked in the water, her hair fanning like weeds around her.

"What in the name of God!" It was Sanctissima croaking from high above. Some streaks of sun began tattering the treetops, making one warm hand against Ellen's forehead, another against her belly. A third beam, missing Ellen, turned into the brown quart bottle in Sanctissima's hand and made it radiant. The radiance was the thing to watch, not the amazed eagle face above it.

"Ellen!"

"Yes, Most-holy."

"Is that what they call me?"

"Inevitably."

"Please . . . come out of the water. If someone came . . . if you love me, come out of the water!"

A deep breath, packing lungs nowhere near the size of the universe; and she turned over, face submerged, and kept on floating. She imagined how laughable were her bare buttocks, jutting blank white, like two smooth steppingstones, from the brown water. Despite the water stuffing her ears, she was not deaf to Sanctissima:

"Of course my name is not *really* Sanctissima! I was born a Hart, H A R T—can you imagine the loathsomeness of that? Hard Hart, Stony Hart, Bleeding Hart, Harts and Flowers, Hart of Gold? Oh, for God's sake, come out of that water!" (Ellen sneaked a breath and, through the shine of wet clinging to her lashes, saw the bottle pouring into the mouth, saw her slinky underpants, her rosebudded bra, her yellow unbuttoned cotton being waved like a flag of surrender, or a temptation to surrender, through the air.)

"Sanctissima's Mama's name! Or the name Papa dreamed up for her when he thought her well on the way to stage center at the Metropolitan Opera House. The sweetest singer ever born out of a tree! No matter how the critics carped about tremolo—the sweetest! Is that what you're bound on being down there? Carp? That kind of fish that lives forever? Don't be too sure: I can catch anything that swims; and what I catch I eat; and I'll eat a carp once a day and live forever."

(The brown bottle gurgled; in response, Ellen bubbled out all her air and snatched some more. Her underwear had been abandoned to cling to the mud slope. The mud beamed through it; it was like the skin of Black Mumbo.)

"I was the only little child ever born to lie in its crib at sunset and be sung to sleep by 'Dido's Lament.'" She began to sing it, with strong, tuneless fervor: "'When I am la-aid . . . and-da la-ai-ai-aid in earth . . .'" frowned, broke off. "Aurora Sanctissima," she said, "the sunrise of the Most-holy! A most full-bosomed, most golden-haired little lady, who was taken from us into the choirs of the angels one snowy, untimely December when she slipped in the slush and fell in front of a passing Rolls-Royce that was moving not too rapidly down Fifth Avenue in the city of New York. She had gone out that evening for a fresh bottle of iodine. . . . Some fool had told her that Mary Garden took ten drops in warm milk every night of her life. A martyr to her art! No nobler death than that, if death is what you're after . . . although Papa, our Svengali, our all-round impresario, accompanist, teacher, press agent and occasional provider, insisted it was nothing more or less than a Rolls-Royce that killed her. Papa was very proud of that Rolls. He found it hard to make much out of a wife who never got farther than twenty-five-dollar solos for Jewish and Episcopalian feast days; but *who* could deny the glamour of our close relative beneath the wheels of that pristine chauffeured Rolls?

"Well. Luckily, that night, I was already asleep; luckily, I had got my dose of song in ahead of time. *If only you would get the hell out of that water!* I can see you sneaking in breaths, you know! A most full-bosomed, a most golden-headed lady! There are some lonely old bags like myself who knock themselves out at night with raw gin or masturbation or an ear to a radio full of firsthand accounts of flying saucers—but not me! I've never got what I wanted," she mocked, "so I've never gotten old. No, I listen and I can still hear it coming from the foot of my bed every night of my life: '. . . Re-mem-ber me! . . .' in the sweetest voice that was ever born out of a tree!"

For a long moment, there was silence; then a clumsy sob; then a swift, fresh gurgle of the bottle; but before Ellen could lift her face to breathe, a long, heavy foot was clamping down on her head and forcing her open mouth to fill itself with the stony mud of the stream's floor. Her head could not move; the scream in her head could not get out; but her body twirled and thrashed like a fish half-dead on the line. Then, the Sanctissima hands, hands of skin and steely bone, were inside her armpits, the foot was gone, and Ellen's body was jerking from water into oxygen in an exploding backward arc. The Sanctissima spine scarcely had to bend to take the weight of her. Sanctissima's mouth was spitting words against her closed eyelids. The water off her body was drowning all the air around them. Ellen spat mud and stones into the Sanctissima shoulder and put her arms around the neck and hung there. Ellen's face was cocked up to the treetops, which were beginning to whirl into a green broth. They stood knee-high in water.

Janet Sanctissima dragged Ellen up, by her wrist, up the slippery embankment, like a child stupid with sleep and tantrums. "Little girls wiggling in the water . . . seducing themselves in front of me . . . making me a mirror," she said. "I am a very conventional woman!" she shouted. And Ellen rolled all the last of the mud and pebbles on to her tongue and spat them into the invisibly darned patches of Sanctissima's broadcloth.

"How dare you handle me!" The spurt of mud made it sound like the tongue-tied trying to shout for help; but Sanctissima clenched the wrist harder and heaved until the body she wanted dragged. At the top of the embankment, she let go; Ellen fell backwards against the spongy spring earth that grasped at her, tried to make her a fleshy white toadstool, or tried to drink her like rainwater.

The circumference of the little wood was tightening and drawing in; before long, its edges would touch the tips of Ellen's outstretched hands, and the blue and lighted world beyond would creep up to, then into, make a different thing of, this dark green one. Janet Sanctissima turned her muddied and darned cotton back to Ellen and tilted her own face up toward the green roof. Once more, the brown quart bottle in her hand caught beams and seemed to flash signals off to the world. Some birds sang above her; and out of the emptying bottle, the eagle was released and when it had drunk enough, its sharp beak fell like a knife against Ellen's lips.

The circumference of the wood was shrinking, its dark, thick colors were crushing in against each other, at first slowly, then ever faster. The wood had a heartbeat that skipped, then thudded. Finally, there was nothing to it at all except a single tree, then a single branch, then a single leaf, pale with the white light of the outside world that had slipped in and swallowed whole the rich food of the thick little wood. The heartbeat went on thudding, now inside the single pale leaf. It was something the lighted world could not absorb.

"Now . . . where did I put that sweet bottle?" Janet Sanctissima was on her knees, sweeping her hands through high grass, as though they were combs tending hair, until she found what she wanted, again. Things were getting dim. It seemed that much time had passed. When at last they went outside the wood again, passed by the last trees, and re-entered the grassed and paved quadrangle, it would be a twilit, suppertime world that they would find there. Janet Sanctissima stretched out her legs and drank again; she held the bottle with both hands and stroked its shape, and turned it between her palms, but the sun was not strong enough, anymore, to reach down and pierce it.

"There's been a Janet Sanctissima bottle hidden in this wood as long as there's been a Janet Sanctissima coming here."

Ellen opened her eyes and shifted her head, uneasily, against the Sanctissima shoulder. There seemed to be an established tradition of a bottle in these woods and a Sanctissima, in these woods, to drink it. A little idea began to stretch itself across Ellen's mind, tapping out a message like a little rhythm into her: I am a little cog in the Sanctissima wheel, jangled the little idea; I am not the first naked girl she's seen in that old water down there; this wet ground has not been warmed by springtime alone, not by my body alone. She dug her heel in the ground; its pressure squeezed up hot forms, from the dirt, of teacher and many students, one teacher and many students, all bent on escaping music. She closed her eyes to them and crossed her heel over her knee and tried to retrieve the good dream she'd been having. The dream had been building a house that could have been Sanctissima's house; and in the house the dream had made a place that was unquestionably Ellen's. The dream had been domestic and homely: it had a sober Sanctissima digging around the budding crocuses and Ellen pulling batik curtains against evening; and all these clear, calm pictures were pasted on a hunk of blazing foil that rattled and glared with the storms and hot eyes of sexual drama: tension, quarrel and ecstasy.

Sanctissima moved her shoulder, took it back, and Ellen,

with her head cracking back against rock, recognized the pictures and the people of the dream for what they were: her parents, and their life together.

Still, she thought, through the pain (and the afternoon began to blink its eyes, to draw shadows out of its mouth), if that were my life—if my life began to look like theirs . . . How lucky she was to have it all settled so easily, so early: the long, fat years ahead, full of music like her mother's music, with long, narrow, musical Janet Sanctissima. All this notion of happiness required, she thought, to set it rolling, firm and silvery off into the future, was her acceptance of herself as something she was not: something named ordinary. Happiness, she saw, hinged on discarding the extraordinary self that had strolled down to the water through the trees, hinged on joining the faceless and nameless in the common denominator of the past love that had been made on the patch of warm earth. She saw a flood of lovers sweeping toward her, sinking the hard, dark boats of their individual selves behind them, joining one another until they had built a smooth and heavy wave of kissing and copulation, good for nothing but a mighty crash, food for the sand. Happiness, she saw, was an eternity made of the hot, vacant instant of the climax, when it was not her own name she called, but another's.

Ellen curved her hand around her knee and felt it still good and hard and hers; as hard as the rock that had cracked her head. The relief felt good, was packed skintight with the strength of ten thousand; because of it, she could pretend happiness a little while longer for the sake of the Sanctissima feelings.

"Here we go loopdy-loo, here we go loopdy-ly!" As Sanctissima sang, she got up and crunched into the bushes; when she came back, the empty bottle was gone from her hand. She slipped away, when Ellen tried to fill up the hand with herself.

Sanctissima dug her toes in and lit a cigarette. The match

sizzled for an instant against the stream and then was carried away. Ellen began to watch Sanctissima getting carried away, all up and down—first up, then down—on the supernatural current of her whiskey-drinking; and there was, Ellen thought, a whirlpool at one end of Sanctissima into which Miss Janet Sanctissima—old maid, old seducer, old gadabout music-tickler—would presently hurl herself. It would be a death-defying leap to the bottom, where she would wrassle with crocodiles (shedding crocodile tears) until the rabble on dry land glorified her name. And that's what the wicked bitch really wanted—a crowd of eighteen-year-old Auroras all screaming *Ave Sanctissima* while she performed feats of strength in dangerous waters.

Ellen saw Sanctissima's thoughts begin to stumble across her face, causing her teeth to snap, her lips to wrinkle, her eyes to squint: what she thought was clear as daylight: she was as drunk as she could possibly be; she wanted to be back home playing the piano; there was the mess of getting rid of the kid; then at least twenty minutes getting home; then the freshness of the drink gone; then the power to play like a god gone; she would sound like a senile José Iturbi. So she would have to smash something, something that might be the piano itself this time.

It was boring, Ellen realized, for Sanctissima to be careful with the young, but it was only the young that she coveted. And how quickly the presence of Sanctissima aged them.

"Loopdy-loo . . . *crap!*" Sanctissima's cigarette stub flew sparks, then floated, then shredded and was gone for good. She was going to be Sanctissima, Ellen saw—faster-than-the-speed-of-light Sanctissima with her pretty girl, her dirty girl, and then leave her a drowning girl, push her face down, Ophelia style, into the water along with the match and cigarette, while faster-than-the-speed-of-sound Sanctissima cut the hell out, back to music.

Sanctissima said, "I was thinking, Eleanor—dammit, *Ellen*—of how absolutely individual—interesting, I mean—

you are; but *only,* only, I say—like so very many others that
I've known—only, I say, when you're in heat. I was so very
interested to see what you'd be like in heat and yes—yes, you
are very similar. What a similar person you are, Eustacia.
. . . *Yet* it occurred to me that I'd never heard anyone hiss
Sanctissima quite like that before. No, never quite like that
before. Do you think you could possibly reproduce that
sound, that delicious hissing, for me one more time—right
now, I mean, and absolutely unaided and unabetted by
Sanctissima herself? Right now? Do try!"

While Sanctissima balanced herself against a tree (itchy
sticky gummy pine bark; harboring chiggers that make you
itch where you can't scratch)—while she balanced, Ellen's
howling began, howling that sounded like Sanctissima
laughter: a croak-ish, caw-ish, wounded sound. Sanctissima's
blue eyes turned eagle-eyed and swept the lowering dark,
measuring the distance between her beak and the shaking
black head. Her fingers were twitching involuntarily, already tapping out the music they intended to make.

"Sanctissima," Ellen cawed. "Sanctissima . . . old drunk,
old fool . . . you hack, you stinking music teacher. . . .
Going to kill you. I'm going to get *your* ghost, it's yours I
want . . . *not* sweet old Margaret's. . . ."

Sanctissima flattened Ellen against a North American
holly, pinned her wrists behind it, held them there tight: the
Puritan setting the witch on fire, the savage staking the
homely plainsman. As she spoke, Sanctissima gradually let
her loose until Ellen slid to the roots and became a little
image of the curly fetus Sanctissima had made of herself
in the earlier afternoon.

"Papa took our building super's wife to his bed, soon
after the funeral. She couldn't sing a note, but by that time
I was well on my way to perfecting Chopin and was suffi-
cient artistic distraction for him all by myself. What a
round, black, lusty little bundle she was, with breasts like a
sack of melted marbles, all run together, all one color and

53

all still hot as hell! She became my very first sweetheart, with her thirty-three and me sixteen, and she loved me like a leopard. The first time was one rainy afternoon while Papa was out arranging my first recital with the nice Rolls-Royce man's money. What does anybody know about romance, what does Chopin know . . . ? And not a bit of it dimmed, even when father and daughter simultaneously took the clap cure, and both of us swore like good soldiers that we didn't know who in the world had brought it on us. But it hit Papa so hard it threw him off the music for weeks. *She,* dear Betty Brown—*she's* what threw *me* off the music. But I played the concert—played so good with the vision of Betty Brown inspiring me—that I was like a memory of Rachmaninoff to all the newspapers next morning. I dedicated it all to her. *I love myself when I was young!*

"Papa and I finally forgave each other . . . indeed, became faster friends than ever, especially when, the very next month, sweet Betty Brown, darling Betty Brown, irreplaceable Betty Brown got done in by her husband's switchblade. Papa and I were scared to death, even while we were trying to console each other, thinking it was us next, fearing that this excellent Mr. Brown, despite his masterly touch with broken furnaces, had at last gone berserk with jealousy and meant to leave a river of blood and bodies in the basement. But it was nothing so grand . . . nothing the way I wanted it to be. It turned out—as he had sincerely explained to the cops many times—that the truth was he simply couldn't stand the sight of unwashed dishes in the sink for one more day, and that the roaches on the kitchen floor had become too numerous for a man of his simple tastes.

"We were saved; Papa soon forgot, stuck his nose against less complex, cooler-colored hides . . . but I still mourn to this day, *mourn* sweet Betty Brown, and that bond, that camaraderie she made between Papa and me. . . . We didn't forget that in a hurry. Every night for months after she was gone, we cried together after the day's practicing was finished, me into my muscatel, him into his lovely bushy red beard. I used to think . . . oh, I felt denied a lot . . . that the least Papa could have done, before he shot himself out on the Bowery that winter night, was to make a will leaving me that great red bush of his. Nobody ever sees a pianist with a beard anymore. You don't know what you're missing. . . ."

Ellen observed the darkness, almost completely gathered now. If she stayed much longer without speaking her piece, she would miss the fried shrimp and field peas-and-snaps and applesauce that had been her favorite supper all year, and she would starve as she led the chorus of Trojan women. Even now, sweet old Margaret, the star, and their Greek teacher, Mr. Pathways, must be dying to get their hands on her for all the last-minute stitching and painting and keying-up. She was going to speak in a hurry, through all that noise, about Papa. And as she spoke, she began to walk to the path that would take her up and out of the wood. As she walked, she ignored the eagle-eye fastened to her back; it was an itch she could scratch in private, a red mark she could cover up later.

"This afternoon," Ellen was saying, over her shoulder, "my own daddy, a big straight furry man, who never knew one note from another but had to listen to a lot of them anyway, got smashed to kingdom come by . . . *coincidentally!* . . . a car. A fat white Cadillac . . . nothing, I know, compared to a Fifth Avenue Rolls . . . while he was scooting around delivering the letters in his little mail cart. Perhaps the white Cadillac will buy something for me! So be it. I've got a feeling that at this very minute my big furry daddy (his was *black* fur) and your golden furry mama are picking their fleas beyond the pearly gates and listening to us talk about their last moments beneath the wheels of expensive cars. And I'll tell you another thing, you dumb old drunk: *that Betty Brown* . . . how could I ever let you touch me! . . . that fat black ass is roasting in hell right

55

now and cursing your name because you're keeping her waiting. . . . Why don't you go on and get her if you love her so much!" Ellen screamed. "But maybe you wouldn't be welcome anyway, since she's got that stinking Papa of yours to keep her company, with his beard all black with ashes and his balls all shriveled to roasted peanuts! Go to hell, Janet Sanctissima!"

Ellen realized, with pleasure, that Sanctissima wouldn't, after all, get time for the piano tonight. She grabbed at Ellen's elbow.

"Get your nigger-loving hands off me!"

Sanctissima kept on walking behind her, hands in her pockets. "Dah-dah, de dah, de dah dah dah. . . . *Ein feste Burg ist unser Gott!*" she sang. "What's that you said, honey? Can't make out a word you say, honey," Sanctissima furiously mocked.

Ellen's voice went from hot to cold, and when it was frozen, she stood stock-still and lectured: "I know something you wouldn't know, you crumb-bum, about beards. Listen to this: beards are nothing more nor less than pubic hair transferred to the face and deliberately grown there by men with secret yearnings for emasculation and woman-hood. This yearning is most apparent when the pubic-hair beard completely encircles the lips. . . . Then, of course, the classical dream of hermaphroditism is realized: mascu-line equipment tucked away in its little forest below, and a full-blown vagina, complete with teeth, in its identical little forest above."

Sanctissima was huffing and puffing and stumbling be-hind, and she was furious: "That sounds like some more of that shit-ass Sigmund Freud!"

Ellen was rising through the dark tunnel of trees as neatly as a night animal. "Not at all. That observation is entirely the original observation of Mr. Pathways, the most brilliant and unappreciated of teachers on this faculty: Mythology 101. No one else has ever had the sense to see. But what is

even more perverse, we think . . . Mr. Pathways and I
. . . than the *man* who wears the beard, are the people who
admire him for it, who even wish one for themselves, who
see nothing at all peculiar or surreal in a female sex organ
that opens up and starts quoting the stock exchange prices
or lecturing on the Bach family."

Abruptly, Ellen stopped still on the path. Something ran
across her foot, and she tried to stomp on it, but missed.
Sanctissima fell against her and snatched her around to
face her, looming and furious.

"My father . . . my poor Papa," gasped Sanctissima.
Their faces were like pale paper globes burning in the
dark; but one light shook with speech, and Ellen could
feel her wrist beginning to crack in the claw that could
speed so lightly up and down the treble clef.

"My poor Papa! What a sickening little mind you have,
Eleanor . . . Eustacia . . . *Ellen,* is it? This poor man,
with his innocent lust . . . his lust for lust . . . and music!
You'll never see a man slip the barrel of a revolver into his
mouth on a frozen Bowery night while far uptown . . . uptown the crowds are screaming . . . *Brava! Bravissima!* for
some other young, unbearded lady . . . you *stinking* girl,
see me cry? Your sex, your beautiful face haven't ever made
me cry . . . but my father; and you stinking girl!"

"Shit on your father."

"Oh, it was so cold. . . . The beard was frozen, and the
gun went crunch against it when his . . . mouth opened.
. . . His tongue curled around the barrel. I was snuggled
against him in that pissed-in doorway, even all the bums
were gone, out of the cold . . . just room enough there for
two of us and the voice that was singing me to sleep. . . .
Then I heard that dissonance of lead through brain then
bone, and that was the song I'd been hearing."

They were out of the wood. Off away from them, in and
out of discreet dazes of electricity coming through the dark,
girls moved; and they heard an accidental clash of cymbals.

Janet Sanctissima's student was loping across the quadrangle bearing music manuscript, guitar and cymbals, preparing to approximate Greek music for the play. The grip on Ellen's wrist was loosening, and the voice in her ear was becoming less tear-stained, brisker.

"What the hell does any of this mean to me anyway?" Sanctissima said. She backed off completely from Ellen. "At midnight, my dear, I will be taking off into the air in one of those stunning whooshing jet planes, leaving here forever. . . . Can you believe it?" The words spat out of her like mouthfuls of mud.

"Someone—you'd never guess her name in a million years, but, just as a hint, think in terms of Flagstad, Lind, Tebaldi, Galli-Curci—*someone*—with not a single black buttock to her name, for your information—whom I loved twenty years ago, decided just last night—inspired by the gods no doubt—to love me back again. She sent me a telegram telling me so. Can you guess what she's like? She is a most golden-haired, full-bosomed lady with a voice as shining as her head. She sings like something born in a tree! We met in theory class. Oh, *theory!* And now, with her star rising even higher than that heaven where my original golden singer watches over me, she has begged me to come to her, to stand in the wings and hold her atomizer, to shake out her cloak and muffle her throat and play the scales for her morning voice. And at night . . . at night, you know . . . she will stand at the foot of the bed and sing that song . . . *you know what* . . . and then, *then,* unlike that original singer, she'll get *into* the bed, into it! And then she'll sing another song, that song even you can sing: *Sanctiiiiissima!*"

Sanctissima dropped the hurting wrist and threw her arms into the sweet air and into the soft crashing of the disappearing cymbals.

"What do I care about Papa when I've got that? Think of it . . . no more of the likes of you. . . . No more peering at pretty crossed knees at eight in the morning, no more describing Bayreuth to pretty crossed knees at eight in the morning! Papa, you can go to hell and take this one with you!"

Sanctissima tapped Ellen against the ear, folded her hands behind her back and walked off into the nearest patch of light, whistling the opening bars of her student's approximation of Greek music. Ellen folded the ends of her dirt-matted hair against her face and smelled, for the first time, the woods in her own hair: pine needle, fern frond, moss, mold, water, whiskey.

"Oh Ellen! You better come on, you better come on. I've looked all over."

Margaret had replaced Sanctissima there in the dark.

"All right. You better come on, Margaret."

When there wasn't a thing more that could be done to the new library, and all the grass and boxwood had been planted, the faculty nit-pickers had gathered in front of it to pick nit. Their group was composed of the youthful, devilish members of the English department, the Art instructors, and Mr. Pathways, who constituted, in his bony frame, the entire faculty of Greek and Latin. They had gathered in front of the shining domes and teakwood door handles of the Physical Education building, which housed the largest and most active school for female sport in the whole United States, and which had been built fourteen years earlier, while the library was still being housed in the subbasement of the Home Economics building—they had gathered to face the new library and pick nit.

The building squatted bright before them, three stories of T-shaped red brick. The architect, either bowing to the ante-bellum pressure groups or else wishing to remind the readers of the antique past, had built, as his final touch, an oval marble porch supported by six Corinthian columns against the front. Twenty broad steps of marble ascended on three sides. From a distance, and with one eye shut, the effect was vaguely (as the architect had intended) Parthenonian. From another angle (if one ignored the enormous bronze doors that took great strength to open), and with both eyes open, it was strictly Tara Hall.

"But anyway, Pathways," one of the Art instructors said, at last, "anyway, I see a chance for you to get your Greek play off that soggy golf course this spring. It ain't no amphitheatre, not by a long shot, but it won't do any of us any harm to watch the girls drape themselves around that marble in their draperies."

The new library's stoutest defender became the frail Mr. Pathways.

Crouched in the scratchy azaleas that banked the side steps of the library, Janet Sanctissima's student tuned her guitar, rubbed one finger around the edge of a cymbal, touched the bass drum with her toe and handed two tambourines to her assistant, who had returned at last with cigarettes. They began to chain-smoke and to wait. Out in the dark lawn behind the spotlights, hunched on bleachers, the audience blinked like fireflies as they dragged on their own cigarettes. The night was chilly for May; the newly soaked grass beneath the bleachers shifted in the night breeze and sent slivers of damp up into the trouser legs and short cotton skirts. The spotlights had been arranged to keep the library's red brick in darkness and to give the marble a look of white Greek sunshine.

A freshman climbed up through the bleachers with a flashlight and bashfully distributed programs still warm from the mimeograph machine. On the covers was a freehand drawing of a ruined temple; the same hand, even more freely, had printed, below the drawing:

THE TROJAN WOMEN
by Euripides

Presented by the Redwing College
for Women Classical Club

Directed by Dr. Wesley Pathways
Miss Ellen Fairbanks, Student Director

And:

Poseidon (the audience read, inside the program), God of the Sea; *Athene,* a goddess; *Hecabe,* widow of Priam, King of Troy; Chorus of captive Trojan women: Winnie Ruth Evans, Joanne Lee Furman, Mary Louise Henderson, Ola Ray Stroud, Iona Ruth Moye, Alma Jinnette Pringle, Eleanor Jo Graham, Dure Cope Gillikin; *Chorus Leader,* Ellen Fairbanks; *Talthybius,* a Greek herald; *Cassandra,* daughter of *Hecabe* (and, as the audience read and smoked, as the air dried and darkened and the light against the white marble began to glare and grow strong, Ellen was beating at the librarian's office door and calling, "Margaret, let me come in . . . I'm nervous; I feel bad here by myself. . . . I have to talk to you before it starts. Let me in!" But Margaret, becoming Cassandra behind the door, would not open and would not answer); *Andromache,* daughter-in-law of *Hecabe; Menelaus,* a general of the Greek army (Mr. Pathways, hidden behind the dictionaries, was adjusting the robes in which he had played nearly every hero of the Aegean for fifteen years; and he was listening to Ellen and feeling a small eyelet of meaning open. He wished that he were not a man so that he could help her. When she graduated, there would be no student or teacher left at Redwing to read Greek with him); *Helen,* wife of *Menelaus.*

Red gels had been slipped into the spotlights, and someone was causing them to flicker against the white marble: Troy's ruins were still smoldering two days after the city's capture. An instinct to cry *Fire! Fire!* shuddered across the audience.

In the bushes beneath the library's front windows, Sanctissima's student finally put her mouth to her flute and its sound slunk through the heating air from high to low, from high to low, always minor. Two tambourines shook, trembled for three prolonged beats; and stopped. The flute resumed, hysterical, keening: something was dead. Two girls, dressed in gold muslin, pushed open the bronze doors against the flames and then stood guard against them. They pointed their spears at the audience, then raised them to point at heaven. The flute shrieked, then was silent. The play had begun.

Just as the shouting and the sirens and the screamings were beginning, Margaret slipped away from all of it and hid herself in the librarian's office; and there Mr. Pathways found her and there they spent the rest of the night.

It is toward dawn, the rosy-fingered dawn, Mr. Pathways thinks as he lies on the leather couch and watches light break against the soiled drab of the sky. He closes his eyes for long moments, but some thud in Margaret's voice always wakens him and he has to drink again of the restorative brandy to make his heart keep going. Each time, the thud in her voice tries to knock his heart out cold. (When he was a little boy in Atlanta, his mother stroked her hand up and down his back while he sat on her lap in the garden, summers, by her on her bed, winters; and she had taught him Greek—α β γ δ; and the bad neighborhood boys had known, had cornered him, had said, *Sissy-sissy-bastard-queer-smells-his-mama's-underwear;* and he had whispered to himself, then, α β γ δ while they kicked and he sweated with fear. Now, all night long, he had said to himself, α β γ δ, while Margaret's voice kicked at him.) Now he thinks he sees all his dead heroes falling from the reddening sky and clambering over the windowsill to bear him away on his puny shield to the house of shades. And he wishes he could drive away the awful fantasy of flowers' scent that has possessed him all night long; but each time he corks the brandy, the smell of flowers returns.

It stinks of my funeral in here, he thinks; but there's not a flower in the whole building; it is a mystery, it is a clue to my future. . . . But Mr. Pathways has had his eyes on the dark ceiling all night; he has not looked at the floor where Margaret's headdress, her ribbon-garnished, florist-fashioned wreath of flowers, lies against the tufted wool of the librarian's Oriental rug. The librarian would smear his soles with rose pulp many times the next day before he would discover the source of the sweet rotting odor that was clinging to him.

Margaret is again beginning to describe (for the tenth time) the scenes that had occurred to end *The Trojan Women*. It does not matter to her that she is telling Mr. Pathways only what he already knows: he saw, of course, everything she saw; and she does not know, yet, that he was stung with the same celebrating emotion she had felt when the real blood had begun to spurt from real flesh. He must —*somebody* must—see it the way she still sees it, she thinks. At each retelling of the story, she erupts into violent shaking, throwing the story off herself as a retriever shakes off water after his swim for the duck; and she pulls the librarian's plaid blanket so tightly against her throat she nearly chokes on her story.

Mr. Pathways has had many chances to drown during the night from the accumulation of tears and sweat that Margaret has shaken off; but he does not seem aware of it. He listened once to her recital; since that first time, he has not listened. He drinks his brandy, smells the flowers, presses his thoughts down on the shield of the single heroic act of his life. He expects to die before day arrives entirely; and, as Margaret talks around him, he inspects his life from every angle, looks into all its crannies, tries to enlarge it, shine it up, make his swift, instinctual action of that evening enormous and worthy of the rowdy, blood-strewn Greek-speakers who are coming for him.

". . . and if only I had opened the door when she called me," Margaret was saying, "but there I was prissing around in front of a mirror like a whore, fixing myself up like that Botticelli picture, that *Primavera*, because I *am* just as pretty as that droopy-eyed old thing, but how goddamn, damn stupid—it was your fault, you should have stopped me—to dress up like that silly thing to play some broken-down Trojan girl. But that's what I wanted to be—to be *Spring* . . . tra-la, Spring!" Margaret groaned; the sound came up from her stomach. "So I got yards of this darling blue batiste and held it on me with a lot of gold cord . . . did you see just how *smart* I was the way I held that blue stuff on, crisscrossed my breasts in gold cord, my cute little breasts in thin gold frames? . . . And I *did it all* . . . did it all to get hold of Ellen again. I used to do it when I was the Countess and she was Cherubino and I knew I could do it again if only I could be a pretty *Primavera* instead of a broken-down crazy old Trojan girl!" She beat her fist against the rug; Mr. Pathways thought he heard the thud of Death against the door and stiffened, got ready.

". . . and I shot out that door screaming . . . crazy Cassandra . . . like a blue rocket going to fire into her, make her feel for *me* again. . . . And I was Spring itself, I'd dressed as Spring, remember, and I ran off the steps onto the grass and there she was swaying to the Greek and the chorus moved with her, like wind against her, but when she saw me, she stopped and broke it all and her chorus stumbled. . . . Maybe she thought, perhaps she thought . . . that I was coming to burn her down, burn her down with that torch I was carrying, treat her like the most *fabulous* of arsonists would—you know, after he's set the whole world on fire, then he's got nothing left to burn down but his own house.

"And that mountain girl who was doing the music, Sanctissima's student—that goddamn rotten Sanctissima—that mountain girl was forgetting where she was and forgetting her crazy Greek music and she was just strumming away on that guitar for herself, I think, and she was back home on some hill and making us listen to stuff about early spring mornings, maidens so sweet and fair, cuckoos piping, heartless young cads . . . but when I started yelling she stopped for me. . . . And Ellen let me go on and on with Cassandra's speech—maybe she'd planned on letting me, slipping up to the new end she'd made for that stinking play. It was as if . . . it was . . . it was *this way:* I know it. She had secretly gotten up some dance for herself that she was going to sneak into that play—you know she *can* be sneaky and ugly, no matter what you think—going to sneak it in the play so quick it would be over with before anybody could remember that old What's-his-name had never written a line about the Trojans having themselves some girl who rose up and changed history by leading a slaughter of the Greeks at the last minute!

"She was watching my face—but *everyone* was—while I said, 'Come and dance, Mother, dance with me: / Charm the Powers with lucky words, / Loudly chant your daughter's wedding-song! / Wildly whirl and turn in purest ecstasy! / Maids of Troy, / Wear your brightest gowns / Come, and sing my wedding-song, / Hail the lover Love and Fate appoint for me!' See? I still know it. Look at it this way: this poor crazy Cassandra has snapped, can't bear seeing her life get like her city—burn down—and she's raving on about her happy wedding day, and it can't get through to her that she's headed for the slave market, and Ellen's watching my crazy face and thinking, Well, why not? Why shouldn't she have some luck in life after all that prophesying stuff? Let's grab us a Greek and murder the bloody bastard and save Cassandra for ourselves! And all the time her hand was slithering like a snake inside her costume and getting ready to snatch out that steak knife. Have you ever in all your life seen anything so bright, the way it caught all that light and bounced it back against us? It was better . . . brighter than any moon . . . or spotlight . . . and she went straight up with it, straight through all those people, her arm stuck up tall as a tree with that knife growing out of her hand . . . and she was ready to take that murdering Greek in the heart!

"Sanctissima didn't move but must have known Ellen

66

was coming for her and sat still as stone, she just sat and waited, watching her with the rest of us . . . and the lights slid in streaks down the steel when Ellen put the knife in her chest . . . and with all that chorus following Ellen, right behind her—so used to her leading them, blind as sheep behind her while she went to Sanctissima right at the top of the bleachers . . . and the audience moved over and let them all by. What was Sanctissima thinking while it happened? Did that black soul of hers try to pray while the knife went inside and all the girls gathered around, bent over her with all their eyes and mouths painted in gray grease . . . and what did she feel—*repentance?*—when Ellen spat on her, hissed on her: Sanctiiis—sima! Sanctiiis—sima! . . . and her knife went for her heart? Thank God Ellen doesn't know where the heart is. . . .

"How fast you can move when you want to, Mr. Pathways. Right away you were there and the knife was in your hand and Ellen was down sprawled in the dark and your arm held up that old bitch while she bled red all over you. I did—I saw Sanctissima's face when Ellen was killing her: I swear she wouldn't have minded dying . . . she was *terribly* excited. . . . Then so bored when they bandaged her, when the police came, when the whole school got scared to death. *You* saw how dull she looked when they tucked her in the car and drove her to her airplane . . . you saw. No relief . . . no gratitude for being saved, restored, whatever. . . . Her face was happy only when she saw the knife falling down on her. Her face . . . as bright as the knife, the moon . . . all the lights together. . . . It was brighter—she was lighting herself up for that knife.

"And even before Ellen started the play, I was the one who really got it rolling . . . way back in the afternoon. I wanted Sanctissima to leave Ellen alone. That's what I wanted. So there she was in the dorm parlor—and I know what she was doing there, such an *obvious* old fool—and, *and* I didn't say a word, just walked right up and gave her something, gave her that picture Ellen's mother took of Ellen and me when we were five years old. We're standing together in a bunch of hollyhocks higher than our heads. We're wearing puffy bloomers that were printed with lions and tigers and elephants and we're both brown and barefooted. Ellen's hair was blacker then than it's ever been since, and mine was bleached like a bone, and we're standing in the hollyhocks with our arms around each other and our eyes squeezed tight—because of the sun or because we were so happy . . . I can't remember which; I wanted that vile woman to see how *nobody*—not her, not anybody—can upset fate and love and history: what I was destined for, what Ellen is destined for. And then I gave her the *Figaro* picture to see—but we were too old in that one, and Ellen's mother is in it—and what I wanted, what I wanted was . . . to impress her with the *very beginning*. But she took my pictures and stuffed them in her pocket like a dirty handkerchief and she took Ellen and she . . . *took* her dirty . . . *Ellen-seducing* . . . machinery, took it all down to the woods . . . away from me. . . .

"Where did Ellen go tonight? How did she disappear? Nothing of me will ever be any good anymore. . . ."

A weak breeze is slipping in beneath the windows. Mr. Pathways opens his eyes to examine what the morning is bringing: the fact that, after all, he is going to live. He concentrates on controlling the nausea this knowledge stimulates in him. The heroes, he sees, have watched him all through the dark and have again gone away without him . . . again, they found him wanting. He draws back his lips, he bares his teeth at the rosiness leaning on the window. He wants to howl out loud. He reaches out and switches off the dim lamp. In the corner, on the floor, there is the smudged, crushed outline of Margaret in her blanket. He wishes to be in the blanket with her, wrapped up in the dark again, still having a chance.

He said, "You simple-minded . . . slaves. You girls are simple slaves. That's the single conviction that's sustained me all these years in this pesthole—girls are *meant* to be slaves. Even when they prophesy, even when they rip through a tragedy dressed like *Primavera*s trying to promote the notion that it is a good thing to whirl this stinking planet through one more fertility rite. . . . One thing in all the world that I love and I'm not even sure I pronounce it correctly. Perhaps that's why they won't wait for me, come for me—they don't understand a word I say when I call them. *Absurd* girls, trying to act like Greeks—that Mozart fiddle-faddle is certainly all you're good for. A poisoned robe . . . infanticide . . . cannibalism . . . a head of curling snakes—not a chance in any of it for cowards like yourselves. You've wasted my night. No woman ever caused another woman to do anything. If any of you did a thing tonight . . . took action . . . became a stimulus, it was Sanctissima. But she's not a woman, not a man; she's neither here nor there. . . .

"Those women . . . they're outside this seasonal life the rest of us are bound and gagged against. If they have any place, it's back there with my lovely language that I can't pronounce. . . . But it makes no difference. There was a soldier out there, in oversized khaki, with a face like raw beefsteak; and when Ellen fell, he pulled her up and ran with her. 'Disappear'—silly-ass you! But if *she's* on a slave ship now . . . it will sink. I know it—even if she has to drown with it."

Mr. Pathways stood up and pulled his Menelaus costume into place. Then, with a slow second thought, he began to take the costume off, carefully, keeping it neat for another year. He pulled himself across the floor to Margaret on his hands and knees, keeping close to the wall to avoid the long red streaks now entering the room in droves. But, as he crept into the blanket with her, and lifted himself above her, the sunrise caught him full in the eyes; and when the rosy-fingered dawn covered his face—fully, from brow to chin—Mr. Pathways howled.

Margaret, feigning sleep, could see through her eyelids

the red shuffling at the window. The red seemed the color of a shriek, shrieking at her. When the papery, trembling hand was fitted against her breast, she welcomed it and held it down with her own.

Mr. Pathways was crying onto Margaret's collarbone. He was stammering: " 'Soon you will fall, and lie / With the earth you loved, and / None shall name you!' "

Margaret answered, "All right."

" 'Earth and her name are nothing; / All has vanished, and Troy is nothing!' "

"All right."

He said, " 'Farewell, Troy! / Now the lifted oar / Waits for us: / Ships of Greece, we come!' "

"All right," said Margaret.

It's my heart that's running, my brain, my arms, my guts, my nerves that are running, my red and white corpuscles racing each other, disease and health—but my legs are flying! The hard thud that shakes my heels second by second is the concrete of air, soon the concrete will rise and stiffen all of me, the coat of sweat that's poisoning me, my sucking lungs. All day long, my wrist gripped to the bone and me yanked to destinations not on my map; now, off the concrete—bare white feet soaking every step in dark grass —and sleepless children looking out their windows will scream they've seen a ghost pass in authentic white ghost suit: *It's a headless ghost, Mother, with black streamers where the head should be!* How superstition begins: wide-eyed children see running girls; running, mad, flat-bellied girls the mothers of superstition. *She was chasing after a poor soldier-boy, Mother, and her hand was on him, Mother!* Crush. My feet are on fanged stone; it's the town side of the woods. You aren't out of the woods yet. . . . Scented claws, hands damp with eau de cologne slapping, flaying my face alive; the poor soldier-boy ducks, but the branches lift their leaves and slap my eyes out. He can't find the path; "Watch it, water running here!" Witches can't float and he knows it; he didn't rescue me to drown me. Let me out, out, out—I'm back where I shouldn't be, back to the green sputtering, the pulse of this wood. Being pulled again, and things are crawling on me—hard-backed bugs, pale leaves that turn black when they touch me, earthworms that coil, retract, coil, retract over my skin; pollen that sticks to my tongue; and the trees are livid by the light of the moon; my hand will come off in his hand, and he'll keep on running, the one-handed moaning girl will wander through the wood until the goblins come and give her a bucket for a hand and fill it full of her desires; in their underground world, she'll eat and drink from her hand. "Keep on running!" Run me to still-life: the sign says "Teddy's" in dim red and blue, with half the *e* and *y* already burnt out. Not even a college boy would drink there in the high-backed leatherette booths, with ashtrays humpbacked with old butts, with little ladies—top-heavy, bottom-heavy little ladies shoehorned into satin and nylon—cross-legged at the bar from nine till closing, when the cloistered crapshooters hear the rap on their back-room door, leave the cold dice.

They leaned against the wall until their breaths came at least as slowly as the blinking of Teddy's name above them.

"Godalmighty!" he gasped. He pounded his hard-working chest and slung his arms. "Godalmighty, can I take you inside, look at you!" His breath was chugging back, his words chugging out; it seemed to be no trouble at all for him. "Guess I can, guess this joint's seen worse than you, but blood's come off your hand all over mine, and, baby, that's got to be the first thing fixed, the toilet's at the rear, and I'll get some clothes fixed for you with one of the little ladies—you can't screw around no longer in that bright nighty-night—*Estelle!*—she's the one can always spare something for a buddy—and then we'll drink a little, dance a little and who-knows-what, and then split like crazy where

72

no bull in all the world can get to you—you ain't the first little lady I pulled out of a bad spot—goddamned high-tone bad spot I got *you* out of—but scratch the superficial and there ain't a thing different about you from any other hot-blooded woman I ever run with, especially my sister Bethel —didn't I or didn't I not get her over many state lines after she up and carved her husband who was asking for it one real hot day and then bonked her kids over the head with a Nehi bottle—I *did* do it and didn't ask no questions at no time, either, and to this day we still send postcards— I mail to Jacksonville, Biloxi, all over, and still don't ask no questions of her or any other woman. Women love me. I want to know your name."

"Eustacia Vye."

"Jesus."

"What's . . . yours?" The soldier-boy was taking all the breath there was; she couldn't find any at all for herself.

"Uh-*huh*—it was a deal, I don't ask no questions, and you don't either."

"Why did you drag me away from there? I know I didn't kill her; I didn't have to run." But the running had been more wonderful than the killing. She shuddered, and her lungs began moving in the old way.

"Well, why do you think? I come there number one to get you and number two to have a date. After I go to that kind of trouble I don't number three expect the disappointment of seeing my date haul ass off with some bull to get a third degree, I don't care what she's done. That's another reason why women love me, I'm dependable."

Ellen looked straight into his face. It had not changed since her first meeting with it the day before, but now, for the first time, in the blue and red illumination from Teddy's name, she really watched it. There was no trace of irony in it: it was a face composed of thick human meat and plain unvarnished truth according to its own lights. The eyes were shallow wells of bright blue artlessness. His hair was brick red. She was moved to tell him her real name, but did not.

"You think we can go in now?" she asked.

"What are we waiting for? You just light out straight for that toilet at the end of the bar—here's my comb—and make yourself look straight as you can while I have a little talk with Estelle. And you stay back there till she comes with the clothes. Teddy's gonna think I robbed the in-sane asylum as it is."

"Will she . . . will he?"

She could turn and run again; she could throw herself at a policeman, she could bang on the door of the house across the street where the blue glow of television flickered images of cowboys and hair dye out the windows. And someone would come and take her back to the college where she could rest on the clean infirmary pillow and watch their eyes widen at the story of the Sanctissima's wickedness that made her do it, at the story of the criminal soldier-boy and his murdering sister. And the next day, she would graduate with Margaret and be supported in the late afternoon at her father's graveside. Why didn't she run? The running had been more wonderful than the thought of killing.

Through the house's windows, the cowboys were lynching an innocent Mexican; the family was lifting drumsticks and thighs to their mouths, chewing, swallowing, watching. In a second she could be inside, and they would pass her the chicken, and she could watch the inevitable coming of justice while the head of the household made the phone call. She couldn't run anymore: the traffic through the rabbit's hole is downward, and one-way.

She stumbled, and fell heavily against the soldier-boy.

"Now, whoa!" said the soldier-boy; and he jumped back so that she had to dance sideways to keep from going down to the street. "Don't you pull no shit at this stage. Just go on in and old Teddy'll fix you up with his specialty."

Through the padded, swinging door, he held her by the elbow, and her feet slid like the creepy-crawl of the bogyman across the star- and moon-patterned linoleum, feathery with sandy dirt; and her head bobbed through the funk of beer smell. The hand was gone off her elbow; and another, thinner door clicked shut behind her. Inside the narrow cement cell the air was sharp with cold and Lysol. In one corner, the toilet seat was flaking off another coat of white paint, but it was scrupulously clean. Facing it was a dressing table with a round, unframed mirror and a flowered chintz skirt so faded with cleanness that she had to stare hard for several seconds to see that the disappearing flowers were full-bloomed roses and bluebells. The sink ran cold water that halted the moment she took her hand from the faucet. Written on the wall around the roller towel was a hodgepodge of first names, telephone numbers, obscenities; drawings of valentines and cupid's arrows and of erect phalluses as long and thick as her upper arm. All were done in lipstick, in shades ranging from pink to purple. Ellen read them all, wondering, Who's Lynn, who's Betty Nell, who's Bar-Dee, who's Mick the Greatest Fuck in Town; wondering if anyone had answered the scrubbed-down advertisement: "Want Sex Tonight? Call Bar-Dee Simpson the Greatest Fuck in Town."

When there was nothing left to wonder about, and to keep thought and recollection away, Ellen began to use the room, flushing, running the cold water until her hands and face were dazed, combing until her scalp ached in front of the mirror that was vivid with her stunned face, her swift hands, her crackling hair leaping up against the soldier-boy's comb. The cold was beginning to cut bone-deep through her grass-smeared tunic; the Lysol was forming tears beneath her eyelids; the walls of the cell were creeping up, tightening up, inevitably to crush her. There were no shadows anywhere in the cell. She threw her hands around her face and crawled beneath and hunched beneath the skirt of fading flowers. Outside the room—if there was an outside to that room—there was a jukebox against the wall, and someone was feeding in fistfuls of quarters. The bones in Ellen's pointing elbows, the skirt of flowers, the tin box holding the roller towel—all began to vibrate to the ground tone of the basses, began to shake in syncopation against the beat of electric guitars: "I wuzzz the uh-ther woman!" sang the machine. A finger of paint slid gently to the floor from the toilet seat.

"Well, I don't see nobody," said someone to herself.

Ellen crawled out and stood up and saw Estelle.

"Yes, she's here—I'm here," said Ellen.

"There's one thing Teddy don't allow in this here bar, niggers and jail-bait, and you're white as me but sure as hell I think that crazy soldier-boy's swung his ass just a little too close to the cradle this time around, don't you agree? Teddy's going to be mad as fire."

Estelle seemed to be made of chunky but smooth-running, well-oiled machine parts, each fitting tensely on top of the other. Only her red hair was allowed to go free and untamed down from its black roots to swish around the back of her nylon blouse. And beneath the ruffly nylon, a black satin brassière stood up, huge, pointed, and meaning business with its every stitch and hook doing its efficient best. Her motorized hips, curving abundantly and instantly from her waist, were channeled into neat red faille that was lined with something slithery sounding. A long slit up the skirt showed a muscular thigh in black net and the pure white of a garter strap. Estelle carried a black pocketbook as wide and nearly as thick as her hips; a du Maurier cigarette worked its way from one corner to the other of her purple mouth; and its smoke made her eyes wince behind their shutters of mascara.

Ellen, intimidated by it all, began to feel underage, though she was absolutely sure that she was legal for anything at all.

"I'm harmless," said Ellen.

"That ain't what I heard." She heaved the big black bag to the dressing table. "But I'll give you the benefit, but ragging our ass you are, kid. If there's one thing I know in my life, it's how to do a turtle-snap with my cunt, Scripture, and Thomas Hardy. I was born with the turtle-snap—you either got it or you don't—but I achieved the other two holed up with a tired-out drunk for a week-long stretch in this town's lowest-down fleabag. The drunk, being drunk, could not take much advantage of my natural talent, but still he would not pay me and let me go. So while he slept and drank—drink which I do not touch in any form—and ofttimes tried to get it up, I read Gideon's Bible and the smart-ass bellhop's *Collected Works of Thomas Hardy* which I got in exchange for a quick turtle-snap whilst the drunk was in the can. *Eustacia Vye,* shit! That is one chick you are not."

"Estelle . . . you're Estelle?"

"Call me anything you like, just don't call me late for supper!" Estelle's laugh at her own joke propelled her onto the dressing table's stool and caused her cigarette—still deeply embedded in one corner of the purple—to wiggle up a panicky smoke signal.

Ellen clasped her hands together and wished she could use them to stroke the red electric mop that bounced around the nylon back as Estelle giggled. Ellen was being drawn into a warm, slow-heating oven of security. Estelle's professional hauteur, her straight-backed self-confidence were, to Ellen, as restful and as gorgeous as sleep.

"I'm sorry about Eustacia Vye. It was just an idea or something. I'll tell you or Soldier-Boy or Teddy or anybody my name, it's . . ."

Estelle held up her hand. "Just a minute, sugar," she interrupted. "As far as I and Teddy and Soldier-Boy are concerned you just want to go on like you started . . . less you know, less you want to know, right? Who's Soldier-Boy,

77

after all? Just old AWOL . . . long-time AWOL—Soldier-Boy. Just call *him* Diggory Venn—that ought to straighten me up for a few laughs when I hear it. As Jesus Christ said, What's in a name?—Leviticus 4:15."

There was impatient, thick-knuckled beating on the door.

"Don't open it," Estelle said, getting busy pulling clothing from her bag. "That's nobody but old Diggory losing at the crap game and wanting himself a handful of hot tail. You, I guess. The girls know they can take a leak in the men's if they have to."

"What in the fuck is happening in there? Estelle, you've had time to dress her for a preacher's funeral!" Soldier-Boy's army boot followed his fist to the door, hard and loud. "Get a move on, or else this here guaranteed made-of-honey motherfucker is going to huff and puff and blow you-all's house *in!*"

Estelle stamped on the du Maurier butt. Unencumbered, her mouth opened wide and red. "Cool it, you loud-mouth son," she bellowed, "cool it!"

Soldier-Boy, on the other side, shut up. Immediately, the jukebox clicked and whirred; at top volume it spoke: "Shake it up, Baby! Twist and shout!" Thudding, shuffling noises against the linoleum answered it.

"Dancing," Estelle breathed. "Dancing! Teddy's going let us dance." She ran a little finger over her purple lips and smeared her skirt down closer against her thighs. "Honey, listen, I got to go and dance! Get those clothes on and use that lipstick like a grown woman and come on out and I'll dance with you. Can you shake that thing? My best girl friend Annie Laurie can't shake that thing one bit; she is one drag for dancing—hurry!" Estelle's hips rotated as though they were soaked in grease. She slung her shoulders back and let the door slam behind her.

Ellen, in silence, watching herself in the mirror, saw what she was like, like an Easter lily in mid-July, rotting in its silver-foiled pot, its petals blackened and stinking. She remembered the hollyhock flowers bending their hot and dusty heads over Baby Ellen and Baby Margaret. If Sanctissima is dead—*if* she is dead—they'll give me rhinestone harlequin sunglasses to wear and they'll peroxide my hair into a yellow beehive. Stiletto heels, rhinestone earrings, tight black suit. Led into court by fat-jowled detectives: all to make my aspect fit for print.

There was a burst of excitement in the courtroom today in the third month of the trial of Ellen Fairbanks for the murder of Janet Hart-of-Gold. Occasionally crossing and uncrossing her shapely legs, Miss Fairbanks gave her version of the sensational tragedy, to which she pleads not guilty. "I believe that Greek is the most vicious and corrupting course of study to which a young girl can be exposed, especially if the young girl is as innocent about the evils of the world as was I; especially if she has been raised, as was I, on the sweet, unsexual genius of Wolfgang Amadeus Mozart," began Miss Fairbanks. "Let me hasten to say that it is not only learning the Lord's Prayer in Greek that so ill befits the young virgin, but also her involvement—her actual performance in—those grotesque parodies of real life known as the ancient Greek drama. Those plays, which were written by hedonistic, sex-crazed perverts—who have been dead these many years—are highly commended to her by cynical professors who often share the immoral predilections of the playwrights themselves. Urged by her professors to immerse herself in the un-Christian and totally un-American viewpoints which these plays express, the young girl's impressionable brain is soon warped beyond repair. Her mind is beset by lurid visions; her gentle upbringing is snickered at by her professor, who insinuates such examples of *true womanhood* in her clouded thinking as *Medea! Electra! Hecuba! Cassandra! Sappho!* I blush now to name their crimes—incest, child murder, insanity, fortune-telling, unnatural sex. It is not long before the girl has forgotten her true destiny as wife, homemaker, mother of decent American citizens. She returns her engagement ring, she breaks the heart of the clean young man who has dreamed of leading her, radiant and unsullied, to the altar on that glad day when he has made the first down payment on the ranch split-level of which they have so often dreamed,

79

parked together in the moonlight. Her sewing machine lies neglected; she fails her Home Economics course in 'Nutrition for a Family of Six.' How long does it take before she is seen in the company of rowdy companions, tasting, perhaps, her first cocktail? How long is it before she is solely and simply out for a Good Time? How long is it before she is spending her days—and, oh, my friends, her nights!—in the company of females around whom rumors of neckties abound? All unknowing of the hell that awaits her, of the honest tears that are shed for her, she takes her final step into degradation, aping the sentiments expressed by that unfortunate creature—Greek, of course—who pressed her unnatural affections on similar innocents thousands of years ago—and then had the gall to write about it! I do not mince my words—as unlikely as it seems, there is sex forced on this young girl barely out of her mother's arms! Sex everywhere! *Outdoor* sex! Yes, my friends, it has all happened to this wretch who stands before you today. There I was, enmeshed in the unholy passion of the experienced, crafty Sanctissima; and there I was displaying myself in that devil-inspired play, *The Trojan Women!* Did I realize what I was doing when I secreted that steak knife in the brief, immodest garment I wore before the leering throng? Did I truly have a calculated plan for murder? That I cannot tell you, my friends. Redeemed as I am today, it is hard to look back into the monstrous imaginings of the young sinner that I was yesterday. I only know that as I stood mouthing those unrhymed obscenities with my other misguided sisters, there came suddenly a vision to me of purity, cleanliness, innocence—like the sound of Mozart's sopranos, like a vision of untrammeled spring virtue! Before this loveliness—heaven-sent!—I could feel all of a sudden the filth of my behavior creeping through my soul like a giant worm. I turned; there before me, grinning suggestively, was Sanctissima— she who had tipped the scales entirely in favor of perdition; she who had led me that final step into lechery and good times. I saw her: she was Evil personified. My friends, I could not, with a single stroke of a knife, rid the world of Euripides, Socrates, Plato, Aeschylus—and Jane Harrison, Gilbert Murray, H. D. F. Kitto, Phillip Vellacott!—but I could kill Sanctissima; I *could* forestall the corruption of others like myself. So with that vision of sweet springtime before me, I reached out and stabbed Sanctissima in the heart, in her black and shriveled heart! Yes, I plead: Not Guilty! Your real villain, your real murderer, my friends, waits on the shelves of your home libraries, is perhaps at this moment in the hands of your daughters as you pay good money for their educations. Your murderer, my friends, is the Greek drama!" The sensation in the courtroom following Miss Fairbanks' testimony was quelled only when Judge Euripides Aristotle Zenoussi sentenced Miss Fairbanks to the electric chair.

But if Sanctissima is alive, thought Ellen, if I did not kill her—and I know I did not—perhaps she is at home wishing I were with her. Perhaps she has changed her mind, and loves me.

Ellen fell on her knees before the toilet. Vomiting shook her. When she had finished, she drenched her face in the water again and dressed herself in Estelle's clothes.

"May I have this here cha-cha?" said Soldier-Boy.

Ellen lifted a numb arm to clink martini glasses with Estelle, but no sound came. She focused her eyes. Estelle's place, across the table, was wiped clean and dry. Estelle's ashtray was empty and polished.

"She is long gone," said Soldier-Boy. "Sunday is *the* busy night for Estelle. Let's have some of that there fancy tail-work you was showing off with her!"

How simple, how lovely it is to dance on the linoleum with Soldier-Boy and Estelle! I float, I shimmy with the beat; I am Fred Astaire and Ginger Rogers dancing on the ceiling; I am the original hootchie-cootch!

"Cha-cha-*cha!* Oh, shake that thing, sugar!" Soldier-Boy was a great redheaded turkey; he danced with his face lifted in smiles, with arms akimbo and flapping, trying to take off with him. The cha-cha ended in a smash of brass. Soldier-Boy stopped dead, his arms poised mid-air, his head cocked to catch the next sound. Ellen fell forward, hooking her chin on his shoulder; the music came, and he gathered up the rest of her and began pushing her across the moons and the stars.

"That's just what I thought I punched next," he said. The music swayed and went bump every fourth beat. With every bump, Soldier-Boy's knee knocked against Ellen's crotch, a small but important bash against the bone.

" 'Loooo-ve is a manny splintered thang!' " sang Soldier-Boy, as much to the rest of the bar as to Ellen. "This is what I like best—romance music," he said.

First he tilted her forward, then backward; then the knee again in the crotch. " 'It's the Ap-rell rose that only grows in the earrrly sprang'. . . . You should have been here last month. That's when Teddy decided to put on some class around here, so he picked me. Every Sunday night I got to wear this white jacket? And a black bow tie? And I'd start the ball rolling with 'Love Is a Manny Splintered Thang' and then end up with my best loud piece, which is 'Give Me Some Men Who Are Stout-Hearted Men,' which is what I learnt in high school before they said shoo, boy, out of *this* here school because I tried a little something on—well, *raped,* I guess—that English teacher with the big tits, and I had to leave town fast. It went just great for two Sundays in a row but then Teddy said I got to cut it out because the customers wanted to watch the fights then. I said I would sing after the fights; but Teddy said no, and I just happen to know it wasn't the fights was why I had to quit what was going to be my career once I get out of this Service, but old Estelle fucking up my act. She was just jealous, being nothing but a good old piece of tail herself with no career, and she would start yelling out just when I was starting on 'Give Me Some Men Who Are Stout-Hearted Men,' she would yell out, 'Give me some men who are stout-hearted men and I'll soon show you ten thousand *whores!*' And she got everything ruined for me just when they all had got talking about getting me on *Ted Mack's Amateur Hour*. Ain't that right, Teddy?"

Soldier-Boy began to sing all the words to "Give Me Some Men"; but he sang them to the tune of "Love Is a Manny Splintered Thang."

It was Teddy tapping her on the shoulder. He was all enormous beer belly; and it was swathed in a giant-sized wraparound white apron that swept the floor like the hem of a cassock.

"We got to close. Get out, Soldier-Boy. Let me tell you. That there is jail-bait you got there."

Soldier-Boy stopped dancing and leaned close against the beer belly. Ellen, without music and unsupported, sank to the harmless floor.

"You watch out, Teddy," Soldier-Boy was saying. "You watch out what you call my dates. If you look close you will see that this date of mine is wearing one of Estelle's most fabulous creations—it is, if you will look close, not even her work clothes but a nice black dress with a built-in bra that she wears to collect unemployment in. Don't that go to show just how much we trust this here so-called jail-bait? And this here so-called jail-bait just happened to knife somebody tonight, so I wouldn't go around calling that underage if I was you. I'd watch my mouth if I was you."

It was dark not only inside her head, it was dark everywhere. The air was no longer full of beer and smoke; it was scented with the first of June. It was the first day of June; flowers were exhaling night sweetness. A red streak of dawn bent down and touched her.

Soldier-Boy's only window commanded a fine view of Teddy's sign, which blinked once, twice, and then went out. It left, over the world that she could see, a thin haze of exhaustion bloodshot with sun; becoming day. Soldier-Boy yanked down his green shade. In the lightening dark, he became a dancing ghost shedding its clothes; one shoe off, then a hop and a skip; then the trouser leg around the ankle. One shoe on, with a lace too knotted for loosening beneath thick fingers; whimpers of frustration. Bound by his clothing, Soldier-Boy was hopping and dancing; his dog tags jingled in the light fur of his chest. Giving up the dance, he fell, heavily, to his hands and knees.

"Hell hell help me. . . ." He was sobbing against the lavender fringe of the bath mat beside his bed. "Girl? Eustacia? If only the shoe would come off, the pants won't come off without the shoe comes off. . . . Eustacia?"

"In a minute."

The window shade is like a vat of green dye, tinting the light that dips through it pale green. All the light in the room seems green; but the light everywhere, at the window, in the room, is outlined by gray, leftover night: the light has a ghost in its arms.

Soldier-Boy, hunched over his mat, is making noises, responses to the noises the birds are beginning to make—sleepy, bubbling, deep in the throat. Ellen cannot tell whether it is harsh breathing or weeping that she is hearing. There is a color, like the feel of green, of a bird's song painted in her throat; she feels it there. One bird is breaking from the noise, is beginning a song. There is the color of the air inside the room, green air now changing to green water and filling the room and pushing against her skin like a crush of velour. Soldier-Boy will drown first; his mouth is open, inviting the water to let him drink all of it.

Standing there against the window frame, Ellen is dreaming of the long, slow motions of her mother's evenings in the three-personed country that Ellen comes from (the others in the house disappear like ghosts when the three of them, Roger, May-Ellen, Ellen—father, mother, daughter—try to be together, watching, listening to each other). There is a final clank of knife against fork; and her mother's hands hold the heavy silver handles for a second above the china's rim before she lets them drop. Ellen and Roger smile at her, and she smiles back, speechless, before she starts her journey into the evening. Barking begins behind the door into the kitchen where Hortense is waiting, not a second too soon, for the leftovers. Ellen's mother leaves the chair and her napkin falls. And in a moment, there is the rustle of her wide skirt against the piano bench. When the music begins, Roger and Ellen begin to chew again. Never anything in the evenings but Chopin and Liszt. "That other stuff? Mozart, you know? It's just too hard-headed for me after a long, long day." On and on until ten o'clock, when the mailman's newspaper is folded and smoothed and inserted with yesterday's into the magazine rack; and the mailman's wife is folding shut the piano lid and begins to carry her saucer of nearly a pack's worth of cigarette butts and ashes, that have burned for her while she played, out into the black garden, where she pours them over some flower bed, "where they will do some good." And then the last lap of her journey, beginning the expedition to morning and the hard-headed Mozart: the wife leads the mailman up the narrow flight of stairs. Ellen, through the wide-hipped banister railings, watches them go, consumed with the thought of them together at the top of the stairs, in the giant bed, in the giant's room. Will the evenings of the mailman's wife now become much longer, slower, smoother, without the mailman? Without the rattle of the newspaper to hush the piano, how long will the mazurkas and waltzes and rhapsodies go on? This dawn, the saucer of ashes will be overflowing onto the ivory keys, and the mailman's wife will be out of tunes and cigarettes. The giant's bed, this night, will swallow the mailman's wife whole; and, when they go to look for her, though they pommel and pound, shake the linen and beat the mattress, they will never find a clue that her body's been there—except, perhaps, for a nicotine stain where her fingers have rubbed, or the sound of some jittery clicking from beneath the covers—again, unmistakably, her fingers at work, or the ghosts of them, remembering the long runs and trills, forgetting that the piano lid's shut tight. With Ellen in the bed (Ellen dreams) Ellen will weight it: Ellen propping open the jaws of the giant's bed with her own body so that the mailman's wife can sleep easy.

Someone in the street below slams a door and shouts, "Are you ready, hurry!" Another door slams, and Ellen, looking down, sees two men with fishing poles and buckets drive away in an old maroon Buick.

A minute—at least—was up. Her drunk, warm and woven about her since Teddy's second martini, was beginning to shred and let in drafts of anxiety. The fabric's largest hole was between her eyes. The light was stuffing itself in there, heavy as bricks, thick as cotton. It was time to move away from the window and help Soldier-Boy with his trousers;

only when she lay bouncing beneath him would she permit herself to imagine the president of Redwing giving her description to the FBI. And would Soldier-Boy finish, and receive her gratitude, before his door burst open against the shoulders of the men in pin-striped, double-breasted suits . . . ? She hoped that they would pull Soldier-Boy away from her before they blazed holes in her chest with heavy revolvers. . . . It was Humphrey Bogart in a slouch hat pointing the gun at her.

Soldier-Boy's hair glimmered on the lavender; the window shade, flying away from its sill, let sun press against his hair. Sun absorbed his hair and made it invisible. He crouched like a huge, muscled infant asleep in a crib. Soldier-Boy was asleep, his knees drawn up beneath his belly, his arms tucked beneath his chest. Ellen stealthily moved her hand through his chest fur, reaching for the dog tags. What would happen if the name engraved on them was *Diggory Venn?* When she touched the silvery disks, Soldier-Boy hunched himself smaller, sighed, took his tags in his own hand and held them tightly. Ellen sat back on the mat and watched him sleep; then she lay down beside him, joined his sleeping.

M̲r. Pathways, at the open door, spoke in Greek:
"Πoυ μoι τα ῥoδα"
Ellen did not open her eyes or lift her head; but she translated: *Where are my roses?*

"Πoυ μoι τα ία" said Mr. Pathways.
Where are my violets? said Ellen.

"Πoυ μoι τα καλα σελινα" said Mr. Pathways.
Where is the beautiful parsley? said Ellen.

Soldier-Boy slept on, twitching in his sleep like an old hound with dreams of chasing and catching. Three people in the room were awake; all three faces had hungry looks. One looked at the other as though it were a huge meal. Behind Pathways, Margaret was standing already dressed and polished for graduation. She looked as though someone had stuffed her, like a doll, into her clothes, doing the work for her; on her face was the patient smile of a doll. She held up a compact mirror, watching her face, admiring its color, the color of bleached bone about to crumble to dust. When she spoke, it was into her mirror; and she continued to speak to the mirror alone; her lips spoke to her and she answered her lips.

88

Margaret rattled off the answers to the questions: "Here are your roses, here are your violets, here is your beautiful parsley."

She was describing herself; she was the answer to the Greek questions: red, violet, green; but not a trace of those colors lingered on her. She had been Cassandra, garnished head to toe in them.

"Let's go, Ellen; now, before he wakes up," said Mr. Pathways. "I am very weak, weaker this morning than I have ever been. I would loathe to fight this Hercules, this Ulysses, for the prize he's fairly won. Things look black, very black indeed!" He was speaking into the enormous voltage of light being shed into the room by greenish sun, by Soldier-Boy's head, by white Margaret.

Ellen unwound herself from the mat, slowly, first to her knees, then to her feet, finding that legs, even when trembling, can support you when they are your own.

"I meant," said Ellen to the glaring hair, "to go right on belonging to him—or, as you say, teacher, to go on behaving properly as a properly conquered enemy should. . . ."

"He's no conquering Greek. You're no grief-stained Trojan . . . *Cherubino*," he added in a malicious whisper.

"*Je ne comprends pas*," said Margaret, into her mirror.

"I think you're both crazy," said Ellen. "What has she told you about Cherubino? He said he would hide me under a blanket in the back of his maroon Buick until we got across the state line. Then, he said, I'd sit up front with him and we'd start out to find his sister Bethel in Jacksonville, and then we'd get rid of the Buick and wipe off all our fingerprints and we'd steal a fishing boat and live with Bethel on the boat and fish for food. And soon, when he'd got boats all figured out, he could steal a yacht and take us to Paris, France, where he'd keep us, Bethel and me, as swell as he could in perfume and in dresses with built-in bras; and he said he'd lock us in at night while he was out learning French."

"The wine-dark sea . . . " said Mr. Pathways, blinking his eyes against the light in the room.

"*Je ne comprends pas*," said Margaret into her mirror. The sun, shifting, hit her mirror and began flashing signals around the room.

"I mean it, you're both crazy! Here I am a murderess!" Ellen shouted.

"Sanctissima's far from dead," said Mr. Pathways. "But, even so, to us—to Margaret and me—she doesn't exist anymore; so why should she for you?" (He tugged Margaret to him; her shoes scraped to him like the sound of a wooden plank being dragged over the floor.) "Things are quiet, very, very quiet, back at school. They're simply, very quietly, waiting to give you a degree and say goodbye forever, you silly girl. They agree with me—that you should have spent more time on your Latin and less groping about for tragedy, like all the other adolescents . . . *Cherubino*," he added slyly. "But why should I complain? Look at me: it's taken me this long to learn that even I am not worthy of tragedy . . . worthy of the heroes. That boy on the floor will absorb it with his food and air and not even know its name. He'll be a hero and not even know the word— exactly like the real heroes. Did I, after all, run with you? Look!"

He was holding the steak knife high in the air; Margaret's signal flashed against it. He twisted the knife; the signals flashed faster.

"I want to kill my enemy with this knife," said Pathways. "While he has nothing but a lavender mat for a shield—before he earns even more honor and can cover himself with . . . I don't know . . . bronze! . . . beaten gold! . . . I want to kill him."

He held the knife toward Ellen. "Here," he screeched. Tears inched down his long gray nose. "Here! You do it. Rise up and slay your conqueror. . . . It's your duty as a captured race. You won't? And I can't. . . . Did just a little blood kill your appetite for freedom, Ellen?" He dragged his seersucker sleeve across his nose, crushing it.

"*Je ne comprends pas,*" said Margaret into her mirror.

"Look at him," whispered Mr. Pathways. He flourished the knife in a killing motion, increasing the signals. "He lies there like a dog, drunk, snoring, secure . . . like any conquering hero. Won't you kill him?"

Pathways sighed; Margaret sighed with him, clouding her mirror. He opened the closet door and threw the knife among a pile of rusting hangers on the floor. The room grew dim and green again. Pathways took his shabby trench coat off and draped it over Ellen's head. He pulled it tight, buttoned it in front, pinning her inside; only her face showed.

"There," he said. "Wolf in sheep's clothing. Come downstairs now, ladies, to my miraculous all-black Morris Minor. The play is over. Never tell a soul you've seen me cry. Ellen, you looked so ruined. . . ." They were leaving without a last look at Soldier-Boy; they were struggling down narrow stairs, with Mr. Pathways balancing Margaret by her elbow, helping her keep the necessary mirror before her face.

"Ellen, you look awful. Look at Margaret . . . all clean and shiny and golden in her darling little . . . what is it, Margaret? Voile?"

They were outside the front door. The first of June blasted them. "*Je ne comprends pas,*" Margaret whispered. "*No.* Dotted swiss," she added, loudly, irritably.

Mr. Pathways chuckled. He rubbed his hands in the sunshine as if he were before a fire. "Dotted swiss," he repeated. "As you say, my dear."

They were folding themselves into the little car. "And, by the way, Ellen," he said, slamming the door behind her, "you owe not a thing to anybody . . . not a thing. Understand? Not a thing for this rescue. Margaret and I have already paid your debts, haven't we, Margaret?"

He began to drive.

"*Je ne comprends pas,*" said Margaret.

Traveling home, back to where the funeral is, back to where people, when they mean to murder, accomplish murder. *Je ne comprends pas,* Margaret kept saying; but I do: Sanctissima is alive and well and she is not my corpse and she will never be my ghost. Sanctissima, like me, is alive and well and traveling through the middle of the night.

Sanctissima is traveling through it; and it is beating at her from the bottom, compressing against her from the top and sides. The jet, as she knew it would, is wooshing. She is facing the night through her porthole's thick glass and trying to arrange her mind around the stars beyond it. The attempt is making her shoulder throb and the bandage on it tighten. The wound's heat is rising and seeming to bake her face; the rest of her is shivering in the cold monstrosity that's carrying her where she wanted to go, through the middle of the night. She is missing my knife. If I could give it back to her, the hole in her shoulder would be filled; her flesh would reknit itself around my steel. Soldiers and gunfighters can carry bullets, without harm, in their brains for years. She is turning her mind back to her pain..

This lessens the pain and seems to protect her from the menacing beams the stars are turning against her. Sanctissima thinks that the universe at night is the essence of hell. It looms, biding its time, waiting to suck her up to float forever in the stars' swill. Sanctissima questions, as I do, the sanity of those saints who are pictured praying with uplifted eyes.

A knee, taut in its nylon, is touching hers.

"Excuse me." The knee withdraws, and Sanctissima takes her vodka from the little tray. They stroke on through the middle of the night so steadily that the ice in the drink makes hardly a sound until Sanctissima stirs it: she is putting her forefinger between the ice cubes and stirring. She is drinking and, over the rim of her glass, peeking at the stewardess. The face she sees is blank and pretty and seems to her like all the faces of students who happily fail her courses and go off to lead happy lives. Now she leans into the aisle to watch the girl move away. The ankles, unlike the face, appeal to her. Indeed, the stewardess is very much like any old student; Sanctissima feels at home there. The ankle is turning and wavering above its high heel as a flower occasionally—rarely—does when blown in the right direction. Sanctissima's neck is stretching farther around her seat, longer into the aisle. Sanctissima's neck is becoming a lengthy white serpent; the serpent's tongue is flickering out, feeling the distance it must cross before it can taste the neat package of bone and skin and stocking.

The plane is dipping and Sanctissima presses herself back hard into the seat. She fumbles in her briefcase, draws out her album of Bach *Inventions* and begins to beat her fingers against the page in a silent performance, casting Bach's spell against the erotic, the romantic. Her sniveling, lying papa has told her many times that nothing drowns a thirst for flesh so surely as a Bach Invention. She is hearkening to her papa's words; and she is finding cause to doubt them. Her fingers thunder on; the music is thrusting aside the ankle, the ankle is thrusting aside the music. Her fingers are stumbling, making mistakes that sour her mouth and twist her stomach. She knows what's wrong: there is a flaxen voice inside the music, weaving itself around the hard black notes and pushing her hands off the page. It is singing "Dido's Lament"; it is no respecter of Bach. A pointed bosom goes with the voice; it rises and falls with the song beneath Sanctissima's cupped palms; her teeth unclench.

She slams the album shut, smashing the bosom, the song, the voice and Bach's Invention into one thick mess. She lifts her drink because the ankles will not return until she wants more.

Pathways, I imagine, gave her a parting gift, bashfully shoved it at her while he giggled, giggled the way a cat whines at a door. She will open it now while there is nothing else to do, tearing at pink tissue paper, balling up silver ribbon, throwing it beneath her seat. It will be a little book of only thirty pages, with lavender covers, a gold-stamped title: *The Collected Poems of Renée Vivien*. Renée Vivien: Pauline Tarn; American girl gone French and depraved; Lesbian affairs reeking of black satin sheets, statues of Buddha, hothouse violets; living relatives who refuse to unleash her poems on the public until the year 2000. But Pathways is resourceful and she is his favorite poet (save Sappho). Crap. Pathways is a silly old man giving this Sapphic bull to old skirt-twirling Sanctissima. Sanctissima hates the French. She is up there right now, miles above the solid English-speaking earth, thinking that there is nothing like the French for shut-tight windows, a lack of briskness, a tendency to moon and not get on with it. Pathways, she is thinking, with his interminable need to parallel life and literature. . . . Then why, after knowing the crazy bitch for so long, didn't he present her with the war diaries of General MacArthur? The feel of crisp khaki; the snap of riding crops; dramatic dirty trench coats. That's the style that makes her heart rejoice. I've heard her say before to him, Isn't there enough trouble in this old world without the poems of that Renée Vivien? A smell of chocolate is drifting off the fat man across the aisle and I hope it will remind her, painfully, of the smell of me that day the Hershey bar got crushed, then melted in my dress pocket. But it won't. It will remind her of the letter that was responsible for bringing her to this great height. So sweet. The letter she got, the little lost lamb she'll find now, there in the awful middle of the universe. I see what it looks like, pale blue and skimpy, flourishes and scrawls in purple ink:

Darling Saint Janet!

Written from the Peak of Parnassus! Written on the verge of fame and glory! To you, sweetest J-issima, who believed when others scoffed! Who comforted me with Madeleines and lime tea, with whipped cream in my cocoa in far off Ann Arbor while others selfishly fiddled, bassooned, pianoed only for their own *ugly* self-advancement! Or are you only some *diabolic dream* wrought to torment my sleepless nights with sweet fantasy??? Sanctissima, sweet love, come to me!!! Play for me! One artist's soul cries out to another. My voice shall vibrate only to thee. Sweet Sanctissima, *I* shall vibrate only to thee! Drop everything (*whoever she is*) and fly to your first love, your one love! Twenty years are but the beat of a swallow's heart between true lovers. You will find me as lovely as you once told me, passionately, that I was. The Steinway! How sadly silent. It gleams beneath its Spanish shawl wanting only your hands upon it—as do I! Listen! I am singing for you: "When I am laid . . ."

Tendressement—Ever!
Your Gloiryeux

Sanctissima will love the filthy thing, will press it tenderly between the third and the fourth of the obscenities by Renée Vivien. She will have to remember to remove it, re-place it with a tidy handful of signed checks before she rewraps the book as a present for . . . Gloiryeux. Gloiryeux. Sweet crucified God.

The plane will begin its descent about now. She will say to herself, Sanctissima, you're no fool; smile, sigh, close her eyes, imagine what it will be like. And now I am home.

Now cuddle me," said Pathways.

Margaret tightened one arm around his neck and spread the other across his oval paunch. Pathways, digging his bare heels into the sofa cushions, inhaled deeply in an attempt to decrease the paunch and increase the squeeze. Margaret put her head on his shoulder, but he shrugged it away so that he could lay his beneath her chin—which was, of course, more the thing. Across the dark room, the television set pointed at them, bathing them in a pale blue glow that made them look dead, or like plastic replicas of real people. They stroked each other with flattened hands, like paws, as though one animal, weirdly, were petting another. Their hands had no effect on their faces; they stared, blank and unaroused and still, at the moving picture. A tiny woman, about the size of Pathways' foot, was dancing before them, wrapped from bosom to ankle in silver sequins that flashed a coded gibberish across her body. She was singing, in a loud, happy voice, "Come to Me My Melancholy Baby."

Margaret unstuck her hand from the paunch, unraveling her fingers from its folds and hairs. She waved it at the tiny woman.

"Is this necessary . . . I mean, for it to work?" she asked timidly. The truth of these matters was difficult to come by. Hours earlier, Mr. Pathways had told her that women under thirty, to achieve orgasm, had to hold a teacup in their teeth during intercourse. Pathways had been astonished—but he was becoming less so—at the success of this spur-of-the-moment scheme. But it had been his last remaining piece of Limoges; and now, naturally, the handle was gone. Margaret had not seemed at all surprised by the idea; he might hope for even greater things before night and energy gave out. Down in the pits of his belly he was feeling wonderfully dead tired; he had to resist the impulse to sigh, "Wow!" over and over again. But he was, presently, searching the hollowed pits of some old fantasies —those uncured plagues that had festered in him all his life—that he might now pleasantly express with Margaret. Sodomy, of course . . . but he hoped to save this—since it was so much in the great classical tradition—for some time when he was entirely fresh, for some moment of overwhelming tenderness—perhaps after he had confessed to Margaret that he, too, had been a virgin until the night of *The Trojan Women*.

"Oh, very necessary," he answered solemnly. He put her hand back where it belonged. Perhaps it was necessary. He didn't know, not for sure. The song was over. He plunged the button on the remote control. There was a flash; then there was a young woman, with hair even longer and lighter than Margaret's, being systematically beaten by a large man smoking a cigar. The young woman wore spotless white boots and a tiny dress, and she struggled and screamed. The man seemed to want her to be still so that he could burn her with the tip of his cigar.

There was that, of course. Mr. Pathways had a small collection of photographs (of men and women and men and men and women and women; and some dogs, and one stuffed tiger), some of which featured sadism. During his preshower morning ritual, seated on the floor of his coat closet, Pathways had often wondered if there might be enormous pleasure to be had in stringing a girl up by her wrists in a doorway and beating her black-and-blue with a cowboy belt—as a man in one of the pictures did. He snuggled closer against Margaret; he decided that the thing would be more exhausting than exciting.

"I shouldn't have let her go like that," said Margaret; and she suddenly felt much less cozy with Pathways. "My mama and daddy, I know it, were upset because they couldn't take me home, and it was cruel of me to let Ellen be without me at that funeral this afternoon. Do you think I'm fickle?"

Pathways pressed closer.

"You silly. Your parents were simply delighted to let you stay and begin graduate work in classics with me this summer. And I've already explained about Ellen. . . . How many times do I have to do it? She's beyond me and you. You'll never touch her again. She's caused blood to shed. That funeral will be like eating ice cream off a plate for her. Pretty Margaret! Blue-haired, golden-eyed, pretty Margaret!"

He tickled her and chuckled; and she became afraid that he might want to do it again. He pressed his hand against his chest and sang out: "Upside down rendition of flesh! Upside down, inside out—that's what girls are. A man's old coat turned at the collar, rewoven in the tail—and all the buttons missing—*girls!* Blast your petticoats! Touching just one of you, all my suspicions are confirmed—" He began crying; his cheek became stringy with tears. "—old Pathways is nothing but a girl's furbelow. Look at my old friend, that old bawd who fancies herself a Regency rake: Sanctissima—working hand-in-glove with that powerhouse, that Soldier-Boy who's taught me so late in life what a hero is: a blind, involuntary actor who memorizes virtue's script at birth—and the play is lifelong. When he hears the bell ring at intermission, it's only us, the audience, taking a piss in the aisles! *Unh* . . . be careful with your elbow, dear! And I thought it was Pathways those Greek brutes were waiting for. . . ."

Margaret eased a cushion between her arm and the paunch. She was terrified. Pathways, with every word, was shuffling her reverence for her own history—the twenty-one years' worth of painted days in which she had expressed nearly nothing but a need to become like Ellen, while Ellen was becoming like . . . was *becoming* Cherubino. He was shuffling all those days into a dirty deal of catastrophe. The music she remembered was being snarled, turned upside down; melodies were being shot down into out-of-tune zig-zags; simplicity was over. She would curse the man, and leave him, were it not that this country where he had taken her, this wet country of games where the geography could burst out of shape in a moment, where there were new rules for every new hour, was the best place to wait for Ellen, to find the right way to become like Ellen . . . to *become* Ellen.

Ellen no longer wished to accomplish friendship, so Margaret would learn the distinguished feelings of the body, aping Ellen's every breath, gulp, twitch until, when they finally met again, Ellen would know without a doubt that they were one and the same. It was right that she have Ellen. Be Ellen.

"I'll read you some Homer. Don't be upset. Do you want me to read Homer?"

"What's the point of Homer anymore, Sweetie Pie?" He lifted a handful of her hair and rubbed it across his tears; he let it go and was left with a patch of mysterious beard and an oily smear. "Once I had a little calico pussy, and I took her everywhere I went, and she loved me back; but Sanctissima, drunk again, smashed my pussy's left front paw, and I could never love it again, and I had to put her to sleep. Homer's like that now—he has a smashed left paw; he's been my wrong teacher all my life."

"Samuel Butler says a woman wrote the *Odyssey*," she whispered.

"Horse *shit!*" Pathways shouted. He jumped up and jiggled across the room. He was shouting: "Go to it, Sanctissima! Glory Hallelujah, old friend! When you get to this one, lock her in a little box, keep her in a reliquary, like the foreskin of Christ—keep her pinned to your pocket with her thighs taped shut if she doesn't learn to amuse you! A buxom lieder singer—to tease Sanctissima's nostalgia —to give her back the bedtime song. Sanctissima, you are a sleeping prince bound in a century of ivy! Awaiting the kiss that'll come wrapped in 'Dido's Lament'—there's one song you'll never hear again from the foot of the bed. But a dream—and an end to a century of dream—is got most satisfactorily for money, and you know it, old friend! There's no other way . . ."

He leaped back onto the couch and whispered the rest into Margaret's ear; her eyes squinted against the blast she heard.

" . . . but the singer had better watch her song. . . . It's a mean piano Sanctissima plays, and she can sing a snatch with the best of them. Ah . . . you're dripping tears down your belly—you think I'm betraying the conversation—but it's Ellen I'm talking about to you. Look into my mouth and see Ellen coming out, while Sanctissima, in her honest trousers and Inverness, gets into bed and sells herself for a song. You're pretty as the Aegean, but you're the soul of a department store—you think Ellen's on all the counters, at half-price. But when the customers that mob you for your wares tear off the string and bend to kiss their bargain, their lips barge up against thin air. You'd better take your merchandise and run! I'm it, Sweetie Pie; run to me! When the customers try to lynch you for the shoddy goods you've sold, you'll see at once where you belong. Your home's with me and the likes of me."

"I expect it's more brandy you want," she said.

"And while you're at it, pour some on your own snuffling. There's more to come. I've just thought of something."

Pathways held the bottle against Margaret's mouth and forced her, with his hand clamped against the yellow silk skull, to drink more than she wanted. Pathways swallowed even more, pressed his thumb on the remote control, annihilated the victorious young woman in the white boots. They were in pitch black. He found his mouth with the rim of the bottle and drank more.

He murmured, he nearly sang: "Here's to thee, Sanctissima, with the happiest wish I can send you: that our blithe spirit, Lucifer, will choose tonight to get the gate and, on his way down to a sweeter hell than the one you're flying to, grab you from the air and take you with him —you're never more of an angel than when you're in the arms of the devil—Old Janet, you could carry him yourself! Astride your broad shoulders to an eternal damnation with no doubts about it! Could sitteth at the left hand with desire ground beneath your heel. Think of it, Sanctissima! No more hot nights full of Bach *Inventions*—and you can thank your friend Pathways. I should have packed you a bomb instead of a book—you would land on hell with such a dowry of burning flesh that Satan would in gratitude wear white and be your simpering bride through the ages. He'd supply you with so much of your Jean-Marie Farina—'the cologne of Napoleon'—that you'd stink to high heaven with enough conquests and neckties and blessed riding crops to quench even your enormous need. . . ."

He held her tight.

"I'm Margaret. . . . I'm not old Sanctissima, that old fool. You're hurting me. She's gone forever. I wish Ellen had killed her."

Pathways forced more brandy down her throat.

"Ooooooh!" he screamed. "I could laugh like a maniac for the rest of my days over that! *I'm* the fool, trying to explain the ways of heroes to cowards—to a pretty patch of the Aegean! You sail the Aegean, not talk to it! The time for sailing is now."

He felt for the floor and set the bottle carefully down. He moved into the dark, stumbling, making the furniture groan.

Later, he called to Margaret, in a high, sweet voice, to switch on his goosenecked study lamp and to twist it until it spotlighted his bedroom door. He stepped into the light, coyly, like an amateur on his first night. On the top of a thick auburn wig, trained into ringlets to his shoulders, he wore the rough sunbonnet of a countrywoman. He had decorated it, easing the effect of the cornfield, by wrapping several broad ribbons of pink grosgrain about its crown and tying them beneath his chin in a flopping bow. His chin was just beginning to sprout whiskers for the morning. His padded brassière was of blue lace; and the panties that matched it had one word stitched, in script, above the groin: "Monday."

"Now turn off the lamp," he sobbed. He pressed his arms to his sides, trying to make hips. He shook and undulated. "Come on now, undress me, gently, as a loving mother would her only son. Lay me tenderly on my back and sing softly in my ear, 'When at night I go to sleep, fourteen angels watch do keep.' Say I'm your bad bad boy, but mommy loves you best of all, and when you put your breast in my mouth, say, Eat mommy, sweet darling, eat mommy all up!"

Before Margaret could take a step, Mr. Pathways fell to the floor and lay there shaking and crying. Before the sun rose, his bonnet was torn to shreds and her face was drenched with his tears.

What Ellen saw, as she opened the front door, was the front room—*living* room—of her own home suddenly looking strange, suddenly frozen into a tableau, contained by a proscenium. She feels she's never seen anything like it before; she stands still and watches it:

Cold as twelve full fathoms deep in that room with the white shades pulled to the sills and the heavy curtains (with their unfurled peacocks, partridges, purple grapes in bunches big as partridges, repeatedly stamped up and down the muslin until the lesson is dinned unforgettably into the brain, like the alphabet, like her own age at this moment)—the curtains clasped together against the light, which entered anyway in surreptitious slits beneath the heavy door, to strike an uplifted shoe sole, to cause the dust to dance on the thin-slatted floor edging the rug; and all cold from the whining air conditioner, turned up to a new pitch of cold every few hours to preserve what flesh was left in the house, to annihilate the memory of the room's outside: June's lambent second day, with its birds fat as cherubim, its leaves' collective growth as polished and anonymous as an army of new-forged breastplates converged and still above the hapless enemy head below.

All summer nature—but shucked stillborn from its tender husks and limned in dark lines of silk-stitched embroidery, raised patterns of upholstery tapestry—was in the room: flowers in circus colors woven into rings the size of school-girl hoops across the rug; inside each, a true-lover's knot. China plates, painted by someone now dead but dear and near long ago, with magnolias and lilies of the valley, chattered on hooks against the wall (pale green like new buds) from the cold. The whatnot in one corner began on its topmost shelf with a sanguine china robin and descended to its broadest, nether level where carved-in-ivory biddies, canary yellow, were breaking out of dark-gray eggshells.

To keep it clean, the fireplace had never had a fire; for twenty-three years, even during sick seasons, it had roasted only a brass bucket of dried hydrangeas, whose old dragging heads had been propped up for half that time with a handful of peacock tail feathers, tail feathers with eyes that had collected the comings and goings, the mutations of the room, and had shunted them like smoke up the decent white of the chimney.

Violets, white and purple; the tree of life, marigolds, hummingbirds, a cat with a mouse beneath its paw—all long weatherbeaten by the flux, swifter and more harmful than nature's, in the family's seasons—had been plied in chain stitch, cross-stitch, French knots across linen cushions, and then piled helter-skelter in the sofa's corner until the casual eye could catch only the grinning mouse mouth and the finery of the cat's paw.

Half a dozen squirrels, painted gold, climbed a golden tree stump, forever on their way to hide their silver nuts. The gold stump grew out of the broad mantel above the pure fireplace; and, around it, swamping it in a marshfire of glass colors, were twenty-three paperweights, all shimmering with millefiori, collected, one each year, by the mailman to commemorate his marriage to May-Ellen. Above the mantel, tilted to make forty-six paperweights, was a mirror as wide as a bed and so tall that it reached the ceiling. Its frame was baroque, gilt; and at its top center, with their curls barely clearing the ceiling, sat two fat cupids, with little ankles crossed and reflected in the glass. Perfectly round, and simpering, their cheeks resembled tiny golden buttocks.

The tableau came to life, began to move, make noise; became tableau vivant: on the sofa, with cupids smiling down on her, encircled by women wringing their hands, May-Ellen was sobbing into the embroidery, nudging her face hard and hungrily into the thread. Occasionally, on a perfectly regular schedule, she lifted her face to breathe and to scream. The screaming started with a broken gutteral humming and advanced into something that sounded like the moaning blasts from a horn that calls men out to a fire. She ended the scream choking out the mailman's name: Ro-ger, Ro-ger, *Roger!* and fell back again into the cat, the mouse, the birds, the flowers.

Then (Ellen noticed, from the doorway, where the sun burst so hugely against her back that the front of her was black shadow, a black that so much matched the spirit of the room that none of the women in it had noticed her)— then, the women bent low over May-Ellen, with motions so smooth and accustomed that they seemed to have been at them for hours, or years: the arm of the eldest curled around May-Ellen's shoulder; the hand of the younger lost its fingers in the knots of her hair, as wild as a nest of snakes. The other three stood at May-Ellen's feet (which, Ellen could see, were clamped rigidly into brand-new white satin mules) and held each other's hands and said, in chorus: "Lord God, Lord God, honey, you've got to *stop* it!" None of the women recognized a change in the room's climate: Ellen was letting in the heat.

Beneath the hum of the cold and May-Ellen's groans, something growled at her. Under the baby grand, whose top was closed and loaded with vases of babies'-breath, fern and roses from a hothouse, was the dog, Hortense, her black hide sifted with gray hairs and her legs sunk deep into a goosefeather bed pillow. She did not recognize Ellen, but she saw the black shadow Ellen had become. A feather clung to her whiskers and trembled, with her loose old skin, as she growled again. Hortense had come back home, too.

Ellen backed out into the heat, easing the door shut behind her. She stopped long enough to pry off her shoes and drop them into the shrubbery beside the porch. She listened before she ran: from the big sun porch on the side of the house, and through the oily leaves of the camellias that shaded it, came the sound of too many voices. When only a few southern women talk together, they always sound like many. On their breaths would be the smell of iced tea, thick with lemon and sugar.

Ellen's feet took the gravel driveway, on the other side of the house, nearly running, her intentions plain to her: she was going out back and climb the big willow there, and she would sit there and not move until her place in all this was made plain to her. Next door, from their upstairs window, Rudyard and Merrilee Blue, Margaret's parents, leaned out and whispered, "Ellen! Ellen!" but she hung her head, would not hear, and hit the gravel hard enough to hurt.

Up in the willow limbs, she was too big to straddle the forked branch any longer. She squirmed, scraped; at last squatted, with her knees drawn level with her chest. She leaned and relaxed, reminding herself of some stuffed relic of an extinct bird race; if the willow tree were only a museum. Had his fellow mailmen come and reverently gathered his pieces and then arranged them in the box so he could be seen whole one last time? The tree shook. She counted the pale green slivers, the willow leaves: forty-seven leaves in a space the size of her hand, in a tree as tall as her house and half as wide, counting the porch where whispers and ice cubes rustled. A very old tree. The tan bark gnawed against the soft wrinkles of her instep, and she answered it by rubbing her foot back against it. The center, the trunk, soared straight through her arm's arc, wide as human shoulders; and when it slimmed and stopped, an endless distance up in the sky, the snake-colored leaves, thick and fine as hair, began their long rain to the ground.

Hunkering in the willow, as yet undiscovered by anyone but an old dog and still unexpected by the comings and goings of death, Ellen's mind roosted, languished, after the long trip home from education and lovemaking.

She must be careful where she walked here: any ground might be hallowed ground, even the billiard-table green of the grass beneath her. Buffalo Creek Cemetery, where the eroding stone of angels' wings and Jesuses and weeping girls guarded the monstrous lengths of her kin's graves, was not that far away. Who could tell how the dead behaved? How many, discontented with the swampy old ground where they had been left, might have burrowed their way home again where, in their rotting, they could continue to cultivate their own bought-and-paid-for-and-tended lawns? Any ground might be hallowed ground: the weight of one foot on a grave, marked or unmarked, might burst it like a gas-filled balloon and you would find yourself wrapped in the bones of your great-aunt's arms and struck with the splintered timber of her box.

Invisible graves, but a house plain to see. Soused in sunlight and heat, it sat up straight in its vegetations, green and flowers, begun by hands gone to Buffalo Creek dust. Now that Roger's gone, not a single man left for the house. The bugs hummed in the willow hair, about Ellen's hair. When there's no more of a family left to be born, then its women begin to live forever. An old-fashioned belly laugh from the porch, and a hasty crack of fresh ice from the bucket to cover it; and: "Miss Nina? Miss Nina? Use this fan of mine and calm yourself. I do declare you'd laugh at anything, Miss Nina." The voice slow and easy to keep the powder on its bosom dry.

The mailman dies and leaves a gap as wide as a canyon, and six feet deep. How many females do you need to move in and fill the space so the wind won't whistle in the corners, so the dust won't collect on that side of the bed? Ellen's mind, up a tree, filled with the problem, was sinking to a drowse, to a good idea of herself as a mean, booted giant in tight leather trousers, with manners common as clay. . . . "Here's me banging on the front door so hard the china squirrels break their silly heads against the hearth; here's me spitting in the peacock tails and—if I miss!—on the carpet. I *disdain* to lift that toilet seat! Where's my supper? I want it fried in grease! Bang goes my warty fist! And Great-Grandmother's silver (Miss Harriet Love!) jumps a mile and stabs your permanent waves! Quit swishing your skirts and pawing your cameos: come scratch my crotch for me—my hands are busy with this here joint of beef! When I finish I'll throw it at your heads! All you women run to bed—now I go to get drunk and smoke black cigars, curse and swear, have my hounds in the house, fornicate with purple satin women, scratch up the furniture, rattle the dice, deal the cards, piss on the preacher's backside and take the name of the Lord in vain. At dawn, you'll find me puking in the rose bed. . . ."

Ellen's head drooped. The same power that holds the body of a sleeping bird high but safe in a tree held her. Well, gentle Roger, your letters are scattered God knows where, your smoky blue uniforms gone north to the government; well, gentle Roger, meek and mild—you don't watch out, they'll bury you in a feedsack skirt, ribbons and Woolworth pearls tacked front and back. . . . Well, gentle Roger . . .

"Well," he said, hefting her up onto his arm, as though she were an organdy-ruffled mailbag full of letters, "it is one thing for your mama to have the sweetness of temper to let me bring you way out here, but it will be another if I get you home with chicken doo on your patent leathers."

So she rode, easily as a bag of letters, six years old and her big sash fluttering behind, from the running board of Miss Nina's Buick over a yard gray and firm and stamped all over with the witless three-pronged messages left by chicken feet. Nothing grew out of that dust but signs of chickens and a chinaberry tree, old and thick as night. She rode Roger's arm, so close to his face that the wrinkles of joy that were shedding from his eyes' corners as they went beneath the tree (there was a house behind the tree, so tiny it was nearly lost in the light) became her joy, too, though her heart did not feel the joy's reason; nor did her mind understand it. Nothing more to see on that trip over the yard but the flash of the tin roof that took the summer morning, broiled it, then tossed it back to fry the sky a deeper blue. But out of the corner of her eye, still glimmering with the flat reflection of Roger's joy: a small patch of tobacco leaves being cropped by two fat women, one white, one black; a mule, still as stone, draped in the ropes of his sled. The women's faces, flecked with sun breaking through the brims of their straws, lifted and looked for one impassive moment at Roger's pristine thing; then they turned down again to their leaves. And there was a rusty Royal Crown Cola sign that had been tacked down on the third step to the porch to keep a foot from going through thinned old wood.

"This is my granny who raised me up from nothing when my own mama had to leave me to go to God." That tiny creature, shrunk inside her wrinkles, crouched in her starched envelope of dress, trembling from heat that was too cold for her; or else she was trembling from the sight of something. Eighty years of sun and work on a face the size of a walnut, and when Roger made her bend and kiss it, it was like rubbing a cold Christmas walnut. And then the thickest wrinkle—like a mouth—opened, commenced laughing with a sound more like some bad boy tuning up to cry than a laugh: *Hunnnnh hunnh hunnh!*

Thin streams of snuff juice, let out by the noise, hastened down her chin, all ready to blot the stiff bosom, but Roger caught it with his free hand, then held that hand against his heart. The laughter gathered like a wind rising to shake the flesh from the dress, and Ellen was remembering the story of a cyclone and all the dead people it left behind. So much laughing might kill them all! Her chair rocked like a disaster, and Ellen listened for the answering rattle of the silver roof. Roger's hand left his heart, and Ellen moved her knee to cover the stain.

"She's just laughing because she's so proud to see my dearest, she's just laughing because she ain't had a thing to laugh at in her whole life." His joy left both of them; his bewilderment at his own remark replaced it. "Stay here," he said, "and—and you tell her you love her!"

The RC sign called out beneath his weight. Ellen watched him stand at the edge of the tobacco and take dollars from his wallet, and she saw the white woman take and tuck them deep in her bosom. Then Roger put his hand on the woman's arm, and they stood talking and staring down at the gray dust between them.

When the old woman couldn't see Roger anymore, she stopped laughing, shrank back inside her trembling. She became the only thing, as far as the eye could see, that moved at all through that blaze. Ellen's foot, moving back, struck the thickness of an old Maxwell House can potted with a red geranium; and the sound was a chill across her back. To see into the dark house she had to cup her hands around her face, and all the while the red flower nuzzled against her leg like a cat's cheek. A greasy smell of salt pork simmering in the collards: it was the smell that clung to colored people, the smell that America brought with her into the kitchen at home every morning. Then the dark inside took shape beneath the smell: first, the white of the bed with its little impression of old woman; the smaller, rounder white of the chamber pot; then the deeper, cumbersome dark in the shape of the parlor organ, with foot pedals worn long ago nearly to splinters from the heavy pressure of hymns. Above the organ, another frame, but round and deep beneath its glass to make a shadow box; and it held inside a hank of hair, so black, so long in its coil that spread out it might have reached from Ellen's shoulders to her feet. It was twisted around a wreath of flowers that were dead and tissue white. In capital letters curved to fit the frame's circumference, plain as the three bears, were the words: DAUGHTER AND MOTHER REST IN JESUS.

Ellen pressed her face deeper into the lax old screen, the summer door. A wad of cotton, tied there to ward off flies, leaned against her cheek with the same light touch of the flower against her leg. She needed to open the door and pull the organ stool against the wall, needed to climb up and press her face on the dusty glass and look deep into the black hair. What old flowers, what an old room, what an old boy, Jesus. And what old black hair woven into the old things; but a moment in Ellen's hand, waving through the fresh outdoors, and it would be hair so young it could skip and scamper! Her fingers moved to the thread spool that made the door handle. A claw had her by the arm, was pulling; fingernails dug deep enough to stroke her wristbones!

The screaming was coming from her own head, but Roger was running back to her, but not fast enough. The old woman held on, though Ellen squirmed and danced at the end of the arm enough to shake the dead alive. Though she knew it, she knew that the jumping white thing with its flying black hair was enough to jostle her from alive to dead, the old woman held on to it.

All around the rich shade of the chinaberry tree: Roger flying through the brilliance, scuffing the chicken scratches, nearly falling on alarmed hens; the black woman and the white woman rubbing their hands down their fronts, as though cleaning them for some task.

Never to twirl on tiptoe and shake the black hair in a circle around her—no, never! The old woman's got Ellen! Roger, stuttering "No-no-no," bending between them, had his hand with theirs, made it a battle of three hands. But it was not Roger who prized open the claw, nor Ellen who pulled away: it was the old woman, letting go, that ended it. Freed like that, Ellen fell back; again she heard the thud of her heel on the flowering coffee can.

Roger had to bend double to put his head inside the starched lap; and to wrap his arms around the old woman, he had also to encircle the back of her rocking chair. The old woman's shaking included Roger; Roger also seemed to tremble.

"Dor-thea! Dor-thea!" The old woman seemed at first to choke on her word, the name; but then she spoke loud and plain: *"Dorothea! Dorothea!"* above Roger's head, into Ellen's face. The old eyes, swirling in the nut face, would not leave the sight of Ellen; the claw reached out again, began to grasp thin air, and, touching nothing, it began to push with all its strength against Roger. Feeling it, finally, he stood up; in the rich shade of the chinaberry tree, his misery stripped him to pieces. His misery branched through Ellen like a tree, and her heart was like some rotten fruit hanging on that tree. He took the old woman's face in his hand; he could have cracked her skull by bending his knuckles. He said to it: "That's not her. Dorothea's dead, my mama's dead, and she's buried yonder in the woods. This one's mine, my baby, my dearest. Sometimes I've sat and brushed her black hair, many times. She is not your little girl; she is your great-granddaughter. She is such a long time away from you, ma'am!"

Comprehension took the old woman's face, and Roger moved his hand away. Ellen came close, and it took the old woman no time to gather the juice around her gums; and though she aimed at Ellen's face, she seemed satisfied to have hit the stiff white waist where the organdy was gathered to make the skirt. The spit struck and burned like a thunderbolt, and in an instant it had spread through the cloth to the size of a hand, and there it lay, pressing warm like a hand against her belly: someone should say,

Is this where it hurts? When the old woman screamed, it was a scream intended to wake the dead; but it did not.

The white woman, before Roger could move, was there with the old woman up and cradled in her arms. So it was Ellen Roger hefted again to his shoulder, where it was, at last, safe to begin her own crying. The white woman caught up with them at the door to the car, carrying her hat in her hand as a man would. She pressed the can of geraniums into Ellen's hands, would not listen to No. Ellen pressed her face into the hairy stink of the flower and did not lift it until they had gone a long way.

Nearly home, Roger said, "She thought I had brought my mama back to her. She thought you were my mama, Dorothea, and she was all ready to love me at last because I had brought her back. I loved her and loved her and stayed with her until the day I went home with your mother, but she never loved me back because she loved Dorothea and Dorothea is dead. I can't hate her for loving my own mama so much, can I? Did you tell her you loved her, like I said to? I don't know. I don't know. It's a funny thing, because America's a colored woman, but sometimes America strikes me so much like my granny, or like the way she used to be. Well, you know America, and that's the way my granny used to be." And then they were home.

Y̵ou better get down out of that tree. Mama says you ought to be ashamed of yourself perched in a tree and you know what's happened. I can see up your dress."

"Kiss my foot, beige nigger."

"The time for that kind of talk is over. I am sixteen and on the verge of the N-double-ACP. I am the first colored person that got in the white high school. Next year I am going to be a cheerleader, a drum majorette, president of the Latin Club, queen of the Junior-Senior, where I will wear pink net over taffeta, and valedictorian. Then I'm going to Radcliffe, big mouth. You wait and see."

"I'll wait and see what I see."

She was going to wait and see Venusberg. As long as her eyes were closed she could control the heat and bear up to the creeks of sweat that were running the flesh off her bones. Opening her eyes, looking down, would reveal Venusberg beneath a waterfall of willow limbs, looking cool in something that could almost be a green rush of water; and Venusberg's brown eye, thick with the intelligence of what she saw, would be staring up at her. That other eye of Venusberg's, that pale blue eye, the walleye, would be there again, cut off to the side as always, its cool gaze frozen on the future.

Venusberg had second sight; or, rather, her blue—her walleye—had second sight. Venusberg had never claimed responsibility for what that eye saw. When it made known a future event to her, she would write it all down in the form of a letter to the person whose future the eye had seen; and then she would deliver the letter. The walleye's vision was always about someone in the family: Ellen, May-Ellen, the late Roger, Welch and Darwin Waters, Miss Nina; her own mother, America, who was the color of the Mason & Hamlin Miss Nina had brought, on the same day she had brought America, into the house to help May-Ellen bear up to being a mailman's wife.

Venusberg, from the time she was six, and could write, had been handing letters to people and saying, in a surly way, "Take it for what it's worth to you"; and they always did, for Venusberg's blue eye saw nothing but the truth, and the truth was worth agony or pleasure to the person it came to, and even more agony or pleasure about a year later when the truth became fact. Venusberg was surly about the visions her eye saw because none of them was ever about herself; so, since the beginning of her visions, she had been making up gorgeous compensating stories about herself—like becoming a drum majorette and vale-dictorian—and her stories about herself never ever came true.

On Venusberg's sixth birthday, her eye had seen its first sight; and that very afternoon, Ellen got a letter. It said, "Dear Ellen, Soon you and Margaret will start calling me beige nigger and I see this fact will turn you one day long hence to a bat so watch out yours truly Venusberg." And sure enough, soon Margaret and Ellen took a close look at Venusberg's cream-and-coffee coloring and started calling her beige nigger.

Where had Venusberg come from? America had never

had a husband, and was too upright to have ever had a lover. When Ellen was old enough to understand the origin of babies ("We all start out from between our dear daddies' legs," some girl at school had told her), she took a good hard look at America, and then at Venusberg (who was only two then and saw nothing beyond the next meal), and said to her mother, "Where in the world did Venusberg come from?"

"*I* don't know! Don't ask *me!*" May-Ellen had answered, rolling her eyes and rushing back upstairs for something she'd forgotten. It was a Sunday and Roger was still in the Men's Bible Class, which went on and on; and Miss Nina had beat him back to the house, arriving with Uncle Welch and Uncle Welch's beloved, Darwin Waters. Darwin Waters had been Uncle Welch's beloved long before Ellen had been born. He wore a hearing aid disguised as a giant pearl earring in his left ear, and he had a green thumb. That Sunday, as always, the whole family would sit down to a good dinner cooked by America and featuring Beloved's delicious lettuce and vegetables. Darwin Waters was the only one who, when asked, did not reply, "*I* don't know! Don't ask *me!*" because his earring, as usual, was turned off. He smiled mysteriously at Ellen's question, but he smiled mysteriously at everything.

Miss Nina did say, "Well, I know, but I'm not telling," and she didn't, but went on reading *Swann's Way* while she ate. But she had already read *Swann's Way* ten times at least, practically knew it by heart, and could concentrate on the question enough to add, when dinner was over, "But I'm the one who named her Venusberg." She marked her place in her book with her long, silvery fingernail and got up from the table. She was a tiny woman, and as elegant and as fragile-looking as her son, Welch. But Welch was really fragile. The rest of the family, a little sturdier, had always maintained that the two of them could get up and pose on the mantelpiece and who could tell the difference? Miss Nina looked down at her plate. She intended to stay tiny: out of the eight butter beans she had taken, there were four left; and only one neat bite had been removed from the little chicken thigh. She had drunk her iced tea straight, no sugar. Now, above the lacy dinner table, with its mahogany showing through in the places where bowls and platters did not cover it, Miss Nina threw back her white and lacy head and laughed, as she had always done over the naming of Venusberg. And beneath her laughter there was the shuffle of food and forks and murmurs of "Oh mama, you didn't eat again" and "Oh, Miss Nina, you've got to eat *more*." But she didn't; she only laughed more and let the four rings of diamonds on four fingers wink over the steady eaters while she held the battered green Proust to the precious flatness of her bosom.

Miss Nina laughed, and said, "I named her Venusberg, yes, indeed I did. For my own private amusement. I am the only member of this family with culture enough to understand the joke. Despite May-Ellen's brilliance at the Mason & Hamlin I bought her, despite Welch's library of modern French masterpieces in plain brown wrappers, despite my granddaughter's ability to read and write through some incredible triumph over her paternal genes, I, and only I, am truly cultured enough around here to appreciate a name like Venusberg for America's baby and the only one with charm enough to laugh regularly at it!"

Miss Nina's voice then grew tender and humble. She put her hand on Welch's curly black hair and drooped her eyelids at him. "But I owe it all to my only son, Welch, don't I, Welch?" she murmured. Welch took her hand from his head and kissed each ring on her fingers, and he did not answer. With his other hand, to express his agony, he reached under the tablecloth and clutched Darwin Waters' thigh. Darwin Waters, with his earring turned off, misinterpreted Welch's grasp and thought Welch wanted to go upstairs.

"From the moment my son Welch got his full growth and brought his Beloved into my house, I have been a woman of letters. The literacy of that boy! With the greatest aplomb, he eased me through the lesser lights and into Marcel Proust. And here I have stayed for the past five years, and you all know it. Isn't that right, Beloved?"

Miss Nina leaned across Welch and began tugging at Darwin Waters' free earlobe. Darwin Waters smiled mysteriously and scraped up the last bite of America's fantastic homemade strawberry ice cream. The rest of the family murmured, "Bless his heart!" and asked America to bring them second helpings.

"America, where did Venusberg come from?" Ellen asked her in the haze of the Sunday afternoon. Even the world seemed dead to the world.

"This is my nap time. Go talk to some of your white family. You don't know what a Sunday is around here."

There was nothing upright about America in her appearance. Through May-Ellen's castoff satin slip, with lace at the breasts and lace at the hem, America's body curved out like handfuls of plump fruit, going brown and sweet in the hot weather. In the swollen heat their voices seemed to take too long to reach each other. The room above the garage was a little hotbox. It had a white iron bed where America lay, a rocking chair where Ellen rocked, a table stacked with old Dream Books and a Bible stuffed with Sunday school pictures and yellow newspaper clippings that told the progress of America's second cousin from the county jail to the electric chair. He had killed his best girl friend with forty-seven knife wounds in a marijuana frenzy, the clippings said. On the opposite side of the room, there was a smaller bed that had once been Ellen's; on its pillow lay an eyeless rabbit that had once been Ellen's.

"They've all gone to sleep."

America sighed and sat up. Her breasts leaned heavy into

the white lace. Her two window shades, beaming yellow, seemed to sigh with her. America took her Bible up and found the place which had been marked by the first of the news clippings, which reported the discovery of the mad-dog killer in a church belfry. She read, ". . . there were in the same country, Shepherds abiding in the field, keeping watch over their flock by night. And, lo, the angel of the Lord came upon them, . . . and they were sore afraid. . . ."

"America, I asked you a question, honey! Stop reading that. It's not Christmas."

"It makes me feel cooler. It reminds me of how nice and cool it is when they start reading this at church." She shut the Bible and laid it on the slippery hill of her belly. "Your daddy's not asleep, I know that. I happen to know he's at last back from Bible class and is at this very moment sitting on the porch eating ham biscuits." America sighed again; the satin shuddered. "I just wish somebody would fix that eye of hers. All the colored people see her coming with that eye shooting off the side like that and they say, 'Witch girl! Witch girl!' Ignoramuses! There is none sweeter than my V.B. Nearly seven years ago to this day . . ." Ellen stopped rocking and held still. ". . . here I was like I am now, laying in the heat dog-tired from working the stain out of your best white organdy, when *Lo!* I dreamed a dream that a big white angel like a church window appeared by my side shining and stark-naked in the raiment of the Lord and this angel fell upon me and folded me in his wings and lifted me to the glory of Jesus like I never felt before and out of the throat of the angel came a multitude of heavenly hosts singing Glory to God in the Highest and this angel carried me wrapped in the splendid wings the color of night and the color of white and like the feel of water through the Valley of the Shadow of Death and to the pit of Hell where we wrassled with the Devil and won triumphant and then I was uplifted, uplifted even unto the pearly gates where I heard the voice of God say This is my daughter America who I am well pleased with and the angel's singing came upon me softer and softer and then I woke back up and there I was alone, still with your stained little organdy. And in the fullness of time Venusberg was born to me in this very room while Miss Nina held my hand and wept with me and read to me out of one of her books. 'This Child shall be called Venusberg,' Miss Nina said. 'Her name shall be called Wonderful.' "

"Praise the Lord," Ellen whispered.

"Certainly praise the Lord," said America. "My sweetest V.B. came unto me in a way not unlike the infant Jesus came unto Mary, *the Virgin Mary*. Now go find your daddy and let me rest. Let me rest. Take the poor man a glass of tea."

But Ellen did not. She nearly stumbled over little Venusberg, who was sleeping in the thick grass beneath her mother's window. Her head rested in the nest of her two little arms, and with her eyes shut, she could have been any pale little nigger, half angel or not. Ellen went off from the sleeping house to find her friend Margaret and tell her a story.

I wish I had gone to find him. I wish I could see him eating ham biscuits on the porch.

It wasn't that hot anymore. She opened her eyes. Shadows were growing stronger on the grass, and the grass they covered was brightening. Venusberg lay flat on her back in the bright grass, her arms beneath her head as though no time at all had passed. The brown eye was still on Ellen. There was a soft sound of fingers ripping through bean hulls coming from the back steps. America was there, thinking of suppertime.

From the grass, Venusberg said, "You better."

"Better what?" Heat, sleep, the past gripped her tongue.

"Come on down. The limousine's coming in an hour. You have to look at him in the funeral chapel before they bury him. You got to go and look. I'm going. Didn't you love him? I loved him. Your mama don't even know you're home. I have a prophecy for you."

Ellen shuddered; the willow leaves rubbed and shuddered. What else was coming true?

"Tell me."

But Venusberg was on her feet, standing in the imprint of her own body.

"You'll get your letter sometime." Then she lowered her head, and her eyes, and went off to the garage.

One deep breath, Ellen thought, and I'll get down, go into the air-conditioned screaming, my mother's grief will wind around me like one of their bed sheets, will stick to my skin, tear my skin off in shreds, I'll bleed like a stuck pig, run like a chicken with its head chopped off, fall like a shot bird, get mashed like a runover cat. Dirty old woman, get your nasty hands off me! *Mother!*

"Granddaughter of mine up a tree! Unclench your teeth, child! Show a little aplomb."

"Miss Nina . . ."

Her hair, white and soft as soap lather, was tied at the nape of her neck with blue velvet ribbon. The skirt of her blue dress, as gathered, as huge as a ball gown, hung exactly to her ankles; her waist was so thin it had almost disappeared. The book she held was thicker than her waist. Her feet were bare; her toenails carmine.

"Miss Nina, how's the Proust?"

"Ah! So you know about him now? So education's taught you something of my world? We have another woman of culture in the family. But you're still behind me; you'll never catch up with me!"

Miss Nina twirled on her toes, her skirt flew out like a real ball gown. She held her head back, smiling up to some partner. It was for Ellen, up a tree.

"Proust is all over—there's your answer, grandchild. Except late at night when Darwin and Welch and I have finished with the TV and they take turns reading me Marcel's letters to his mother. I can't say I take to Marcel's mighty nonsense for his mother—it gives me the hopeless feeling of being overloved." She held up her book for Ellen to see. It was royal blue, stamped with gold. *"Now* for me it's Madame Récamier—stunning, immortal female, so much like *me!* Do you know what Sainte-Beuve says about her, I mean about her *and me?* He says that Madame

Récamier and I listen *avec séduction!* Can you imagine? Listening *avec séduction!* It would thrill my soul if *I* could find someone to listen to *me* like that . . . *avec séduction* —besides Sainte-Beuve, of course. *He* does already. I listen to him *avec séduction;* he listens to me *avec séduction.* Ah!" She struck her flat chest. "Ah! but I am doomed to nothing but fawning Welch, who loves his mother, and to dear, deaf Beloved. A woman like me with a deaf listener . . . are you appalled? Monsieur de Chateaubriand once wrote to me: 'I must never leave you again. Adieu, adieu. Always adieus: life is made up of them.' Perhaps my condition in this *comédie humaine* strikes you now as fallen, as incredibly fallen for a woman like myself; but I tell you, my dear Guermantes, I tell you: *I have a past.* I am a woman with a past!"

Miss Nina held her fingers before her eyes to let the sparkles from her diamonds hypnotize her. "Do you know that the mailman's dead, dear?" she asked softly.

But Ellen was at last down the tree, leaving Miss Nina to pace the shadowy grass, to whisper to her book. She stepped up past America, whose tears were salting the beans she shelled into her lap. She went up the back stairs and, dressed for a funeral, she came down the front stairs.

Someone had decked May-Ellen all in black and had hung pearls at her throat; but May-Ellen kept taking her shoes off.

"Honey, stop taking your shoes off. You're going to have to walk any minute," one of the women was saying.

"I won't," said May-Ellen. "They can't put him in any hole. He wouldn't go in any hole without me, and I won't go. I won't walk."

"Oh!" all the women gasped.

Ellen, at the bottom of the stairs, joined the female species. The room was full of cotton fresh from the iron, wavering crepe, pleated lace. Beneath all this, nylon in all its shapes slithering from shoulders to knees to toes; and sweating rubber girdles, reshaping. Above all this, lipstick, pink or red, some almost purple; and powder, caught in eyebrows. A jingle of necklaces, rub of pearls, pinch of earrings.

The women were turning to one another on heels elevated three inches off the floor. They turned from one another and touched May-Ellen with glove-tipped fingers; the widow fell forward against each touch, and moaned. Out of her mouth came breath heavy as a male foot. Roger was not dead: he was curled in her stomach, he was marching off her tongue to kick the female room apart. The widow had swallowed her husband alive.

Ellen, watching it from the stairs, swallowed delusions alive.

Then, into them, through the room, came the chimey treble of Miss Nina's voice: "My own daughter acting like any other woman! How much more will I be called upon to bear? She's like a corpse herself and you, you ladies, are vultures descending to dress up her rotting!" Miss Nina twirled around them, making her skirt float in the cold. Her eyes, thickened with much black mascara, seemed heavier than her body; they batted as she moved. "Anyway, she *thinks* she's a corpse. She *thinks* her pretty little body's going to rot! That's all it boils down to when, all in death-face, shaking, and *can't eat a thing* and *come on back to me, dear husband, dear husband, come on back* the widow woman tries to cover the genuine article of grief—and you *all know* what it is!—*not* the hole in the ground she fears getting filled, but the hole between her legs she fears never's going to be filled—nevermore! Oh, go on, scream, draw back, shake your hoary locks, your hoary bosoms at me, just a poor old vulgar widow woman myself. Not a soul of you has the gift to see I'm Proust's mother, that I'm Madame Récamier, too! What's that at my elbow? Twin blessings of old age—the two dearest sodomites known to God and woman: green-thumbed, pornographic, sensual beyond your wildest dreams, my precious daughter! I've seen them myself tossing off an afternoon on my own bed—why, they've dented every candlewick I've ever owned! Name me another old woman with such sweetness at her elbow. Oh, for Christ's sake, you little thing—stop that howling! There'll be another mailman who'll bring you a letter every day—I guarantee you one will be ringing your bell by evening tomorrow. In the meantime, let's get it over with so you can strum some Chopin, this time for your daughter, who's home at last. I think she hankers for women bent over keyboards. In the meantime, if you get a letter meant for me, tear it up; if I hear a song telling secrets about me, trying to dignify me with some music, I'll plug up my ears and maybe I'll sneak in and whack off your fingers when you're taking some lonesome sleep some night soon. Just leave me alone! As for me, I intend to *drink* henceforth—and here's the oldest wine in the world, here by my side. Take down your pants, my boys, and show them the cobwebs on your bottles! Welch! Beloved! Pour me a glass! Yes, watch out! Indeed, a little bit of common mailman has come into the bloodstreams of all of us. And there's the one with the biggest dose of all, hiding in the corner, her thoughts elsewhere, on bells of her own to ring, on a whole city of mailboxes that will know her hand alone. Precious child! She's in her pretty dress and her high-heeled shoes. Get her, Beloved! Welch, get your mother's shoes. Let's bury the mailman. The king is dead. Long live Cherubino!"

Ellen was thinking, from the stairs, So here I am, and I can see through the window what they cannot—that the limousine is here and the funeral man, with his dearest sweet-mush of a face, is buffing his fingernails as he hurries up our walk. Cherubino is what she thinks. I'm wilder than that, they'll see; wilder than boy or girl, bird or beast, you name it: born in the boiling mud of the boiling jungle, carried to land on the hippopotamus head, raised with a cutlass between my teeth, I've come here red-eyed and stinking with the blood of a thousand weakhearted adversaries; I have a mat of black greasy hair that sticks like spikes down into my shoulders; I have a coat of many skins. I have a red moustache that curls around my ears, and in my ears are gold earrings I ripped from the severed head of Charles I. There're two pistols against my thighs and another in the dark, stuck to my belly. You won't believe it, but beneath this scum and stain on the skin of me, my face, washed clean, is as romantic as an empty theatre. And the face nothing but a dim reflection of the romantic, lusting brain where my real scenes are played. I'm decorated, head to toe, inside and out, with souvenirs of my march through history. I've collected them here and there, taking a little something each time a day, or a person, or a love, has moved me to tears: regard the earrings. That rust you see is Charles's blood. Even the clothes I wear are delicate with time—this shirt, my soiled rag, once hung on the panting chest of the Phantom of the Opera. These trousers have holes for knees, the cloth all gone from the praying of Joan of Arc. Even my heart's not my own. Carved from the chest of Catherine of Russia while she still was warm, it took its first leap back to life in my body: hence my tainted, ungovernable Romanov manner. It's time to bury the mailman: don't listen to me anymore. But before I step into your arms, mother, and let your tears wear holes in my eyes (and let me catch them with this silver phial I carry, where they'll join the last tear shed by Héloïse), notice the sheen of my boots—they were licked this clean by the tongue of Jesus Christ—his first act of humility. And notice that my shoulders are strong enough for the weight of the mailman's bag. Just let me have it, my new treasure, and you'll see: you'll have your letters before your morning is over. The feel of the letters I'll bring you will warm your hands day in, day out. I'm coming.

All the way to the grave, the June day increased its gold.

Pots of yellow were being gathered above, then dumped down in bursts of bright heat that made the passing scenery of town, then country, that the little line of cars floated through livid, rich. When the mailman was buried, and when all the living mailmen had passed by to touch his family; and when May-Ellen's veil had been lifted for kisses too numerous to tell; when each survivor had tried to penetrate, unsuccessfully, Ellen's huge sunglasses with bare, quick looks to see what her eyes would say; when Miss Nina had been forced by Welch and Darwin Waters away from a trembling minister ("I saw," she said. "He took sensual pleasure in mouthing those banalities, his whole little fleshpot self grew stiff, absolutely, and stiffer with each penny phrase: resurrection, life-without-end, Jesus' bosom—I wouldn't bury my *jackass* underneath that language, much less my daughter's mailman. You know me—nothing delights me more than a strong, first-class perversion—but God in Heaven! That man's bound for the pit for exciting himself with mediocre language! I'd rather see a necrophiliac at work any day")—when they had all regathered at the cars, each like a slab of darkness against the brightness of the day, of Roger's flowers, in their somber clothes—all somber but Miss Nina, who still floated in her powder blue, so light she seemed invisible, a ghost herself —the bright day disappeared. Clouds rushed to hang above Buffalo Creek Cemetery, and they were gray. And when the cars began to move, the clouds began to soak everything; and the rain beat everybody home.

America, still in her funeral hat of black straw and red roses, worked over supper. She dangled a fish head by its clean, dainty spine before Miss Nina.

"They brought all this fish from next door. They have to be eat tonight."

"Excellent," answered Miss Nina. "Ages ago a goddess, who shall be nameless, shed all her pubic hairs into the sea. That's why fish have so many bones. Cook plenty of corn bread to go with fish. Choking to death on a pubic hair is unlikely in this house, since Venusberg has not foretold it, but her grief may be causing a breakdown in her vision. Be sure they get plenty of corn bread. Where is Venusberg? I've already made the rest of them go to bed. Where is she?"

Miss Nina split open a pomegranate, her only nourishment from morning until night, and began to lick the seeds into her mouth. The juice trailed down among her row of pearl buttons like a pink thread and made her dress prettier.

"She's someplace out in the rain, crying." America bent her head down to shed her own tears into the glaring eyes of the dead fish.

"In that case, we're all accounted for. I'm off to my own bed." And she tiptoed across the floor, careful, as always, to step only on the white tiles, never on the blue.

The rain fell; the clouds moved in gargantuan stumbles above the roof. The rain fell, and, with a little wind behind it, pushed uncertainly at the windowpanes. Miss Nina had got them all to their own beds behind their own doors, but whether they slept or not, even breathed or not, Ellen could not tell. She climbed to the top of the attic stairs, then turned around and went back down. She meant to cover all the house in her bare feet, from attic to basement, collecting every sense, every color, every sound; then she would stir them, mash them, boil them and hold her face in the mess's steam and hope to breathe in sorrow, to eat it, to become so stuffed with grief that she would vomit grief and lie doubled up, screaming, while too much grief ripped out her bowels.

But nothing touched her; she collected nothing. From beneath the first of the doors she passed came the sweet, numb scent of marijuana and the soft gasps of Welch and Darwin Waters squeezing their lungs tight against it; then the quickening creak of their bed. Ellen sniffed, listened, then went on. Behind the next door, there was Miss Nina, talking to her book; the book spoke to her. But before she put her hand against the last door, Ellen went down to the end of the hall and lay flat down on the cedar chest beneath the window there.

She watched the rain come down; she felt her thoughts trace themselves through all their content—animal, vegetable, mineral. First: Margaret, the soft rabbit reflection of Ellen's own lion self; mad-as-a-March-hare Margaret being trundled by her ankles, like a wheelbarrow, through the terrible predicaments of Pathways; trembling bunny Margaret, frightened by the dogs, and stupid enough to want a lion's solace. And Sanctissima, weak reed with traces of oak in her brain, mahogany in her wrists, the look of an old crow set between her eagle eyes, could even now turn on Ellen the secret look that made her wish to cry out. And the mindless steel of the nameless soldier's arrow, on a course due north, speeding dead ahead for the moving Ellen target. She closed her eyes and imagined herself withering inside her skin; she imagined that nothing of her self lived except some center in her belly.

Welch, a long time ago, had joined the Navy to see the world; after a short time, he left the Navy under a cloud and was welcomed home still sweet and alive, thank God. When he unpacked his duffel bag, he brought out red silk robes that snorted and huffed and slithered with the snouts and tails of countless gold dragons. There was one for everybody. And in the pocket of each robe there was another thoughtful gift, a silk fan painted with cherry blossoms. The pocket of Beloved's robe was much heavier than those of the others: besides the fan, Darwin Waters had received various Oriental honeymoon devices that made him blush in front of the family and caused Miss Nina to throw handfuls of rice at him.

Ellen's dragon robe, which, when it was new and she was

a child, used to trail the floor and make her an empress in her courtyard or a whore whiling away the afternoon, now hit her clumsily at the knees; and the sleeves were tight at the elbow. But she lay naked inside her robe and watched the rain.

She moved an arm, and a dragon rode across her breast and her nipple stood up to meet it. She smiled up and out at the rain and thought of fire. The fire was licking at the roots of the house, leaping over the dark basement, lighting it, eating at the shelves beneath the jars of jelly, corn, gherkins. In the kitchen, the fire was taking America from behind and making her shout until she crackled and was as crisp as her own cooking. The vases of flowers, the peacock feathers, the perfect pitch of the Mason & Hamlin, all the embroidery threads, were burning alike in the parlor and humming as they fell. Ellen, cool, while her family choked with smoke in their beds, opened the door to her new home, the only home henceforth, the home of her self. Childhood burned around her; and mother, father, all the attendant blood that had fashioned the color of her eyes, the texture of her hair, the nature of her games until this moment, went, at her command, into the blaze with no greater value than carved sticks of walnut. Beneath her eyelids, Ellen set her house on fire. When she opened her eyes, she was grown and free.

She stood up. The dragon's gold was scarring her skin; it was too tight, too tight. She took Sanctissima, Margaret, the nameless soldier and her own benign future all in her arms and leaped, so slowly it was quite like flying, from the burning house.

All right. Come in."

"I wish you'd turn over and look at me."

"What a daughter! You don't even know when your own mother's not crying." May-Ellen chuckled into her pillow, then rolled over.

For something to do, the neighbor women, especially Margaret's mother, had cleaned the bedroom, then cleaned and cleaned it again. The day's wet light flew over May-Ellen's dressing table and then collapsed on all the crystal and silver engraving and swansdown she had there: no mail-order beauty on that table. Miss Nina's long-dead husband had owned not one, not two, not three—he had owned four jewelry stores, all the jewelry stores in town; he had outfitted the houses of all kinds of brides. His last words had been, "It takes me to get a girl started on life in this town, rich and poor, black and white. It takes me." Then he spat on and polished a silver salver the size of his head, then dropped dead: May-Ellen had told him she was marrying a mailman. Then it took May-Ellen no time at all to be married. Before old August was cold in his silver-embossed casket, the contents of his best store glittered and glimmered and pretended to make an Aladdin's cave around the bed where she went with the mailman. Moved, polished, replaced, rubbed, all her crystal pots doubled themselves on the mirror-topped table and shot rainbow glances at the widow and the orphan child.

Ellen looked hard at her mother. Even during the burial, May-Ellen had still been plump and rosy inside all her black; but now, up and cross-legged on her bed, her bed alone, she was shrinking beneath her gold dragons. The naked eye could almost watch it happening. Beginning with little nibbles, the dragons were growing fat from huge chunks of May-Ellen. Soon the room of rainy, of glinty lights would be full of very fat little dragons made of thread. Or perhaps the food May-Ellen had loved to eat was turning on her, was eating her. Ellen imagined the kitchen cupboards swiftly filling with meat and jelly and corn and bread, all sweetly flavored with the taste of May-Ellen. Ellen tried to close her own robe around her, but the sides would no longer meet.

"Look at all I've got here," said May-Ellen. She moved a hand, a foot, across her bed and rattled all the papers there.

"Where did it all come from?" Ellen sat on the edge of the bed. Anyone could see that the robe was useless to cover her.

"That's neither here nor there." May-Ellen's face would not dry. It was wet as the air covering the house, muddy as a fresh-turned grave. The tears did not seem to come from the eyes; it was a face replenishing itself with water, leaving the eyes out of it, leaving the eyes hot and dry.

"Who's this?" Ellen picked up a snapshot: a slim woman with a dark cap of waved hair, a bow mouth nearly black with paint; a very short dress showing stockings that gleamed with leg. One of her long hands lay on the piano keys; the other reached up to the face of a man whose muscles seemed to bulge through the paper, seemed ready to roar away the entire idea of the young girl and her piano with the huge laugh that was covering all his face. In the margin of the picture, there was a blur of one ghostly hand. It was trying to snatch something back to itself: that much was clear.

"Me, you nit," said May-Ellen. "And my mailman." Her daughter was no longer in the room; she hadn't even been born.

Ellen tried to say something, say something to a woman who was neither lover nor schoolteacher; was not black, was not crazy, was not the girl next door, was not blessed with second sight. She could think of nothing to say.

She said, "Mama? You want to talk about him? What he was . . . like?"

"Oh . . ." May-Ellen picked at the red thread in the quilt; she looked through her daughter. It was as if a child had never been born, because something was coming loose—like a mouth opening, lips parting—in her head; something speaking to her.

"Oh . . ." she repeated, like a sigh. "He was . . ." (*It was the afternoon, the voice was saying to her, you told everybody of your engagement and your papa had just dropped dead from the shock of it all but you didn't know about that yet. . . . You weren't at home, not you!*)

"Oh, he was a good man; I'm sure of that. . . ." said May-Ellen. She began binding her little finger with the thread. (*Down through twilight, dim, green—though it was noon above the trees—he pulled you, your daddy's daughter, your brother's sister, your crazy mama's girl, the beauty who played pianos—pulled you outside the old witch's sight . . .*)

"Old woman! Old witch!" May-Ellen shouted. She kicked at the bedpost. She knotted the thread tightly. Ellen moved back, stumbled on her mother's shoes; fell, said from the floor, "Mama . . . ?"

"Old crone leaned around the porch to watch us go. . . .

Old thing spat brown juice on the hens' feathers, put her nose in her stinking geraniums. . . . Oh, she *scared* me!" (. . . *begrudging you your dear boy's love, though all she ever did with it was spit it out. . . . Saw your hips grow loose at the sight of each other, so she shouted: "Where's my girl that died screaming you never heard such sound from hell to . . .*)

"People die all the time, don't you know it?" May-Ellen cried. Tears hung on her eyelids; she shook her head and they stained her robe. The tip of her finger was growing cold and purple. She pulled the red thread tighter, cutting off more blood. (. . . *push you out, your big shoulders, heavy head, murdering fists that tore up her little belly; then nothing all these years for me but you and those big shoulders, and one turnip could make you stronger than a full meal could most. I see what you're after now, but where's my girl? My girl!" until you couldn't keep your mouth shut any longer, begged him right there in front of her, Please, please get us out of here; she hates you, loves death—look at me, loving you beneath my dress, waiting for one word to give up, give in, allegro appassionata . . .*)

"Loves death! Loves death!" May-Ellen shouted. She still had her pearls around her neck; with a single jerk, she broke the strand, began pitching them, one by one, against her daughter. "I tell you! Hates you, loves death."

Ellen held her, held her hand down, shouted into her ear, "Mama! Come on, Mama—let's talk about him some more. Yes, he was a good man. . . . Then what, Mama?"

May-Ellen's eyes were shut, her head rolling. "No, Roger," she screamed. "It's too late now, just too damn late now, I have you now, I have you, you can't go back there, you sonofabitch, Roger. . . ."

"Mama . . ." Ellen slapped her.

May-Ellen opened her eyes. "Oh yes," she said absently. "Went to church, believed in God, in the resurrection and the life . . . baptism. . . ." She closed her eyes again.

"Could not stand to look at another woman. Could *not!*"
(*. . . spat on you, got that mess on your new white frock;
you could have taken that scrawny turkey throat in your
pretty polished nails, squeezed and squeezed till you popped
him free and clear out of her and he could be truly yours.
But he said, "Grandma, grandma, how you hurt, how you
hurt! But here I am, loving you forever and I won't ever
stop."*)

"Loving you forever and he won't ever stop," May-Ellen
groaned. Ellen let her go, began collecting the pearls from
the floor. There would be thirty to find. She stopped listening; her mother was whispering, in a voice that sounded
like her own; but Ellen stopped listening and found the
pearls.

(*. . . and you saw then and there that nothing made
her sicker than him loving her; and you only smiled when
he kissed her goodbye, grabbed your hand and raced you
through those chickens, the only things that grew in her
yard; across about fifty hard dusty feet you had to run,
gladly, in your high heels and him just laughing to see the
city girl trip, stumble, straps breaking, white pleats bouncing to catch up with his sauntering. Sauntering's the word!
Oh, he rolled. He rolled like Jordan in and out of those
blue jeans he never wore another day after he came to this
house; and he rolled in boots, English riding boots he got
from God knows where . . .*)

Ellen found the twenty-second pearl inside her father's
left mailman shoe. Her hand was full, so she put it on her
tongue and sucked it. She imagined it tasted of sweaty foot;
it was only dust she tasted.

(*. . . because he never rode a thing but a girl and a
mule. Oh, those girls. All the while he pulled you through
the woods, in and out and roundabout—pines, and fox-
glove and fern to your knees, sun coming through less and
less; ground, damper and older, smelling of spring water—
you thought on those girls you knew about from the day*

you decided to get him: the first when he was just fifteen and more like a brother than any other thing to his black-haired son he'd got on that pretty girl who's now gone to rotted teeth and grits-bloated belly, greasy hair, a three-room shack and a mean man who got her ten more when your Roger was done; and the second, the third, the fourth —you thought on them while you rolled after that rolling river Jordan; and they got it, too; though you were the first he'd take off those boots for when he was doing it. It took a long time through the woods. In and out, as I said, and how many rocks tripped you and vines snared you till he took off your high heels and threw one east, one west and kissed each and every pink toenail, took you up in his arms then and there and ran with you, ran till your head hung back and pine boughs up above spun your eyes till they could see not a thing but his running, his green running that made you smell flowers and turpentine and water.

(Ran to his mother's grave. Where he took all his girls, soft as moss; all moss, the old hump twenty-two years old, with a Mason jar of pure white fire behind the stone, drink he poured down your throat and so you let him put you down flat on never such a narrow, such a springy bed. One cold spot through that afternoon of lights and heat, the cold spot of tombstone that pressed your head, hard as ice, pushing you deeper with him. A cold place through your head. . . .)

With her free hand, Ellen covered her mother with the quilt. "Freezing, freezing," May-Ellen was moaning; but Ellen did not answer; her mouth was full.

(Just now, you feel it all over you. The old woman watched. She'd watched from his very first girl; and he knew it, because, just as evening came and all your lights were going dark, he sprang up and called out into the trees, "This one! Granny, this is the one I'm going to have; wait and see. Look! I have her even now!" And you know, though

*your eyes were swimming in the sweat from his face—it's
a gaze that's half-blinded you ever since—that you saw
that old flowered feed sack flash out from the hiding place
and scurry home, laughing with pure meanness. You never
said a word ever about it. He didn't. She—that Dorothea
mama—she certainly didn't. Something between the three
of them—though nothing, certainly not you, ever got her to
love him back.*)

"I want him back, back," May-Ellen sobbed. "He *told*
me he felt like he was going to live forever, he told me!"

"Just shut up, Mama," said Ellen, around the pearl in
her mouth. The thirtieth pearl was in her hand.

(*Oh yes, he believed in the resurrection and the life: so
this is what you've figured all these years when you've
thought about it at all—that he thought, when he rode his
mother's flanks, time after time in those good boots, that
he was bringing her back to life. She did, she let him in,
let him out again. She did. But he did take off those boots
for you. . . .*)

"I said, just shut up, Mama . . ." Ellen dropped twenty-
nine pearls in the toe of her father's shoe. She swallowed
the one in her mouth and walked to her mother's bed.

(*On the way back, he saw a rabbit in his trap, but you
made him let it go. The old woman had to do on salt pork
and black-eyes that night because that night you made him
come home with you, made him listen to you and all
the rondos you could play half that night until you looked
and found him asleep, curled like a big dog on the rug.
Before that, your mother had snapped this picture and
sent the news to your papa, and your papa'd been dead
before Roger fell asleep and you'd finished with your
music. . . .*)

The rain had stopped midway between the sky and the
grass. Somewhere below the window it hung as mist, soften-
ing the air. A bird with a throat like a creaking door
opened it, closed it, stopped the voice in May-Ellen's head.

May-Ellen lay back in her bed and crossed her endragoned arms over her forehead. She gave Ellen a look from beneath the sleeves that meant she was wondering what her daughter had been hearing.

Ellen had heard nothing; but she felt talked out, as though her tongue had been rattling with words for hours. It was holding the pearl on her tongue that had tired it, she thought.

She had found a leather autograph book in the stuff on the bed. It was gold and blue: "The Paragon Autograph Album." Its cover was engraved with ribbons and forget-me-nots.

"Why can't you, all of you, leave me alone?" May-Ellen began to cry.

"Then let us part," said Ellen, moving toward the door with the little book, "on these fine words: 'May-Ellen, Do not forget me: The hours full-freighted with a joy too deep for words, have flown too swiftly by, Oh keep That Joy undimmed: And though henceforth we two may dwell apart, I ask that some sweet Memory in your Heart You'll keep of Me. Signed, Clifford R. Mills.' "

"Hush a minute! Read that again."

Ellen, with one eye on the book, with the other watching Welch and Darwin Waters stretching and smoking and putting on clean shirts out in the hall, read it again.

"He was a nice boy," May-Ellen murmured, her voice surfacing a little, "but he had skinny legs, was part bald when he was twenty and went to Harvard Law. We used to play four-handed Bach together and Papa loved him. He didn't do a thing for me, though. You know what I got! You wanted to hear about your daddy? Well, your daddy's what I got!"

She rolled over. As Ellen left the room, dropping the little book behind her, she heard her mother laughing into her pillow, her soft laughter made softer by the crushing down.

Ellen, honey?"

"What, Welch?"

"You sure have grown. I just don't see you wearing that dragon robe anymore. We can still get into ours, but you had to go and grow. But I bet that's all right with you. I bet you're ready for black lace and pink satin ribbons is my guess. You want to see my new autographed picture of Count Dracula? I guess it's decent; funeral's over, he's buried now. Look."

"Very pretty."

"Well, not *pretty!* More like me, don't you see? Style, elegance, upper class?"

"America says she's going to call the law one day if you all don't stop smoking so much marijuana up here."

"Oh America! Oh *law.* Lawsy muhcy, don't scare a soul to death lak that!" Welch rolled his nearly lavender eyes, weak renditions of Ellen's, laughing; then he laughed over his shoulder to see if Beloved had got it. Darwin got it and laughed back, a true-to-life, sound-reflecting mirror, Beloved was. Their fingers twinkled; they whipped their neckties into Windsor knots, "in honor of our beloved *divorcée*," they said together.

"Next time you hear America getting any black thoughts about our habits, you just ask her again where Venusberg came from!" Trying to laugh, Welch sucked air into his skinny chest and forced out a loud bray. "But I forget myself. How's little sister, how's little sister bearing up? I declare it's a shame to think there'll be no more answering cries from those bedsprings across the hall. Beloved and I will bounce, to be sure, but bounce lonesomely. I mean it, how's little sister?"

"She, too, is laughing," Ellen answered. She let the dragon robe slide off; she made a naked procession of herself up and down the hall. Welch watched, his eyes as slow as her footsteps. "Ask me how am *I*, Uncle Welch, his daughter. Why don't you inquire after the state of the mailman's daughter?"

"Babiest love, your daddy! I *know* you grieve, but I was just standing here thinking, *So young!* And even if you did cut your hair short you'd still be too round to look like Count Dracula. Correct, Beloved?"

"Correct," Darwin answered.

"But Count Dracula might like you a lot the way you look, and that's a huge advantage in life, to be that type. Correct, Beloved?"

"Correct. Please, Welch, I'm going to turn off my earring now, so don't say any more. It's time to go eat, anyway."

"Yes it is, Beloved. That girl had better put some clothes on. That girl's a piece of fancywork. That girl's going to distract my mother's peace of mind with that fancywork—cause vibrations!—then there'll be hell to pay. I don't want it." Welch shouted, furious: "What daddy are you talking about, anyhow? That mailman lived here exclusively for your mama's bed—allegro appassionata, as your mama has so frequently pointed out—and unfaithful! Even unfaithful when he had all that! And how could he help himself? . . . although he *was* helping himself all the time to anything he wanted . . . with his hand dipping so many times a day into so many mailboxes. But, as Mrs. Carlyle said of Thomas, he had the 'habit' of preferring your mother to other women. You're no daughter, naked girl, naked-as-a-jaybird girl! They barely stopped long enough to look at you. But I've observed sister being a good mother, if you can call all that singing and play acting over love being a good mother. But you're no daughter. What would you like to be instead?" Welch came close to Ellen. She smelled violets in his thinning black hair.

Ellen thrust out her breasts, made her uncle back away.

"I would like to be the resurrection and the life of the mailman," she answered, believing it as she spoke.

"A fine choice," said Welch. She had pushed at him until his back was against the wall. He stammered, "Your body's deft, like his—although the stingy, common thing would never let me find out just *how* deft!—and I can see your fingers easily sending and receiving messages, just like his did—the good news and the bad news. Come here close."

Welch grabbed Ellen's hair and yanked her head to his; he whispered in her ear, with a strong scent of violets: "You'll find the riding boots and her first Christmas present to him—the Inverness cape, the one he used to wrap up in, in the middle of the night, to go downstairs and eat ice cream after sex—all in the red box in the hall closet. All yours now. Put them on and go find out about Venusberg."

In the evening, in the grass, beneath the moon, beneath the thick sky that upon occasion rumbled with thunder, everything happened. Things began to come about so easily, so surely, that Ellen of the flashing knife, Ellen of the burning home, fantasy-haunted (she could be, at once, crude seducer and pink Camille), became soon undone.

For two weeks she had slept away the days on her bed, and had come out at night: in the evening, in the grass, beneath the moon, skirting her family, who shored themselves up against the night behind May-Ellen's music, safe behind her fast fingers, although they rattled magazine pages and shuffled books when May-Ellen, mischief-making, lingered through, sometimes even repeated, andante passages. They wanted her doing her music fast and loud, with no signs of sentiment or misery. There was nothing else to worry about but the single burden they all carried, May-Ellen's unaccustomed, awful chastity. They could not cure it, but it worried them less when she was loud and fast at the piano. And Ellen left it all every evening, when it was dark, when the music had started, when America was sleeping above the garage and Venusberg was out wandering niggertown hunting for a boy friend (with a letter to Ellen in her pocket, a letter getting dirtier by the night because Ellen would not appear and allow a delivery) —Ellen left it all to rush into the black wet grass, a tall moth-human in flapping white shirt (a Roger castoff), in shiny underpants, rushing to rid herself of even those few clothes and lie secret and naked behind a curve of boxwood that had been planted to hide and sweeten the mailman's vegetable garden that had flourished privately there for twenty years.

It went on, the same way every night, for fourteen nights: Ellen lay flat on her back where she fell. The grass bent against her skin, tickling and itching; and Ellen, gritting her teeth, refusing to scratch, imagined that the irritation was the thin line of sensation that separated her living from her dying. And she imagined that the dew, passing and dampening her, carried, like any river, a mess of trash: cardboard, rubber, glass. She read the mess for omens, as though it were the entrails of a sacrificial animal. She meant to see, and saw, symptoms of her next-day dreams and images of her future: dreams and future all about nothing but love—love in pink-lit dark, herself rolling with a silky shadow, neither a her nor a him, but strong and causing pleasure that would not stop; an endless dream, an endless future of nothing but endless that. She imagined that the lightning bugs sought to trap themselves in the thicket of her pubic hair. When one wavered above, she raised her hips to its red-hot tail, but she never got near. She imagined things with segmented bodies, many colors, many legs, breaking through the grass to arch themselves up into her body, to stamp with many feet up her long bright passage until they found a warm curve to burrow in. She kept her thighs tight shut. She was ailing with lust, day in, day out. She kept her hands locked, one beneath the other, under her head.

And all of this lasted fourteen nights, the same every

night: fourteen nights followed by thirteen days of swaggering or swooning through dreams. On the last night came her undoing; and the beginning of the future.

On that night, as on all the others, she lay against the earth and felt it slipping and sliding her across its back like some brown beast she'd been tied to, to lumber her across the universe. Her fingers full of purple smell went inside her nostrils, and the smell of purple jogged also into the universe. Why don't I move and get up? Act alive. Because my two feet stick up heavy as two tombstones down there. Two of us dead to the world, and to light; and I was meant to be the resurrection. There has to be a limit. *Think:* How long does it take death to rub the skin off the bones? How long does it take for a dead man's hair to grow as long as his daughter's, for bones instead of hands to cross his breast?

Ellen, quickly, uncrossed her own hands and rubbed them back to life. Her head had been killing them with its weight. Something was growing across her chest and down her belly; but it was not her own hair spreading out, it was the night's, with a breath like the rub of hair: it seemed out to tangle up any naked soul it could catch. Night was sitting on its haunches all over the world pointing and shouting: *Something's new in the rude man's, the mailman's vegetable garden—boxwood's perfumy fence won't save us from the smell of it—burn it up!* Night, first with one stick of lust, then with one of death—with an equal number of each and with many of them—built a funeral pyre as tall as a tower for the naked soul. Ohio Blue Tip from head to toe, Ellen struck herself, went up crackling smoke and fire that fanned out her father's name; it seemed to be her own name.

About midnight, cackling to herself about the witching hour, Miss Nina went outside and sat down on her side of the boxwood fence, the side that was a paragon of a rose garden, all yellow and pink in the daylight and changed by the dark into bunches of soft unfurling fists. Her garden was guarded at either end by gnarled crape myrtle trees with blossoms that had been faded by rain into lavender, Miss Nina's favorite color. As she settled herself down, she imagined what the color of lavender must be in the dark. But she was thinking mostly that there was someone on the bad side of the fence, someone lying there pretty still but breathing hard. She was afraid that it must be Roger lying there on the bad side—he could breathe like a hurricane—but she decided it would do no harm to talk to him. But in case he might want to come over and talk back to her, maybe carry her off over to the bad side, she took the precaution of hooking her arm around the strongest of her rosebushes, the Dorothy Perkins. Then she lay down, comfortably, her head in Dorothy's sandy bed, to converse in safety.

"Roger," she said, "when I was a bride, scarcely deflowered, August and I got another wedding present: it was a trip to Paris, France. Did I never relate this story to you before, Roger?"

"Not a bit," Ellen answered.

"Well, in that case. But at the last minute, August got his bad hemorrhoids, through neglect, into such a state (I've always felt they came on from too much handling of diamonds and silver; and some people I've known wear magic metal rings for arthritis cure) that he had to be rushed off to the hospital bed, not Paris. Loath to cast all joy out of me, however, he said he'd let me go on without him if I'd take his sister Lilac with me in his place; a woman with a hard head on hard shoulders: she'd look after me. Sister Lilac was as fat as two hogs, and if there's anything I hate and despise it's fat. Also, she never bathed but would still take up the bathroom all the livelong day, lock herself up in there to smoke cigars in secret while you stood outside with your kidneys rupturing, and then she'd come out and declare some filthy man had been in there smelling up the place. If you think this is all a lie, Roger, and that I've never been to Paris, you just go ask Ellen. She'll tell you. You can imagine how Paris looked to me after crossing the Atlantic with that Lilac. And in Paris: nothing, nothing, nothing all day long but eat and sleep and criticize and go look for a Presbyterian church that spoke English. That's Lilac. But I fixed her wagon. She'd just got started on her after-breakfast (postprandial!) cigar (you know what she'd eat for breakfast? She got them to get it for her—a big bloody steak, potatoes all fried, an egg salad sandwich, toast and jelly, two pieces of chocolate pie and then complained because you couldn't get grits out of Frogs!) and it was our fifth day over there, when I just calmly up and pinned on my hat and pushed and pulled like a mule until I got an eight-foot highboy up against the toilet door. Then, by God, I went out, saw Paris and, before the day was over, fell in with a gang of fetishists. And if you're thinking you can pass them in the street and not know, and that they look just like you and me, you're right—to a certain extent. I had on these gloves, you see. Nobody without my slender arms—they're paper-thin!—could get away with gloves like that. White kid all the way up to the elbow, and with some very fancy puncture work on all ten fingers so that it looked like every finger was entwined with little roses and violets and leaves. And sixteen pearl buttons. It wasn't any time before I was sitting there drinking champagne with these three fetishists, very refined, too, and before much longer I was realizing what I'd been missing all my life: *appreciation!* I won't go into any details. Enough said that they kept showing me their gloves and I kept showing them mine. This with all the romance of Paris abounding. But what I'm really leading up to, Roger, is about the one fetishist that genuinely took my fancy. I'll just go ahead and assume that you've never read that great work of romance and intrigue, *Psychopathia Sexualis?*"

"Of course," Ellen answered. "But of course I like some parts better than others." (Especially, she thought, very still among the reeking squash that not even America would touch now, that part that so delighted Janet Sanctissima, Sanctissima's ideal you might say: "Case 166 . . . this ostensible Count Sandor [who] was no man at all, but a woman in male attire—Sarolta (Charlotte), Countess V." Countess V.! Of ancient and noble Hungarian lineage, growing up with a pack of females who gave balls from their sickbeds, who cried "Bewitched! Bewitched!" at a particular table, who carried a key to a Black Chamber and who might closet themselves up for two years without a single appearance—and all of them, without exception, "intellectual, finely educated and amiable." But Countess V. herself: her mother could not bear the light of the moon; her father admired the horsemanship of his daughter and the muscle in her arm. Countess V. She fell in love at least once a year with persons of her own sex and, indeed, boasted that once in a brothel she had held a girl on each knee. In love she had no constancy. But of all her "marriages" to that long series of passionate, weeping, clinging women (the first, at thirteen, to a redheaded English schoolgirl), Ellen thought, I'm most fond of the relationship with "Miss D.": "That S. (Sandor!) also had the power to excite passion in other women was shown by the fact that when she (before her marriage with E.) had grown tired of a Miss D., after having spent thousands of guldens on her, she was threatened with shooting by D. if she would become untrue.")

It's my hard luck, thought Ellen, pushing her thumbs into the throats of rotting crooknecks, that I choose knives instead of pistols. Those with a preference for aiming and firing spend a lifetime being showered with thousands of guldens. Ellen gave her eyes over to the dark and her ears to her grandmother. In her heart she was shouting, Sandor! Charlotte! I love you.

"You must realize," Miss Nina continued, "that this particular charming gentleman told me his story *himself*—told it himself, there in the precious avenues of Paris while we strolled and cast glances, while Lilac beat upon the toilet door and no one came. . . . Just because you, Roger, have read his story in a book does not mean that it really didn't happen and that I didn't get it first-hand! If only you had beheld him, then even you, Roger, would have remarked upon that charm of his, that fatal charm that ate me up, that made me swoon. I think of him—his wide blue eyes, brilliant, spinning with hot fire —like August's diamonds. His hair was curly and black; he was graceful and thin—wasting away, really, he said, with that constant gnawing inside him, that would not give him peace, for the sweet female hand encased in tender kid. Mine, he said—oh, he couldn't get enough of them—twin de Milos! Goddesses gracing a world full of clumsy mortals! Well, we strolled and strolled, but his pleasure would overcome him every second step: in ecstasy he would grasp my hand—there, among all the Parisians— and kiss each violet-, each rose-strewn knuckle, bear down with his teeth into my leather palm, rush his lips up and down the sixteen pearl buttons and, quite often, really, he would snatch his coat to the front of him and rush inside one of those numerous French conveniences to emerge shortly, exhausted; but smiling and calm and ready to begin loving me again."

"But what do you mean by all this?" Ellen asked. She could hear footsteps scrunching, could hear someone set-tling, rustling into the bean-vine leaves at the other end of the vegetables. It could be anyone. It could be love down there. Miss Nina must go. Ellen's grass bed was getting hot; the sight of stars, tiresome. The air was close and pressing; she must find some new space of it to breathe. Ellen rose up on her elbows, careless that her grandmother might see not only Roger but a Roger increased—Roger himself and Roger feminine: Roger as Ellen. But Miss Nina did not take her eyes off the dark. Deep down in the dark, her hands moved beneath the Dorothy Perkinses, piling and patting the sand into castles as high as her hands; her amber hairpins, hanging by a thread, drooped, then fell and got lost forever. She murmured, about something, "It's a sin and a shame." She made tunnels as narrow as her fingers.

Miss Nina kept talking. "It was only that one afternoon. I never saw him or any of them again. Soon we had to come home. Lilac was rip-roaring mad about the toilet and bound and determined to tell August and everybody but the dogcatcher what I'd done to her, but I said you do and I'll tell about the cigars. What cigars? she said, dumb as ditchwater to think she could fool me; but she never told on me. Oh, I came home full of a dream! And the next thing you know August crowded Welch in there beside it: full of dream, full of Welch, and Welch came out of me tailfirst all wrapped up in it. How can he help being his mother's son? For a whole year I nursed him, changed him, rocked him: always up to my elbows in those same sixteen-button gloves. I was always hoping against hope, and who can blame me, that he would become . . . but you see what he became. Not a bit of that lovely Paris fetishist in him. First of all, an ordinary onanist, having fantasies of me sitting in the nude and rocking him; dreaming of his daddy polishing him like a silver cake knife. Common stuff; not what a mother wants for her son. Then he brought me that lengthy, boring time; me tending your wife-to-be's piano lessons—enough Czerny to float a battleship and unnerving the entire neighborhood, and him pulling home every ragtag and bobtail that could get its hind legs inside a pair of tight blue jeans, and eating me out of house and home and messing up I don't know how many sets of percale. I bless the day of beloved Darwin Waters' coming! We all settled down from that day on; but, too, no more dreams for me except the kind you get out of a book. But after all, what living thing—either son or Paris gentleman—can compare with Monsieur de Charlus? After all, perhaps, I have the best. . . ."

Ellen listened to the sounds of thorns tearing a yard-long rip down her grandmother's batiste; of hands slapping off the sand.

"I'm going, Roger. I hear your wife commencing the *Appassionata*—with which, as you well know, she will finally wring the night dry and wear herself out enough to sleep. Soon, silence will be back. I'm going now. . . . Besides, I'm not all that sure it's you, Roger, I've been talking to. But if it is you, Roger, it's high time you came back inside, went to bed, and gave us all the peace we so sorely need. . . . Hurry to bed, Roger—if it's you."

The thunder of her mother's music rolled out the back windows; it was like an electrical storm, frightening and dazzling and seeming to mean too much. As either art or nature, it seemed to mean too much; and Ellen was as positive as she'd ever been about anything that down there in the butter-bean vines, Sanctissima was crouching, beating her oily, heavy wings and ready to fall upon her. Ellen eased into Roger's shirt; then into her underpants. She began crawling toward Sanctissima between the vegetable rows, her hands and knees ruffling the dirt, leaving the signs of struggle behind her; her bottom rose behind her like a shiny double of the real moon. Midway through the squash, she stopped. Not only Sanctissima: the nameless soldier was also sure to be lurking there. Without a doubt, he was lurking with Sanctissima, both of them identical twins in a single egg of their love for her; ready, both of them, to be born with her. She stood up and began to strut, propping a hand on a hip, pointing her breasts as though a real built-in bra was there to keep them in step. For the nameless soldier, she made her body into a movie-girl, fleshiness swiveling out of a machine;

and for Sanctissima, she made her eyes languid, old-fashioned, musical. Here I come, ready or not. They were down there, ready. She'd been burying her daddy; they'd been making plans—and nothing was beyond people full of desire. It was easy to see their design. Her left foot crunched through a squash; she went on, and the gray dirt covered and made a cake of the seedy pulp. Looking up, she could read in the stars what her lovers had in mind for her. The small wind rustled the myrtle leaves behind her, telling the story plain and simple. The other tree, in front of her, stood still, leaned quietly over the boxwood. It was under those branches, she understood, that appetite sizzled and sent out the steam, hoping to roast her before she was fairly in the oven.

She was nearly there; the music was running ahead, then chasing its tail around her ankles, hurrying her up for them. Her skin crackled in the heat and smelled delicious, like perfume to eat, like roses to drink. In a moment now, they would have her. Janet Most-holy, Nameless Soldier—between them, they would grasp her, tear her, eat her up. She crept on tiptoe. She knew what they really wanted: not her body, but the two weeks' worth of fantastic erotic growths inside it. They were going to shell her like a hull and eat up her dreams, eat up the flesh of Roger there inside her. She went ahead, ready to give it to them.

"Reach me one of them tomatoes before you come here. I am so hungry. Please."

"*Venusberg?*"

"Call me anything you want, just don't call me late for supper." A light laugh; hard crying.

"Venusberg? It's you there, no fooling? Who's with you?"

"Who would be with Venusberg? Not even her own mama. Even her mama's got herself a man. Ain't no man for Venusberg. Just witch girl, witch girl!"

Ellen knelt before a vine; what she thought was a vine

or the beany shadow of one, with the moon above and to one side of it. No, not a moon; a head. Below the head, the shadow. Not a shadow—flesh and bone, and Ellen's own, and wanting Ellen. Someone had come. Ellen moved one arm to hold back the vines, and Venusberg fell through the clearing and onto her.

"I love you, Venusberg. Cry it out on me."

She was as light as dust. Every cumbersome sob that fell out of her mouth made her lighter. The moon was behind her, its light growing thicker and stronger by the second. It pushed against the little backbone and drove Venusberg deeper into Ellen's arms.

"The night after you all buried him, my mama stopped spending nighttime reading the Bible and figuring out the Dream Book. The first night after, we went to our room and she said, 'You want to do something for me? Take out the iron and iron me that yellow taffeta in the back of the closet.' I did that; I didn't know what to do. While I ironed, she sat and rocked and smoked a cigarette. I never saw her smoke a cigarette. Then she put on the yellow dress over nothing at all but her bare skin, and combed Dixie Peach in her hair and put red lipstick, brand-new, on her mouth. I started crying, I cried, 'Mama, Mama, don't leave me! What's going to happen? What are you going to do to me?' She never smiled. She just said, 'I'm going to leave you for a while and leave all that white mess, too, for a while, and what's going to happen now is the truth. I'm going to go stop making real people into dream things.' Then she turned around all of a sudden with her face all worked up and mean like she hated and she threw the scissors off of the table right in my face. My lip got cut."

Ellen moved her fingers along the lips. There was a tiny ridge in the mouth's corner; she leaned and kissed it lightly.

"Mama said, 'Shut up that crying, I never want to hear

that crying again, you're going to stop having a mama just like you just stopped having a daddy. Get on out of here! But don't you come following me. Go find yourself a boyfriend, one with a knife in his pocket and rowdy and mean and drinking and gambling, something *real like that!* Shut up with making things up. All day you do it and all night you call out music! piano! castle! book! drum majorette! *love!* Shit shit shit! Nothing like that is ever going to happen to you—or to me either! You hear? You hear me? And when some night you get flat on your back and think you hear angel wings, you better be in your right mind quick enough to know it's just a man's pants getting throwed across the room!' She yelled and yelled at me, then tore out, and I stopped crying, because you know what? I'd just heard a piece of news about me, Venusberg, and it wasn't about nobody else. . . ."

She lifted her head from Ellen's shoulder. The moonlight was covering Ellen's eyes; and Venusberg couldn't see whether there was anything to fear there.

"You mad?" she asked shyly. Her tears were all over Ellen's face. "You mad? What I found out was your daddy is my daddy, too. That's my news."

Ellen's eyes did not move. They looked straight into the light and would not come clean for Venusberg. Her hand slid up and down Venusberg's back, pausing at each little knob. Someone was loving Venusberg.

"Why have you been crying so hard?" That was all Ellen answered.

Venusberg hardly knew. Whatever it was had happened so far back that it didn't count anymore. Someone was loving her, Venusberg. She sighed, spoke softly and slowly, relaxed and in pleasure from the end of the weeping.

"She said that all I ever did was wrong, that I couldn't do any of it anymore. Those words she called out to me —I think they're the names of things I been wanting. But she said no more; she tore out of there and showed me the way it's got to be. So all that first night long I just sat there, said to myself, Stop wanting all that, V.B.; stop it, V.B. But what do you do? Can't stop just like that. All life long you think up names of mess you want, and the names get stuck inside you—can't shit it out, can't vomit it out, ain't no doctor that can cut it out. What do you do? So right before daytime, when she came back home, I took this letter out that I been carrying for you seems like forever, and I wrote all the names down on it at the bottom. Once I give you this letter, they're going to be your names; you got to take them over. All the things I want are going to belong to you then."

Venusberg's back, beneath Ellen's hand, shuddered in peace. Her mouth spoke words, soft and wet, against Ellen's shoulder; full speed ahead, Ellen felt them dive through her body.

"You read me the letter now, Venusberg."

"It's too dark; moon won't stay still to light it up."

"Then say it by heart."

Venusberg cleared her throat through its fog of old tears. She lifted her face. She said, "Dear Ellen: Through a death you'll see your life and your need clear before you. Get rid of that death and inside you you will find great change that will be great joy. Nothing will you desire but this joy. Another change: You will become like unto a bat! Another change: A child will come and will make lasting change. Sincerely yours, Venusberg. *Book, Castle, Music, Piano, Drum Majorette, Valedictorian, Up North, Good Eye, Dresses, Beauty, Rock Hudson, Home, Love*. That's all."

Venusberg pressed her cheek against Ellen, where all her things had gone.

"Look back up here at me, V.B."

"What? You got them now. You can't give back."

"That last thing. Say the name of the last thing to me again. That's what I want most."

"What?"

"You say it."

"Love?"

"Say it."

"Love."

Ellen stood up, shaking little Venusberg from her gently, as though she were dropping her doll or her dress to the ground.

"Where you going?"

On her feet, Ellen felt herself expanding; bliss was blowing her up. She rose from the earth; her feet dangled in thin air. She pressed a hand on her chest where, inside, something was kicking her heart over and over. She opened her mouth; she expected to see the word JOY, spelled in big letters of white vapor, issue forth. It did not. She whispered, Fuck off, Sanctissima! Take a flying leap, nameless old Soldier-Boy. Stay dead, Daddy: I got better things to do with my time.

"Listen, Venusberg! Wait for me. No matter how long I'm gone, you wait right here; don't move, you hear, until I get back. No matter how long. Do you hear, Venusberg?"

"No matter how long, I'll be here." And Venusberg was left with a moon that was sinking to her feet.

Here we go, baby! Use the back door, sugar pie, your mama's winding up the Old Favorite now—Appash-a-snotty's what I always wanted to call it, but it always turned her sexy as a rabbit— The *back* door, I said! They'll never hear you through that last loud mess—the faggots are trimming each other's toenails, the old bitch is having a nervous breakdown over some book— Hurry up! The *back* door, baby, I said!

"Daddy?"

Sure-nuff, sweetheart—who'd you expect, Franklin Delano Roosevelt? It's your old man, here I am! You've done it, I'm back! Back for a bigger time than ever— All that sexy stuff you been stuffing in your bonnet these last weeks—you started going at it right, but I was right there with you pushing, shoving it in, all that sugar candy that got you so hot—*it brought me back!* You got my number all right, baby—first time you thought *Fuck,* old Roger started crawling out of that grave. You said you'd do it, you did it—my sweet Resurrection-Baby! Now we goin do something feels good—the *back* door, now you heard me!

"Daddy?"

You heard, sure.

"Stay dead, Daddy—I got better things to do with my time!"

No way to talk—besides, it's too late now, I'm back—and all those things you got to do with your time, you ain't goin do one of them without me with you. Understand! I'm the *way,* baby! Call me Roger. Here's the closet. Watch it, the door creaks. Listen at your mama go! She's going to be hot as hell tonight. Let's be sure not to forget your mama tonight, whatever we do. Careful how you handle them boots, baby. They're purer-bred than anything in this house and they've seen a lot more action.

"They don't fit, Roger; not me. . . ."

Now they do—feel now. Don't wiggle your toes so much; I tickle easy.

"Now they fit fine, Roger, fine. . . ."

Told you so. You look first-class in my britches, baby; never saw nothing like the way you fill 'em out, except for the way I filled 'em. Now for the fool cape; only bathrobe I ever owned and still stinks to high heaven of my sweet prick. There! Your mama's hushed, and they're all goin to bed. I'm ready now; *we're* ready, sugar. . . . Let's go!

Down the block, baby, run like hell! Smell that air, smell that moon! First stop, Miss Betty Lucas; bang hard on her mailbox —brand-new last year algebra teacher, blond on top and black below and I ought to know! She'll come like a hornet when she hears that bang. Bang *hard!* Her mama's deaf as a post; she's just sick to death *she's* too dried up for the good old me, but we'll bring her young'un down to her marrow bones begging for it— Bang *hard!*

"Daddy? Roger?"

I hear you talking, but *bang* and hush! Don't shilly-shally, here she comes, that yellow-topped harridan's hurrying like hell, she's coming, she's coming, she's here! Now run some more, and run and run and beat those heels of mine hard like I beat 'em for a million years up and down these streets to keep you fed and clothed and strong; to keep you ready for just this night. I'm exploding! To rise, to rise again! No more narrow grave this night! To feel my britches snap and slide, and a greasy yellow moon up there for me to slide on! Look inside the pocket—the silver flask, her #2 xmas gift for me, meant to wean me from homespun jars of lightning, God bless her, how dumb can you get? Thinking to filigree me! Feel it, baby? You feel it? It's stars scratching your tongue then busting in your belly. One more sip, then run some more—there's a widow on the block with nothing to live for but church work and me. Listen at her sing hallelujah! Jesus H. Christ himself is goin to have to raise more than the dead to get a hallelujah like that from her. Lord God, how many have we had already? Fifteen? A hundred? Just two? More filigree lightning now—there's nothing more wearisome than a night of special deliveries. Down there to that vacant lot, walk slow. My ankles ache—Lord God, is it death that makes me so tired? Bad girl, bad girl, what did you raise me up for? And it was only yesterday, or a year ago—or a hundred years ago—that I coulda tore apart a mountain of female arms and thighs and then stuck it all back together again with honey! Now, I'm tired; cain't remember anything but you and how sad I feel for that big monster man I was, all trapped now in this sissy-prissy girl walk of yours—no big shoulders to swing back and forth—I'm so tired. . . .

"Does it hurt, Daddy?"

Nothing hurts or feels like anything anymore, fool girl— Hold your shoulders straight, my breath is cramping! All those doorbells we rung—God, God, let's sit down. Sit me down, baby girl —here's the vacant lot and here's where we'll sit: on the big stone steps that didn't get burned down with the rest of the place. Now I'm remembering another thing: I'm the one that made this lot vacant. It was Halloween, and all these trees that're green and thick as I was then were blowing and creaking, and red leaves thick as my blood were covering all these steps. I was fifteen, was with Roy, and the sassy mean old bitch here in this house-that-was turned us away, said, "Not gone give you big ol' boys any candy! How come big boys like you are out Halloweening 'steada out working for your mamas like you should be? Go on! Shoo!" she yelled at us, "you don't, I'm callin the police this minute!" *Mad!* I was mad to beat the band! So I said, "Roy, you just wait a minute." Old witch had gone back behind her big old door, slammed it right at us, and all her lights'd gone out, too. Couldn't't've told there was a single soul in that great big old house. So I said, "Roy, wait a minute—that old bitch ain't so mean that she can keep me from sittin on her steps one minute to have me a cigarette. Nobody's that mean." But Roy wanted to get back to the girls we had waitin on the sidewalk, giggling and grabbing at each other, thinkin Roy and me was so cute to trick-or-treat, thinkin how we was goin to trick-or-treat their fannies fore old Halloween was done. So I said, "You just go on, Roy, keep em quiet any way you can till I have myself this one cigarette." So Roy went, thinking I was crazy to sit there in that howling scary yard all by myself, but I stayed. Couldn't get the butt lighted, though, in all that big wind, so I had to step up in the porch shelter, and five packs of matches caught on fire, don't ask me how, I don't know. Just did. And her front-room window was cracked open—got cracked open—and the lace curtain was blowin out some and somehow all those packs of matches went in at the window and got caught in the curtain. Nothing I could do. Nothing. But for a minute, I stared straight past the fire into the room: There it was; and there was my granny back home eatin mashed-up turnips by a kerosene lamp—there it was, and I was burnin it all up: big piano with a Spanish shawl to hide it; big glass cases on both sides of the fireplace with red and blue leather books in em; rugs on top of rugs, all of em the color—and more—of the books. Chairs and settees covered in flowers and birds. And all very warm; and my granny back home startin to freeze at night. Summer was gone. It got warmer, so much warmer I had to shut my eyes to keep from seeing what was making it so warm; and I nearly broke my ass gettin down those steps and back to Roy and the girls. I nearly broke both them girls that night, then turned around, did it all over again. And here we are. Sit me down, honey; stretch me way out in the leg—

though God knows it still ain't good enough for a man the size I was. These stones are still warm; summer's here. There's a draft down my back, though—comes from all them empty rooms that ain't there behind us. Tell me why I'm here!

"Daddy, you might be tired, but I'm on fire! Let's move, Daddy; let's ring some more doorbells! Let's do it to a *man's* doorbell! Mr. Jimmy Cornelius down the street: *him!*"

Honor thy father, fool girl! And you wanta know what it'd be like with a man? Huh? Just like old Welch with that horse's ass, Darwin, and I oughta know because I watched them at it one time and it was horse's-ass dumb! Catch *me!* And I'm tired and gettin tireder, didn't I tell you? Bend that elbow of yours and take some of the tired outa my bones—and tell me why I'm here. Go on and do it—I keep forgettin everything.

"Jimmy Cornelius is the son of Mercy Cornelius, Daddy; the one who was the witch, who lived in this house you burned down, all thirty-two rooms, Daddy, and he's pretty and has a red moustache and is forty years old and has read Latin all his life and's been to Europe three times, and he won't sell this land nor do a thing with it. Let's have him, Daddy!"

Goddamn you to hell, girl! Won't you remember that as long as I'm here with you in these boots *you're a man!* I give you the time of your life tonight, like no other girl alive's had it, and you turn out to be nothing but a serpent's tooth. . . .

"Daddy, won't you remember that as long as I'm here with you in these boots *you're a girl?* Try hard, and you can remember that. Tell me how you got here."

Ellen felt a long helpless sigh escape her, a sigh she'd never dreamed of feeling; never felt. A story coiled up tight inside her loosened itself, and, in her father's voice, jumped from her mouth. The night in the vacant lot— though green and rank with old moss, old rot, old box- wood, old wisteria, new blooms spreading over shabby blooms, though it was June—was cold. Or perhaps it was the stones, mortared together to arc elegantly below an arcing porch, that made her cold. Behind the steps, for a distance of thirty-two vanished rooms, nothing grew but old weeds and vines, close to the ground. Through all that space, a little wind was blowing up and making them hunch further down inside their Inverness. The night, though it was June, had a Halloween scare about it.

Here's what happened. It was nothing; it was like falling off a log: but I don't recommend it. Death, it upsets everything you can think of, ruins your habits—all of them—both sour and sweet, both rotten and delicious. . . .

Ellen's body began shaking with sigh after sigh, all of them beginning to sound like moans, like groans and rattling chains. But the ghost went on talking.

I ain't talking about the first part of it—what happened when that rich bastard's hound-dog of a son's wad of a car flew through the air at me—that wasn't nothing but a big body explosion, the biggest I can remember, and that wasn't anything I object to so much. It was everything else: first, at the funeral home—Dickie Crumpler with one of my arms, Ernest Crumpler with the other one, both of 'em cramming my arms down a pair of black sleeves, then working an hour to get my feet pointed right, in line with my head. Then prettification, prettification half the night long! Swabbing, powdering, dusting, rouging, draining, combing—sweetening enough to make a whore blush. It was even more than that—like a bride using every trick you can name to make herself ready for the wedding night. Then they covered me up, left me all alone, and there I was, sheer craziness itself and wondering when hell or heaven was going to start. Nothing started. I kept myself—sane? . . . alive? . . . what?—kept myself going by saying One, two, buckle my shoe and Lucy Locket lost her pocket and There once was a whore from Tibet until—*Jesus save me!*—there were new hands all over me. Not Crumpler hands. *Un*dressing me, rubbing me; something whispering, something kissing. I couldn't move or shout. When it climbed on top of me, I couldn't fight it off. Couldn't say No, get off me! It's not supposed to be this way! *Oh, Jesus save me!* It was all over me; it was me getting raped —I couldn't fight it off. It took a long, long time down in the hole in the dark with it; and it was chuckling and hissing and cursing and whispering: *More! More!* Oh, girl, listen to me: I never raped once, not anything in all my life. I figured it out at last, and it was hard to figure during all that, but I figured it out. I figured, this is hell forever, what I get for all I did to women. Finally it stopped. A light started somewhere around me, and I saw its face. It was like your mama's diamond with the sun on it; it was like a maggot in a dead cat's bowels; it was like the head of a rose in a woman's hands. It was the outhouse floor at the end of a week-long July revival. It let me look at it. . . . Then it said . . .

The ghost's voice of sighs and moans changed, became harsh and distinct and filled more with stink than sound. The words became old.

Then it said, "Ah, my beloved, my own! You have come unto me, my precious, my darling, my jewel; your love is to me the taste of honey and the sweetest of wines, your touch is the caress of summer, your passion the fire that dispels all frozen winter from my flesh; I have lived eternity to crush your lips, I fell from Paradise and the voice of God to create you; forever I will lean on your breast and love you, forever will my love pour over you; name it, my darling, name your dearest dream, name your gift from me and it will be yours for one whole night long before you come to be mine forever. . . ." I tried to struggle from under it, I tried so hard, but I was froze there, held down with cold despair that hurt me more than death itself. But then its voice changed to yours and its face became yours—your face, fresh and simple and full of a lust I could understand. It was you against me, not it; and I knew what my wish had been, knew it exactly. I began to rise. Then I was home.

The night stood stock-still. The wind that had been blowing through the missing rooms behind them was gone. A bird chirped through the thicknesses of the camellia bush beside their steps.

Morning is coming. Soon it'll get me again.
"Will it get me?"
I don't know. If you say so.

The voice of her father was cracking and falling away from Ellen. She was beginning to feel lighter. Her feet moved back and forth inside the boots. Her toes were all alone, by themselves. The stink of old rooms, of old ground turned up too many times, of old women's dresses, was going away.

"Daddy?" she said, one more time.

Oh, what, oh what! Why don't you look behind you?

Ellen looked behind her. It was dawn coming, pulling itself up over the vacant lot and flushing the porch stones.

"I looked," she said, "it's daylight almost here."

Yes, goddamn it!

"What I was going to ask . . . what's going to happen now?"

She was cool and vacant inside, like the land she sat on. Had it been a night full of ghosts or had it been a night full of imagining a night full of ghosts? Neither terrified her. She felt nothing but coolness, vacancy; and there was a beginning rub of warmth down her back where the day was falling from the sky.

Back to hell, you ought to know by now; back to hell to be the devil's mistress time without end to pay for all the beds that went before now; and I used to believe, without a doubt, while I was going back and forth with the big bag and the white letters, that when I died all this would stop, all this sex, and *finally* it would be nothing but *my mother, my mother, my mother* forever and ever! And never nobody else. Dorothea . . . Dorothea! I didn't dare name you for her, didn't dare. And for all I know, for all the old woman would tell me, you might be the image of her! You might be—don't you see?—the one face I wanted to look down on all the times I rode the grave and that old thing watched from the woods. She'd never say nothing. I carried you to her straight from your christening—me drunk as a coot and wearing that vanilla ice cream suit your mama got me for the day in church, and behind me a pack of women

164

baying like hounds: "Where you going with that baby? Bring that baby back here, Roger!"—your mama wouldn't sleep with me for a week after that—but I went on anyway, laughing my head off, and you were yelling and tangling your long dress in my legs; how I drove it I don't know, but I did, straight out there and got to her door somehow and said, "Look what I brought you, granny! Who does she look like the most?" And the old woman just grabs holda my pants leg and pulls us down to her, squinches up her face and sucks in her cheeks and lets go with a wad of juice all over us. "Not my girl! Not my Dorothea! Git it outa my sight!" And she hollered and hollered and fell over forwards in her chair and wouldn't stop till I got you back in the car and was pulling away; I looked back once but there was nothing to see but what I could make out through the dust and the heat and my own whiskey tears. Nothing much. Oh, Jesus! The sun! Look at it fall! Here I go! My baby girl, don't be like me—if you love me, go to heaven and find my mama. Find my lovely mother!

A spray of water, a few drops, fell against Ellen's face. She hardly felt it.

I christen thee Dorothea! I spit upon thee and christen thee Dorothea!

The ghost had gone. With the sunrise, a light rain had fallen. Ellen took a drop from her wrist on her fingertip, but before she could carry it to her mouth it had dried.

Halfway home, Ellen pulled off the heavy boots, left them on top of somebody's garbage, then sauntered barefoot the rest of the way, twirling and floating the heavy cape behind her. She hummed several tunes until she hit on one that she liked. She entered her own yard, soaking her feet good in the dew, then knelt and washed her hands in it. She passed beneath the willow, through the squash, into the tomato vines.

Venusberg was asleep, curled close against the hedge, hugging herself against a chill. Waving her cape up and down in the rhythm of her song, Ellen stood above the girl and finished it, loudly enough to wake Venusberg: "The *ba*ron is drunk! The *bar*-ron is drunk!"

Venusberg, opening her eyes, started to scream. She was seeing a giant bat above her, flapping its wings, readying itself to swoop down and suck her blood. She did not get to scream; Ellen's foot came down over her mouth, arched hard there, pink and wet, holding the mouth closed until the warm brown eye that stared up at her had lost its fear and revealed nothing but happiness.

"I'll take my foot off now if you'll shut up."

Venusberg nodded, grinding her head deeper, beneath the foot, into the roots of the vines.

"I'm real cold." Her mouth hurt coming back to life.

"I'll warm you," said Ellen. She took off the cape with a flourish that Roger had never accomplished and spread it over the girl. Venusberg huddled; then she relaxed and waited. The cape's heavy braided collar covered nearly all her face; one of her pigtails, bristling into a rotten tomato, was becoming soaked in yellowish juice.

"I'm not cold at all." Ellen was warm; she felt herself part of the sun, which was making her transparent, which was making of her a narrow canyon through which its current of heat could pass and spread in a bright flood over Venusberg.

"But you'll *catch* cold."

"From you?"

"Out there. From the sunrise chill. In here it's sure warm."

With two slow movements, with one harsh clumsy movement, Ellen went beneath the cape.

Venusberg whispered, through her sighs, into Ellen's shoulder: ". . . Sincerely yours, Venusberg. Book, Castle, Music, Piano, Drum Majorette, Valedictorian, Up North, Good Eye, Dresses, Beauty, Home . . . home . . . home . . . Ellen, Ellen, Ellen," finally she gasped.

Ellen's feet jutted from beneath the cape; her toes dug

into the gray vegetable earth. Before long, their pink wetness became thick with dust. The cape rocked.

On the other side of the hedge, Beloved snapped a leaf off with his fingernails and began nibbling it with his front teeth.

"It must run in the family," he said.

"Whisper," Welch screamed, in a whisper.

"If it hadn't been for your hair, we wouldn't be here at all. It makes me mad for you to say *whisper* like that." His hand moved up to switch off the pearl earring.

Welch had had a dream just before dawn. The dream had told him that he was losing his hair. Just before he was completely bald, he had awakened sweating and trembling. Since then, he had made Darwin pace the yard with him, barefoot, their robes twirling silk gardens of dragons around them. Occasionally, they would stop and Beloved would peer again at Welch's scalp through Miss Nina's magnifying glass.

"You take your hand off that thing and listen to me," Welch whispered. "First all my hair going and now this! I should have known, I should have known! It's that mailman coming out again in her and bound and determined to ruin my mama's peace of mind. I have never been able to impress on you how delicate that woman's peace of mind is; and she finds out everything and she's going to find this out—something she'd never think of by herself in a million years. . . . *Take your hand down!* . . . That bitch of a girl ought to be in reform school!"

Beloved turned off his earring and put a heavy hand around Welch's neck; drew his head down to his shoulder.

"You come on, honey," he whispered into the thinning curls. "We're going in the kitchen and have us a Co'cola while I have a good look at that hair again. But I *swear* I've never seen it prettier or thicker."

The two men turned from the hedge and pattered silently away across the drying grass.

167

"You wouldn't lie to me, would you, honey?" Welch murmured.

Behind them, the cape shook as though a little wind had found a way inside it. Then it lay still.

Toward noon, the smell of butter beans simmering in salt pork slid beneath Miss Nina's door and woke her. As her stomach turned and shrank away from the food smell, she remembered she'd been awake a terribly long time the night before. She had been remembering, during the night, a great deal.

Across the room, clinging when they could to little chairs, were scattered many dresses. All were in the fashion of 1920; all were silk, voile, lace, batiste. Among them glittered garnets, diamonds, turquoises, pearls set in old-fashioned lacework of platinum and gold. Piles of long kid gloves, yellowish with age, flocked together in a heap like a nest of doves.

From her bed, Miss Nina stared hard at the pile of gloves. To her the gloves looked pure and new.

"Now I have everything," she told the gloves. "It took me all the night to find everything, but now I have everything and all I have to do is get to Paris."

She pushed her sheet away and began craning her neck to inspect every part of her body. Miss Nina slept naked so that, without a moment lost, she could make instant inspection of her thinness upon waking; so that she could reassure herself that no curl or lump of fat had grown stealthily on her bones during the night. This morning she was thinner than ever. So thin, she noticed, that there was hardly enough skin for wrinkling. She reached her hand, as far as it would go, and felt her back. It was like a huge fishbone, she happily decided, picked clean. "The day is hot," she said, "like every day, it is hot, so I will wear the backless dress and show all those fat people my wonderful fishbone back." She remembered what she was going to do. "Now all I have to do is get to Paris."

She got up and began sweeping her hands through the limp, frail dresses left in her closet until she found the backless. It was white voile, with a high front and long loose sleeves. It reached to her ankles and was printed all over with large brown fish. She had bought it in town the last time, many years before, they had let her leave the house alone. She put it on and stood before her tall triple mirror. For a while, looking over her shoulder, she admired the sight of her great fishbone; and poked at her ribs with a finger. She was pleased to see that all parts of her body were visible through the dress. She had stopped bothering with underwear in 1947. She rummaged in the heap of jewelry until she decided on three diamond brooches, two big ones, one small. She pinned them across her chest, where they hung, too heavy for the thin cloth, beneath her jutting collarbone.

"August was a fool to end all fools," she told her glittering chest. "It is *not* vulgar to wear three brooches at once. In fact, I am so angry with the old fool for keeping me bare all those years that I shall wear the garnet pussycat, too."

There was no space left on her chest, but the cat, with its long tail of diamond chips, fitted nicely above her navel. When she had given herself one more long look, when she had kissed her reflection goodbye, she trampled lightly, barefoot, through the piles of dresses and made her way down the hall. The brown fish floated alive and sinuous around her; she smelled strongly of the closet's pomander-ball scent; orangey.

She could see into all the bedrooms she passed by; all the unmade beds shimmered in the hot June light. But the bathroom door was closed; also, it was locked. She twisted the knob. There was a noise behind the door.

"There is someone puking within," she muttered; she quickly took her hand from the doorknob. "Welch!" she called. "How many times have I told you never to mix gin and marijuana! One or the other, the other or the one—but never both together!"

There was no answer, but the noise went on to its dry, retching end.

"And I have to—badly," Miss Nina said to the doorknob. "There is money in this house for everything but another bathroom." The noise behind the door stopped abruptly; was replaced by sounds of the toilet flushing, of water splashing in the sink. The running water made matters worse for Miss Nina.

"If you're ashamed of your mother's natural functions, Welch, then simply turn your head aside, stop up your ears, while I'm at it. Even Madame Récamier had to sometimes—although there's no direct evidence to prove it. Even Proust. Even his mother, I suspect. Let me in!"

The doorknob still refused to turn. Miss Nina observed it calmly for a moment and took her hand from it. She was gauging the limits of her body's patience. Her words rushed out, hissing and sinister according to her intention: "Very well, Welch. What your mother does now shall be upon your head. Don't come to me when the neighbors complain."

Miss Nina swept to the other end of the hall and climbed carefully, with brittle jerks, up on the chest where her grandchild had lain days before wrapped in tight silk dragons. The old woman swayed for a moment, balancing, then caught the long skirt of fishes up and wrapped it around her shoulders. When she was sure that she was bare from the waist down, when she was sure that no sliver of voile could get trapped and wet between her legs, she grasped the edge of the open window and eased her flesh-less naked flanks into the fresh air. She was just in time. She went downstairs, the dry brown fish floating around her, her mouth stretched smiling over her body's relief and her own marvelous adaptability.

Beloved, below that window, was sitting, jackknifed, on the kitchen steps and listening, across the Blues' picket fence, to Mrs. Blue. Margaret's mother, ever since her daughter had forsaken her family for the Classics, had been lavishing herself on her pet. Beloved watched as she knelt before the albino glare of her old bulldog, stroked her hand through its enormous rolls of short-haired fat and peered seriously into its wretched face. Every few moments, Buster looked alive and dutifully flapped his thick pink tongue over her chin.

"You stop that, you hear, Buster? Darwin, you sure you don't know anything about pinkeye?"

"All I know is what I said, your eyes get pink and it's catching. I wouldn't let Buster kiss me if I were you. Did you just now feel rain?"

Mrs. Blue's knees were beginning to itch in the rough Bermuda grass; it was a strain to lift her face from Buster's and look at the sky.

"Not a drop. One time I thought it was raining but it was only just Buster spilling Margaret's ice tea down my legs and you mention a nice drink of tea at home with her family these days to that girl and all you get back is education, education all summer long and not a word to say what she intends in the fall when everybody and his brother she's known since first grade is getting married. I wouldn't worry so much about Buster's pinkeye except he ate the pinkeye medicine the vet gave us yesterday—*Gave!* *Seven* dollars before I got out of that office, which is more than Rudyard's ingrown toenail cost last year—he grabbed it right out of my hand with that old tongue of his just when I was going to drop it in his eye and swallowed it, dropper and all, and now Rudyard's gone to Climax with the car for four days to see if his sister's all right and the vet is four miles out. That woman has been the bane of my existence ever since I married Rudyard. Won't write, won't talk on the telephone because of lightning bolts, so every six months Rudyard, being the man he is, thinks he's got to traipse all the way over there and check on her. Where's y'all's car, Darwin?"

Darwin watched Buster collapse with a heavy thud and a brief, burbling sigh, and close his pink eyes in sleep. Darwin's head felt wet, and when he put his hand through his hair, his hand came away wet. Sometimes in the summer, he remembered, it rains in one yard and not in the next. He wished that Buster would die right away from the pinkeye so that Mrs. Blue would have to take him off and bury him. There was a city ordinance against burying in your yard, he was certain. Then he could finish his sun tan in peace and get back to the last very thrilling pages of the new paperback he'd got from New York that morning. The book was all about whips; about boys as young as he had once been, who wore black leather belts, black leather boots and had whips up in those New York apartments. Darwin's pleasure in the book had been softened by an occasional, stinging regretfulness: once he had been young enough to do such things and had not, at the time, even known that such things existed for handsome young men to do; but he needed to finish the book anyway, and in a hurry. Shortly he would have to go inside and watch the day's installment of *Living Medicine* with Welch. He did not want to have to sit squirming, wondering about how those whips came out, while the handsome Dr. Hotchkiss was working over a tragic coronary. If he held the book over his face while he turned off his earring, Mrs. Blue would see what he was reading.

Mrs. Blue brushed her palm clean of Buster. "I don't see y'all's car in the driveway, Darwin."

"May-Ellen's gone to the grave in it."

"Will you look at that? How can I look at his poor sick eyes while he's stretched out asleep? Big baby dog! Buster just doesn't take an interest." She grasped his drooping jowls, tried to lift Buster's head, but Buster would not open his eyes again; instead, he opened his mouth and tried to bite, but he was so slow, so sleepy, with a mouth so full of drool, that he could not gnaw the hand that fed him pinkeye medicine.

Mrs. Blue seemed to lose interest in Buster. She wiped both hands across the giant yellow begonias blooming on every inch of her wraparound; she patted her permanent wave. Then she opened her gate and walked across the gravel drive to Darwin. Darwin was quick enough to get the book beneath him before Mrs. Blue got close enough to see it; but the book caught his open tube of sun-tan oil inside its pages, and it, too, went beneath Darwin. As Mrs. Blue talked, Darwin could feel the warm grease squeeze and spread through the knit of his new red bathing trunks. There was nothing to do about it.

"What is it you're reading, Darwin? I wish I had the time for that, but what with that sister-in-law in Climax half the time and Buster's pinkeye half the time and Margaret's education the rest of the time, you tell me when I can read a thing except the new brides once a week. She is like a sister to me, Darwin, and this every day grave-visiting is getting me down about her, but I am not actually a sister, not a member of this family, and wouldn't push myself forward to speak, but just this moment it came to me that you, too, are not actually a member either, so I thought we could talk about her. What do you think, Darwin?"

"I haven't ever felt like a sister to her," Beloved answered. He shifted, hoping to disengage the tube and protect the rest of his suit from the ooze; but the movement brought only a new spurt. It was making him sick to think about it. He heard the spine of the paperback crack. If I ever go to New York City Greenwich Village, Beloved thought, and one of those boys prettier than me, with all his black leather belts and boots and jackets, comes up to me and starts talking about a whip up there in his apartment, I'm just going to turn around and slap him!

Mrs. Blue folded her arms across the bulging begonias and tenderly rubbed her bare upper arms. "What I mean is," she said, "it cannot be healthy, just like I told Rudyard before he left last night, it cannot be healthy for a woman as good-looking as she still is, although we are actually the exact same age, to sit out there all afternoon on that new aluminum collapsible chair I myself saw her buy at Sears' Garden Supply for this very purpose, and cry and carry on and then get back in y'all's only car and come home and eat supper just like nothing ever went on all afternoon. If nothing else, there's always sunstroke out there without a hat on your head."

Over Beloved's head, Mrs. Blue could see into the kitchen, could see America in there stirring pots on the stove. America looked strange, very different; and it took her several minutes to see that the strangeness came from America's wearing a red satin dress over the kitchen stove.

In a minute, Beloved was thinking. In a minute . . . at least it can't be too long before Welch'll come to the door and push it just a little too hard into my back and say very softly and lovingly, If you don't hurry up, Beloved, you'll miss the part where he scrubs up before the operation. . . . Beloved sighed and answered Mrs. Blue.

"We are keeping an eye out, Mrs. Blue, so there's no

cause for you to have to drive out there behind her . . ."

"I only did it that one time! Out of worry!"

". . . but we are keeping an eye out, and we think it's bound to wear off before too long. Something always happens, after all, to people to make that kind of thing wear off."

The ooze through his bathing suit was becoming unbearable to Beloved; and he would never have time now to finish the book before Welch came. And still Mrs. Blue stood, staring over him into the kitchen and looking unsatisfied.

Darwin felt the screen door press sharply, silently into his bare back.

"If you don't hurry up, Beloved, you're going to miss the part where he scrubs up before the operation," said Welch. "It is good to see you looking so tremendous, Mrs. Blue."

"And you have been a rascal flatterer from the day of your birth, boy!" Mrs. Blue answered, looking satisfied. "It is beyond me how you have escaped the clutches of scheming womanhood in this town, but I am glad to say here and now that I, personally, am glad that you have, your mother needs you so much, your sister, in her hour of trial . . . but it is hard to look like anything at all these days, these times, it is an *effort*. Some of us make the effort, some of us don't."

Welch, watching Mrs. Blue squint at him through the screen, imagined that she could see huge bunches of his black curls falling off. In his alarm, he pressed the screen door forward hard, viciously, and brought a short scream out of Darwin. It was a moment before they noticed that Mrs. Blue was almost back into her own yard again.

"You let me know if I can do a thing," she called back. "Women need women in the hour of trial, whether you know it or not, so you let me know! Here I go back to that Buster!"

Through the slats of the picket fence, Welch and Beloved could see Mrs. Blue expose her thick white thighs, which were much the same color and shape of her dog, as she bent back over the sleeping Buster.

"I have never been able to understand how women can't decently keep their skirts low," said Welch. "Your back is very red and unattractive, and you smell funny. Yes, you stink!" Welch slipped out from behind the screen and put his nose into Beloved's abundant brown hair. His eyes grew wide, his face white. Beloved sat still as stone.

"Darwin Waters!" Welch at last gasped. "What have you *done?* Somebody has gone and pissed in your hair!"

Ellen stayed where she was, hunched on the edge of the tub, and tried to still the jumping that would not stop inside her; then she heard her grandmother go away from the bathroom door. There was nothing to see anymore, she felt, inside her own self; she looked instead through her aching eyes outside her self, looked through the tall window, around the green plastic shell-stamped curtain.

In the front yard, below, the sprinkler—no one could keep Miss Nina from turning it on in the heat of the day—whirled furiously and spun ropes of water that all but disappeared in the great waves of light. Below, Ellen's mother was propping a collapsed garden chair in the front seat of the car, and being careful not to snag her nylons on its nuts and bolts; her daughter winced from the glare off the aluminum frame. Before she climbed in the car beside it, May-Ellen held up her ten fingers in front of her face, as though she were inspecting them for dust or counting them to see if all were there. Then she tugged at the tight black linen sheath, got behind the steering wheel and backed from the graveled, noisy drive into the calm hot road.

For a little while nothing moved in the yard but the dazzling water, and the grass, that bent from the spray, then straightened, slowly, blade by blade until it was again repressed. On the winding path of gray flagstones that led from house to road, a little creek was collecting, quietly meandering. It was full of brown dust and drowning brown ants.

Below, the front door slammed shut, hard; and Ellen, leaning forward from the tub a little, could see America there before it, oddly turned, from her viewpoint, from a pile of roundness to a wobbly triangle that started at its peak with black straw and ended, shimmering with red satin, on its three sides. The tears on Ellen's face stopped, collected on her chin, gelled by the possibility of hope: if the triangle would become round America once again, and if round America would stay still there below, and not go to wait under the thick bushes by the road, wait twenty minutes for the bus to town as she had been doing every day since the funeral; if America would stay still and wait for Ellen to go to her, wait to wipe Ellen's face as she had done in the nights of the bad dreams the parlor's scary music had generated, the music that had tried to creep into bed with her and turn into a bear, a snake, an alligator and eat her up, bones and all; if America would stay still, not go, wipe the face clean, then Ellen could open her mouth and say, "America, I am pregnant as my sister Venusberg foretold I would be; I am pregnant by the Nameless Soldier; do something, please, and help me," then help would come.

Ellen's teeth found the ruffle of the plastic curtain and began gnawing it. The triangle that had been America sprouted an arm; the arm, a hand that lifted itself to the black straw and repinned it more securely with an emerald as long and thick as a thumb. Then America went down the steps, into the gravel, skirting the rainbowed spray to stand in the leafy dark, to wait for the trip to town. Ellen could see nothing of her any longer but the new gold anklet that glittered beneath her perspiring nylons.

The key would not turn, unlock the door; Ellen's hands were slippery, would not work. She pushed her mouth against the window screen, tasted its black rust.

"America! America!" Ellen was screaming. "Wait for me to get there, don't go anywhere yet!"

"I don't have time for nothing at all," America's voice called back clear and comfortable from its dark shade.

"You wait," Ellen screamed again.

The key turned; the hall, once a painted, wooden tunnel, became a wind machine to push Ellen forward down its length until her feet struck the staircase and she could stumble downstairs. There was the dark, sullen heat of the hall; there was the icy atmosphere trapped behind the parlor door, freezing the embroidered flora and fauna into eternally summery stances. The air conditioner, hiding behind its ruffled organdy dress, muttered to Ellen as she sped past.

"Halt! Who goes there?" Miss Nina's voice shot out at her from the sun porch, trying to stop her, but not seriously. On the sun porch, Miss Nina and Darwin and Welch were sitting deep in the plastic cushions of the glider, their skins made as smooth and dark green as the leaves of house plants by the heavy bamboo blinds that shuttered the glass walls. Around them, the white and purple African violets trembled in the cold creeping in from the parlor; they watched the expert hands of Dr. Hotchkiss fearlessly saving lives in the luminous, deliberate and eager world performing for them on their television set.

"In a minute," Ellen answered, and no one answered her. There was no trouble with the door to the outside; it let her go with a smooth, well-oiled swing; and it was America who kept it that way, always ready to open. Ellen was across her yard so quickly that the sprinkler had time for only one quick slash of water against her.

The leaves above them, above the sidewalk, made a ledge of thick, watching darkness; but there was nothing in the limbs but an abandoned bird's nest. The looking, listening baby birds had grown up, gone away, two summers before.

America did not take her eyes off the road. Someday, it seemed, she would stare the bus into coming on time.

Ellen watched with her, catching her breath. Their combined gaze slid up and down the road's layers of heat, piercing—then ignoring—the Chevrolets, Fords, Buicks, the Cadillac that passed them by. The bus did not come. America said nothing; she wanted nothing but her bus. Her eyes expressed nothing but dogged endurance of the heat. Sticky black circles of sweat were forming beneath the arms of her dress, outlining the roll of fat that curved out between her brassière and shoulder blade. America did not seem to care about that or about Ellen who shook and sobbed, "Oh . . . I—I—I—oh, I . . ." beside her. The light that filtered through the leaves and through her black straw was making tiny, brilliant pimples erupt on her skin.

"I—America—help me!"

"This is my afternoon off."

"By whose leave!" Ellen shouted, shaking with fright.

"By my own leave."

They were beginning to hate each other; if it would only become cooler, they could love each other again.

Words shouted in Ellen's head: You slave! *Nigger.* You help me. She saw bad and jolting pictures of herself strolling through the market place, costumed in the moustaches, the Panama, the dainty shirt of a planter all set to buy America; and she saw America's back bent and striped with bleeding lashes, nearly naked. Ellen could see herself clamping the shackles around the filthy ankles, driving her home by mule and wagon, giving her to the cotton field, to the monstrous overseer, to greasy collards and corn bread, to the overseer's lust, to years' and years' worth of rickety half-white pickaninnies; and finally, America crawling to Ellen's feet, planting her mouth on Ellen's boot, begging, Mercy, mercy, my lord! And, finally, Ellen could say, Then help me, if you want mercy, then for God's sake, help me! Beneath the dark of her hat, America's eyes flicked from the road to Ellen; but only for a moment. Perhaps she had seen all that Ellen had imagined.

" 'By whose leave!' " she mimicked furiously; but her eyes were on the road. "Smart-aleck missy college girl!" America turned sharply on one stiletto heel and strutted, hand on hip, up the sidewalk to look like what she thought of Ellen: a pea-brained, greedy chicken. Just as sharply, she turned back around, faced Ellen up close: "White girl. White art-y-fact of capytalest impeeralism! One word from me to Black Power and you're dead in your bed tonight." Because of the hat, Ellen could see nothing of America's face, nothing but all the white teeth showing through her words.

Ellen could not tell where her own words were coming from; they simply came out of her, and she was amazed by her memory:

"America," she said, "there I was like I am now, dog-tired from the heat, when *Lo!* I dreamed a dream that a big white angel stood by my bed shining and stark-naked in the raiment of the Lord and this angel fell upon me and folded me in his wings and lifted me to the glory of Jesus like I never felt before and out of the throat of the angel came a multitude of heavenly voices singing Glory to God in the Highest and this angel carried me wrapped in his giant rainbowed wings through the Valley of the Shadow of Death and through the pit of everlasting fire where we struggled with the Devil and won—and then there I was, uplifted to the pearly gates, and I heard the voice of God saying, This is my daughter Ellen with whom I am well pleased and the angel's singing came upon me again and again and then I woke up, and I was alone, and in the fulfillment of time a child shall be born unto me, America, help me, I am pregnant, what will I do?"

"Jesus, Jesus," America whispered. *"Shit."*

Drops of sweat—tears, they seemed—were flooded from the pores of America's face.

"I have to go away, help me get away. . . . If I stay, they will watch me and talk about me. My mother will watch and not know what to do; Miss Nina will talk and talk about it to me—it will be something that happened to her in Paris—Welch and Darwin Waters will turn their heads away when I get big. Pregnant women, fat women, make them sick; they were sick at the sight of my mother a long time before I was born. But my mother didn't care, she was so happy. I will care. Help me get away, America."

"I hate the whole human race, black and white and you and me; and I hate angels and God and every man ever born; and I hate me because I love you, *you* look like your father who didn't die at all, not at all. I come here nothing but a girl just to work, work like a nigger in the kitchen all my life—and all I got was *love*. I am sick."

They stood there under the dark leaves, crying, cursing, until the bus at last came by and America waved it away.

The last bars of *Living Medicine*'s theme music —Chopin's "Revolutionary" Etude rendered on a Hammond half as fast and with half the notes that the romantic Pole had intended—dwindled to a heap while Dr. Hotchkiss, now wearing a manful tweed jacket with leather patches on the elbows, put his arm around the shaking shoulders of the bereft widow. The credits crawled over them. Dr. Hotchkiss's wardrobe was by Pierre Cardin, the credits said.

Welch leaned over and pushed the button; Dr. Hotchkiss vanished behind a shield of steely gray. Welch let his hand brush back and forth over the hairy leaves of the African violets, and he shivered, to the base of his backbone. On the glider opposite, still gently rocking, his mother floated asleep among the brown fish. Darwin Waters sat up straight and alert, smiling a little over the bittersweet ending to the cancer-of-the-aorta case.

Welch stretched his tingling palm out and laid it against Darwin Waters.

"How's my Moby Dick? How's my great white whale? Is it getting big, bigger, biggest? Is it ready to let old

Cap'n Welch chase it through the deep water? Is it ready?"

Darwin Waters blushed, annoyed. He wanted to think about what he had just seen and ponder on life's nastiness to others, its sweetness to him.

"Welch . . ." he said, "sugar . . . sometimes I wish . . ." But Welch pressed harder than ever.

"Be-*loved*. I love you. All in the world I want, all in the world, is to get you upstairs for a nice cool bath to pass the heat of the day; and then it'll be almost time for *Perry Mason*. That's all in the world . . ."

"Have you ever thought your mama might not be asleep? Oh, Welch, I love you, too!"

After they had gone, Miss Nina opened her eyes. The room was smoother, thicker than ever with greenness. The afternoon would last forever. She raised herself up on an elbow, so pointed it could have jabbed through the plastic cushion, and smiled and nodded toward the room's corners. She began her favorite afternoon game: She was Madame Récamier, graceful, fragile as Dresden, on a chaise longue of striped silk. Her little feet, in velvet slippers, peeped from among the infinite ruffles of her dress. Her hair was dressed with jewels, into a pile of little curls; her eyelids drooped, heavy with the direct stares of countless lovers. With smiles, with half-smiles, her round lips punctuated her delicious wit. All around her they sat, balancing the Sèvres cups, letting the tea grow cold while they drank up the sweeter brew of her conversation. Récamier. *Parisienne*. It was so much better to know nothing of people but their names, their cities. One of the shapes around Miss Nina took a face, a form; it bent to her.

"Lennie," Miss Nina whispered. "Monsieur Bern*stein*." She held out her hand to be kissed. "I declare you're tiring of that tea. Reach for the brandy, just for us two—the drink of raconteurs, of intellectuals, of clairvoyants, romantics—just plain lovers! Don't let the others see. *L'Empereur* himself gave it to me, pressed it in my hands, his last act, that night he died in my arms here at Versailles. How good it feels to be back home here in Versailles— to have all of you here to welcome me home!"

Miss Nina let her kissed hand drop. Bending, so low her white hair rubbed the red tiles, she reached far beneath the glider and pulled out a shabby plaid book bag. The ink on the name tag had been caught in the rain too many times; but Miss Nina could still read it: "Ellen Fairbanks, Sixth Grade, Miss Bunter."

"This is the one, this is it," she sang. She straightened up, her head swam, her hair floated. She sat up, fumbling with the buckles, and found everything she had hidden inside safe as ever: the sticky wine glass, engraved with loops of flowers and ribbon and tucked into its thick gingham napkin; the brandy bottle, still half-full. Miss Nina drank the first glass with one gulp, then leaned on her elbow, sipping the second, resuming the conversation.

"It *is* good, isn't it, Leonard? Drink up! There's always more in the basement where August left it all for me to finish . . . for *you* and me to finish—us romantics, clairvoyants. . . ."

Miss Nina smiled on the face she saw. "I declare I don't know what I'm going to do with you if you dedicate one more of those symphonic masterworks to me! How people are talking! And this whole town talks in French. They all talk about me in French, so beautifully . . . very beautifully."

Suddenly, without warning, Miss Nina remembered. The little glass dropped from her hand and shattered on the tiles. But before she could catch her breath, cry out, she remembered that it didn't matter. In Paris she would not need it.

"Dear heaven, dear heaven! How did I forget . . . it

was the damnable TV, damn TV, with its pictures of life; but no TV in Paris or ever again . . . I've got to hurry."

She left the bottle, uncorked, beside the broken glass. Already the room's thick greenery was doping itself on scent of brandy. The violet leaves stretched toward it; it overwhelmed the old, true smells that shuffled from the book bag, still open and flapping its buckles over the glider: of peanut butter, waxed paper, ink, Crayolas, marbled-cover composition books.

The bathroom door, unlocked this time; and through the lavender-coated steam, Welch at one end of the deep, lion's-claw-footed tub, Darwin Waters at the other, in bubbles up to their chins, their eyes drowsily on one another; and beside the tub a tray of triangular, crust-less sandwiches filled with chive cheese and cucumber slices; two green glasses of iced tea, the ice melting to the thinness and transparency of fingernails.

"Dunk your head, sugar, and get that smell out."

Darwin Waters dunked and came up with rainbowish bubbles popping around his mouth and nostrils.

"I wonder who in the world pissed on your head. I've heard of things like that. . . . You better not let me catch you. . . . Dry your hand off and pass me a sandwich, and you eat one."

"Get up from there, me buckos, my sweet boys!"

Miss Nina was shimmering, half-visible, through the steam, thinner, less substantial than the cloud around her. She had torn her dress in her rush up the stairs: her bare hipbone jutted toward her son's face, as blatant, as ill-clothed, as a skeleton's.

Welch looked at the bone for a moment, recalled, un-willingly, that he had once been close for a long time to the bone, inside that woman; he longed, unwillingly, to protect it.

"Mama! You simply have got to eat more. . . . Darwin

Waters, dry your hand and pass Mama one of the sandwiches, pass her two."

Darwin Waters dried his hand and reached for the tray.

"Food be damned!" Miss Nina shouted. "And I don't want to have to say it a second time. Here's what I want: I want your youngish arms to get my wardrobe trunk from the basement up the stairs; I want what you've got for brains to get me out of here and keep me cheerful and get me on my airplane. Get up! I've wasted too much time already!"

Welch and Darwin Waters looked hard for a moment at each other across the bubbles; they stopped chewing.

"Where're you going, Mama?"

"To Paris, France, of course, if it's any of your business. . . . To the man who loves me more than all the others, the man who kissed me one whole long afternoon up to the elbow . . . every single button. I'm going to my lover who is far, far away! Double-damned fool, get up!"

"Turn your back, Mama."

"Nonsense."

"I won't until you turn your back."

Miss Nina turned, bracing herself against the sink. Through the mirror on the medicine chest, she could see her son rise from the water, his whole body covered with foam. She bit her lip to keep the laughter in: *Venus from the Sea?* she thought wildly.

She had closed her eyes as the bus shifted for speed and moved on; the carbon monoxide that shot from its tail coated her tongue. She would not open her eyes; and America, not caring that she wouldn't, led her by the hand like a sleepwalker, protected from all things visible, back into the house.

When they were in the kitchen, America, with her free hand, drew the shades on all six windows, covering the room with dim, washed-out yellow. Then she used the hand to turn the stove off. The low, blue-burning flames beneath the pots popped and went out.

"Nobody ever eats here anymore anyway," she said. "Cooking is just a habit."

When your eyes are closed, nothing enclosing seems to exist; the smallest room, if your eyes are closed, is as wide as a prairie. It surprised Ellen when her knees bent and she was slipped onto the little chintz couch that had been parked beneath the cabinets for America's afternoons. She rubbed her knuckles against its slippery skin and felt the yellow stripes glow into her bones; she felt the brown and red of America heavy against her.

"You can open your eyes now."

Ellen opened her eyes, and there was nothing to see but the four scarred legs of the oak table far across the room; but Ellen was glad to see them, ordinary, as usual. She sat within the familiar, the continuing; and she was outlandish, all wrong.

"I thought he was dead," America began. "I thought he was dead. I saw them, myself, pick up that coffin and carry it to the hearse and I saw them, myself, unload it and put it in a hole so deep he could never get out. And I waited until the hole was covered and packed firm and tight before I came back home. I was so sure. I stayed and watched every move they made: pulling the straps back up, filling all the dirt in, packing it down, covering it with flowers. I said to him, That's all for you, mister. You'll never catch another woman to leave with a walleye baby after your pleasure's done. You are dead and gone and your pleasure's gone with you. And me and every woman you ever drove crazy with dreams are, praise the Lord, still here to tell about it; but not you. No more, not you. I am so damn dumb, baby; how can I be so damn dumb?"

America's hand moved through Ellen's hair, the fingers tightening in the snarls; Ellen felt her starched shirt collar slicing at her neck and her blue jeans tightening like iron around her thighs.

"With all I know about everything, with all I know, I should have seen that kind of thing is never dead, can't never be covered up tight enough. It'll pretend to be dead, lay low for a while, then bust out of its dirt and catch the innocent child and the brazen hussy both the same, again and again! Poor baby, he caught you, too."

Ellen slid her head down America until her ear pressed against her belly. She heard, inside America, the roars of a battlefield.

"You sit up now. That's right. We're going to plan for you now like I planned for me a long time ago."

The yellow shades were darkening, one by one, quickly, like keys being depressed in a racing arpeggio. Thunder was moving toward them. Ellen closed her eyes again. There was no sense in saying, it was not your old lover, my father, my miserable ghost; perhaps America really spoke the truth; perhaps the nameless soldier's name was Roger.

Heavy feet jumped the last few steps; the floor shook. Welch was racing toward them.

"There you are," he panted. "When the doctor gets here, America, you let him in and tell him upstairs. In the meantime, you get yourself up there and help."

"Help what?" She put her arm around Ellen.

"Don't ask questions, fool nigger!" Welch screamed. "My mama's trying to go to Paris!" Welch was naked except for a rose-figured towel tied around his waist. His chest was hairless and a blank white and sticky with soap. He ran back through the hall, away from them.

"They ought to let her go. Don't leave me, America."

"I won't leave you. Yes, they ought to let her go." America sighed and cleared her throat. "Across town," she said, "there is my boy friend. I had an angel and now I got a boy friend. One angel and one boy friend to show for all my life. I love him as much as I can any black man. . . ."

The rain was beginning, and the sky was groaning like the interior of America. Drops as heavy as pebbles struck the windows, attacking slantwise; and Ellen could just hear the long strands of the willow weaving themselves into the noise.

"He's got a car and big plans and a yearning stronger than God to play jazz music on a silver saxophone in front of all of New York City. At night when he sleeps he sweats and his fingers move and he moans tunes through his mouth. He is taking me with him, and V.B. and . . ."

"And me too?" Ellen whined like a baby; the baby whined through her. "America, don't leave me."

". . . and he loves me, as much as any music, he loves me! Oh, don't you think he does love me?" She took Ellen's hand between her own and squeezed until Ellen gasped: "Yes! He loves you as much as any music! And you *will* take me, won't you?"

"You are right, every bit right! He loves me, and I love you and he will take you, too, with us!"

America stood up, quickly, brushing Ellen off her; and Ellen, becoming amazingly light, collapsed into the chintz like a feather descending to earth at the speed of a stone's fall. The extra pinprick of flesh inside her made no difference except to unburden her of her own weight.

America shuffled, like something old, to the nearest window. She shot the shade up and pushed the screen out. She spread her hands in the rain, palms up, then made a cup of them. The rain struck, splattered, slowly collected into a pool; and America drank.

Without turning, she said, "Go upstairs and lock yourself up and don't hear another sound in this house until I come for you. Tonight's the night we go. Don't hear anything until you hear me knock."

At one o'clock the next morning, a morning that was pale rather than black, as it should have been, Ellen and America stood invisibly beneath the thickest and darkest of the shrubs. They were waiting for the boy friend where they had earlier waited for the bus. They stood in a circle of four suitcases that reminded them both of the houses and castles made of wooden bricks in which Margaret and Ellen had spent many hours of their lives. Their feet nudged the sidewalk, feeling for the heavy quilt of stars that had sometimes made the castle's roof, and sometimes a bed for the house. Ellen held America's hand and would not let go of it. When America felt the need to adjust her hat, America used her left hand and Ellen used her right, and the hat was set straight. They did not look up the street for the heavy red Ford they were waiting for; instead, they kept their eyes on the house, which spread and shimmered before them like buttermilk unbottled into a deep blue bowl. The radiant night quivered as though it were preparing to move forward in some sweet direction; and the house trembled with it, breathless and alert. Or else the house was caving in, buckling, ready to fly apart at all seams from the pressure of Miss Nina's silenced insanity.

The old woman had shrieked at her son and called him Lilac, you stinking bitch, as he had lain beside her, holding her to the bed; and, in the next breath, she had moaned to Darwin Waters, at her other side, "Oh, my dear, oh my dear, can you still love me, even with my old and naked hands?" And when the doctor came, she had screamed so loudly, bitterly, "Paris, Paris, Paris!" that all who heard her saw themselves transported across an ocean, saw themselves strolling the Champs-Élysées, with a beautiful woman, in a flowering springtime.

The old woman had been injected with something. When she woke again, Welch would know how to inject her with more of it. America and Ellen could see the light burning fiercely through her curtains; they could feel unconsciousness dimming her light as she lay, dead to all worlds, a pile of tiny nightgowned bones and nothing more.

Ellen was no longer light as a feather; she had become lighter than air, than gravity; and, without America's hand, would soon have shot through the roof of the universe becoming, at last, nothing. The child inside her was nibbling the last of the marrow from her last bone and drinking the last drop of her blood; and he was sinking back to earth alone, a full-bodied, bull-weighted man who had grown strong and six-footed on Ellen. She held America's hand tight enough to hurt.

"Venusberg'll be late," Ellen whispered.

"No she won't. She just had to leave a letter on your mama's pillow. It's her last prophecy because my boy friend won't have it: he says second sight is niggery. You better hush, they'll hear you."

Deep in the pale yard before them, May-Ellen and Darwin Waters and Welch moved through both low and tall clumps of flowers and flowering bushes. They seemed like performers in a midsummer ritual, like heathens propitiating a real and near god. Every strand of May-Ellen's hair shone, apart from all the others; every wrinkle of her dress seemed a chasm in the glare of Welch's flashlight which pointed on her, made her the priestess on whom all depended. She was bending and straightening over the beds, chunking bricks away and replacing them with all of Roger's millefiori paperweights. Darwin Waters, on his knees, went behind her, brushing away the crumbs of dirt on the glass with America's old pastry brush. America and Ellen could hear Welch say, over and over, "Sister, Darwin Waters, the yard's tacky enough without this. How much more do I have to stand!" His words made a chant, a prayer. He kept the beam of the flashlight steady, and the other two, busy with great purpose, did not answer him.

A rustle in the leaves became Venusberg, and then three were in the waiting circle. Venusberg, shyly, would not look at Ellen, but she believed that Ellen could not help but reach out and touch her very soon. Venusberg believed that their trip would end in a place where she and Ellen would do nothing but make love; she believed that her mother had become a bridesmaid. Venusberg thought that she could make the kissing begin.

"You better hurry, run kiss your mama goodbye," she told Ellen. "I hear a car coming now."

"Hush, crazy baby!" America answered her. "You've forgot they won't know we're gone till morning when they get our letters for breakfast instead of breakfast. You hear?"

Ellen said, at last, "I ought to burn it all down before I go, then they can all get out."

"Somebody'll probably do it for you," America said.

And then the car came, silently, and waited for them to tiptoe inside it. The road to the north was open and waiting.

Gritty with either terror or sand—there was no sense in the effort to decide which—Margaret stood in the phone booth and forced herself to compress more and more of the sweating air into her lungs. Trembling, she would surely dial all the wrong numbers, lose the silver coins to a stranger's voice or to the wadded, petrified gobs of chewed gum and beach trash that made the floor of her upright coffin: She thought of it as an upright coffin, a glass box to keep her dead self in, like a saint, on view to the pious public and away from the salted little crushes of the bay's waves against the shore. If she were calm, her fingers would reach Ellen. And Ellen's voice would fold back the glass lid and bring the dead to life.

She dialed, so slowly that the whir of the dial became separated clicks, but so carefully that when the ringing stopped there would be no mistaking the voice of resurrection when it spoke to her. Already she had lost one of her quarters to the sand; the conversation would be shortened.

She had watched the swan disappear into the haze that veiled—that sometimes lifted and revealed—a rich man's island across the bay; then, without a word to herself, she had wrapped her legs in a long linen skirt embroidered with butterflies and dragons by Pathways' own hand and had left the beach for the public library to consult the world's telephone books for the name of Ellen. She was neither overjoyed nor surprised to find the name so close to her, practically on her doorstep. Ellen in Brooklyn Heights, New York; Margaret in Bluebay, Long Island, New York —it was nothing a phone call, a few hours, couldn't cure. She had gouged the number into the back of her left hand with the librarian's blue ball-point and she had trailed back to the beach to the only public telephone that she had noticed in two years.

In Brooklyn Heights, the telephone was ringing; then the ringing stopped.

"Hello," said Ellen.

"Hello," said Ellen again.

"I am Margaret." She was choking. The gray wads of gum, the empty, sticky green bottles; the slit beach balls, the roars of motorboats, the slurrings of the water, the yelling of Italians—all the noises were lodged in her throat, choking her words back. Two years' worth of the beach, loneliness next to water, was choking her.

"I am Margaret," she gasped, at last. "Will you hurry?"

"Where are you? I haven't known in a long time," Ellen answered. Her voice seemed to shine cool from a great height above the stones and greenery of Brooklyn Heights.

Margaret slung the door of the booth open and let the beach inside her free ear, the ear that did not hold Ellen's voice. The sounds rushed her brain, through both ears, met in her brain's center in a loud and full embrace; and there seemed to be extraordinary new noise, the sound of some past or some future: a nauseating distortion of harmonious music. When the silver had run out, she had let the phone drop from her hand; she could not remember talking and telling Ellen how to find her. But when she picked up her skirt with fingers so brown and scrawny they were like dead tree limbs, she was sure that she was starting for home to wait for Ellen.

The taxi driver, in the new morning's most youthful, its blackest time, let Ellen out at the road's corner. Go all the way down there, watch out for ruts and big stones, and at the end there'll be the right house, the last house, the house nearest the water, said the driver. It's nothing but a shack, said the driver. Who could live there? said the driver. The driver yawned. It had been the last train to Oyster Bay he had to meet that night; and the drive from Oyster Bay had been long. Ellen paid him and would not answer and let him go.

She moved to the center of the road and stood looking down it. A wind from the water moved up it to her and flapped the legs of her pants and funneled through the tear in her sweater, chilling her belly. It carried on it the smell of the festering Italian gardens that were climbing and crawling and sprouting all around her and readying green and red food to minister to another day's hunger.

The end of the road merged into a silver, horizontal needle of water that connected two black shapes that faced each other. The shapes could have been houses. The moon rose above it all, an ordered swirl of round light, a ghost of the heat that shook above the white sand all day long.

After the phone had gone dead, without any goodbye at all, Ellen had made the greatest effort, had forced herself into stillness, insisting that her hand keep itself from flinging the door open, insisting that her legs keep themselves from running faster than they ever had. She had forced herself into stillness, back flat against her room's only furniture, a wide mattress that lay huge, curved and unsupported against the bare floor. She had lain on it, knowing that now was the last time she would ever have to.

Her room was coffin-shaped. So long it could have buried a twenty-foot man, so narrow the corpse would have had to lie on its side, the room was made of white plaster and oak floor and three thick glass windows that made a sharp-angled bay at one end. Ellen's mattress was headfirst among the windows, and she lay on it, and the sun came through the glass to sit on her face.

Blinded with sun, Ellen could think of where she was going and how to go there; blinded and thinking, Ellen did not have to look at the room's empty end, the empty foot of the coffin. Down there, the little boy with the head of thick, dark red hair, the little boy whose left eye had seemed determined to shift its gaze against walls—down there, the little boy, Ellen's little boy, had slept at night in a white crib and, upon awaking, had acted out endless peaceable games and fantasies.

"Batman! Batman!" Diggory had growled through his third year, quietly, whispery, so that his sleepy, very sleepy Ellen would not wake from the curly lump she made almost all day under the peach blanket. Diggory would pommel the thin air with his fists, save the city, destroy the villains until the next time they awoke around him. The television set, from a shadowy corner of the room, would answer him, quietly, whispery, with the guffaws of clowns and the chitter-chatter of Bugs and Porky and the speeding Road Runner. Diggory would kneel close to the darting, leaping, speaking little drawings and smear the glass around them with his fingerprints, longing to get his hands around them, to touch them all over. Between bowls of soup and bread and butter and short naps in front of his blue glare, Diggory had showed his life to his darlings from early to late, until the hour when darkness deepened their room and the images on the screen became big, heavy, fearsome; until he heard his Ellen sigh and stir beneath the wool and heard her fingers turn another page of the book that lay beside her head.

Then Diggory would leap on her with hugs that sent his elbows gouging into her breasts, with kisses so soft and wet that his Ellen shivered awake from them. "I love you, dear Ellen," Diggory would whisper, whispering to keep her sleepy; and his Ellen would answer, "Love me? I love you, too, dear Diggory"; and then Diggory, too, would sleep, against her, pinning her arms to him. And then, sometime much later in the night, he would feel himself lifted, feel his eyes half-open, feel the rub of his crib slats. Then he would hear the footsteps of one big man or another tiptoe past him to greet his mother and take his place beside her beneath the peach wool.

Before she reached the end of the road, Ellen had yelped with pain three times: a clump of sandspurs had stuck deep in her bare ankle; she had fallen over the rock; her feet had twisted in the ruts. Nothing had screamed back to her, in answer; but she knew that whatever was waiting for her had been warned that she was nearly there. The water before her was no longer a sharp needle but a flat hand stretched out like the gypsy's palm for the moon's silver. The house leaned out to her, salt-bleached, broken, black-eyed but romanticized by the moon's light and protected, like the enchanted castle, by bristling thorns and weeds.

Margaret was there, half in the light, half in the dark, crouching on the steps, staring at Ellen. Her hair was still flat and gold and long against her face. She wore a long evening dress, of net, and it was green with long, blowing sequined sleeves. Her arms sparkled. She was on the bottom step with her bare feet packed about with sand to make the frog houses that children make to contain their feet when they are tired of pails and swimming.

There was no path from the road to Margaret. By the time Ellen reached her, her hands were bleeding, her corduroys were slashed, her legs stripped. Part of the way, she had had to crawl to her. She dropped her straw satchel and fell down next to Margaret, panting.

"Even here in the dark," said Margaret, "I can see that your hair is cut and looks trashy; you're thinner—your bones stick out of cheap clothes; your face has lines in it."

Ellen took a handful of the gold hair and pulled it back. She kissed Margaret's cheek and left a bloodstain there.

Margaret looked down at her buried feet, stuck her big toes up through the mounds to make tiny entrances to home for the baby frogs.

"All right," said Margaret. "The soldier-boy?"

Ellen caught her breath, to speak. "I don't know where. My mother wrote a long time ago that he had come looking for me."

"That woman?"

Ellen laughed. The weeds rustled back at her; the moon came from behind a cloud and its every silver scar was clear. "That woman," she answered, "spent all her money on a song; and when the song was over, there was no place for her to go; there was nothing but noise in her head and no work for the likes of her. For a while, she made enough to drink on playing the piano and leading the tambourines in the Church of the True Bleeding Vine Our Savior Jesus until they found her with one of their Puerto Rican chicks and nearly skinned her alive in broad daylight on Amsterdam Avenue. My mother wrote me all that. And my mother wrote me a long time ago that she had come looking for me."

"And me?"

"I heard you were a scandal. I heard that Mr. Pathways' mother came and threw you out and took him home with her."

199

The taffeta beneath the green net rustled, like the weeds. Margaret was standing up and twirling around and around, breaking up the watery light and her frog houses.

"That's right," she said. "Now I remember. She was a wonderful lady who came busting in at three o'clock one morning (just like you've done just now) and all in long tight black satin and pearls at her neck and pearls on her fingers; and she came busting in and threw herself between us and she took my face in her hands and kissed me and said, 'I wish I'd had you instead of him, but I know when to be realistic. Now that I got me such a swinger in the family, it's going to be home with Mama for him.' She said she'd got a fix on him right smack in the middle of the third act of *Aïda* in Atlanta and without wasting another minute had got herself flown out of there to go to his side. She made me take the key to this house because it signifies her humble beginnings which, she said, I now deserved, and wrote me a check for two thousand dollars. So I came here."

Margaret stood still above her, blocking a good half of the moon from Ellen; and Ellen believed in a face on the moon. Margaret held out her hands.

"I've been in this dress," she said, "for hours and hours waiting for someone to come dance with me. Do it now."

There were wooden steps beside the house down to the beach. They stumbled, nearly fell down them in a hurtful tangle. They danced across the beach, joggling, crooked against each other like deformed children let out only at night. The wind blew Ellen's bloody scratches dry and lifted Margaret's skirt above her head.

Off the beach and in the house, there was no kind of light for Ellen to see by. The room's windows had been painted black with harsh strokes of tempera; though she panted from the dancing, she was afraid to sit or lean. She felt an enormous clutter crowding around her; she felt Margaret, giggling and swishing around her, knowing her way in the dark. Inside the house, there was nothing more of the sea water, of the bouncing moon that had rocked on when their dance was over, nothing left of the night and its announcements to them in the shape of shells, in the dribble of wavelets over their feet, in the whizz of wind through Margaret's hair. Ellen was inside pitch black without a clue.

"Light a light," Ellen whispered. "This dark is killing me."

The match flared and the great circle of orange took hold and grew and wound all over the room. As the light spread, everything became clear: the glassed-in expression in the huge bear's eyes met the painted vacancy of the rocking horse's stare. A huddle of dolls, with bisque faces and pleated caps, watched them from the floor, their dim mouths unable to smile. Everywhere in the candlelight the toys hung and sprawled, marched, sat, lay. Wooden blocks, their edges worn smooth, their alphabet worn to gibberish, hundreds of them, had been built into a little cave with an entrance shuttered by a thin flannel blanket.

Ellen drew a deep breath that tasted of the salt in her nostrils. Sputtering candle grease seemed to lie on her tongue, weighing it down. Everything she had decided about Margaret, only minutes before, was dead wrong: the lime-green evening dress above the bare feet was *not* a playful gesture, *not* a reminder of the dress-up days when they had been Cherubino, Susanna, the Countess. The dance by the water had not been just for fun. Ellen stared into the light, insisting that her mind and her tongue move. The truth stuck in her throat; but she knew it to be true: the same thing that had made her tired and drab, hurt and grief-stricken, overwhelmed half the time with joy, all the time with reality, had turned dear Margaret into a complete looney bin. The thing was neither love-less sex nor sexual love but something that grew between the two. It was something that had grown like a thick-bodied vine sucking, through its roots, its ferocity; and had taken its passion, like sunlight, through its leaves. And when it had become strong enough it had twisted its arms around the two helpless mysteries (loveless sex, sexual love) beside it, had held them in close so that they, along with the worms, could feed on the vine's fruit; so that they, along with mockingbirds, could nest and sing songs in the vine's greenery. Ellen imagined that the vine's name was Falling-in-love.

She turned, warily, to look at the pretty face glowing at her in the candle's shine. It was half-insane, half-beautiful and not a day older than its childhood. The thing that had brought Ellen to consciousness had driven Margaret mad.

Ellen wondered who it was that Margaret had loved at such a pitch that it had made her crazy. Then, so exhausted that the fact brought on no shock, she saw that it was herself that Margaret loved, insanely.

Margaret was twirling around her toys, kissing them, hugging them, straddling the rocking horse and rocking it fiercely, making the old nag's wood creak, fiercely, between her thighs. She babbled as she rocked:

"When I came to the last of the wonderful lady's money, I got so scared that I hurried to spend it all very fast, to get it over with! I'd seen a poster at the beach, the very minute I got afraid, about an auction at a great huge marvelous house only a little walk from here, so I went, and when the toys came out nobody wanted the toys, so they took my fifty dollars and brought me all the toys here to my house. I've been very happy ever since."

Ellen slipped to the floor and leaned into the arms of the dusty bear. Above her, Margaret flowed over her galloping horse, seemed to flow like the candlelight; but Ellen, stiff with hopelessness, could never move again, she believed. A bad time held her rigid. It was like the bad time before, when she had waked in the dark above Brooklyn Heights to see America, Venusberg and the musician standing bowed and grayed in a row with their suitcases beside her bed. "We cannot stay," America had muttered. "We're tired and we can't stay any longer. They want anything but music in this place and we have to go home. We have just enough money to get us home." Ellen had rolled over flat on her stomach, put her face in the pillow. "Take Diggory." The pillow stuffed the words back across her tongue, down her throat again. But America had heard. "I thought you'd say that. . . ." And, faintly, from the other end of the room, "You come on now, honeypie, it's America here taking you. . . ." And sleepy, surprised: "Ellen da'ling? Ellen?" she had heard Diggory call.

When she had heard the feet and suitcases shift and the door open up for them, she turned over and opened her mouth for more air, her eyes for more dark. Venusberg still hung there over her.

"Ellen, there'll come a time when you won't have a thing left but us and music. You'll have to put up with just us and music because you won't have another thing left for you but us and music. . . . Valedictorian, Drum Majorette, Good Eye, Book, Piano, Music, Love. . . . Goodbye."

A bad time was holding her rigid; the dizzy ride in front of her was all the motion she would ever need. The friendly bear held her tight.

"When did you last eat, darling?"

"Oh, lots and lots!" the yellow-headed horseman called back. "Any time I want to."

Ellen forced herself to her feet, but felt that she had left any life still owing to her in the arms of the bear. There was a second candle, and she lighted it and went into the room beyond the toys. Except for a sagging cot covered with sandy sheets and a vision of the white moon above the white water through the unpainted windows, the room was empty. In the third and final room, an ashen, filthy wood stove, a rusting, bone-dry sink, and two broken chairs huddled against three walls. A trail of sliding footprints in the sand and dust led to an old carton against the fourth wall. There were three unopened cans of hash, a dirty spoon, a can opener left inside. A hill of empty cans, nearly as tall as Ellen, had been made, with a jumble of Coke bottles, in a corner.

Margaret was still astride her horse, her long legs bending, her toes pressed back against the floor, her head against the wooden one. The ride was finished; the girl was wide-eyed. She smiled; her eyes seemed to dance. But Ellen, looking closely, saw not dancing but the spinning of two metallic blue tops. Ellen put her hand on her shoulder, then let it fall slow down the harsh sparkle of the sleeve. She put her hand inside the sleeve, touched the naked arm, and it was like trailing her hand in warm water; she had to resist the impulse to follow her hand, dive clear to the bottom.

"Will you watch me play dolls now?"

Ellen retreated to the bear. "Yes. Go ahead."

Margaret began undressing the old, little dolls and wrapping them in pieces of blanket and holding them each for a little while in her rocking arms. When each doll had been put to sleep, she nestled it in her net lap and stayed still to let it dream in peace.

"Tell me a story," she said.

There was only one story that Ellen could remember, so she began to tell it.

"I used to have," she said, closing her eyes, "a little child that was alive . . ."

"No! The story of Almaviva and Cherubino and Susanna: tell it!"

"*Be quiet.* His hair was thick and dark red. His skin was white and silky, like the piano keys, and his eyes very blue. One of his eyes, though, never looked at me; it made me remember, often, other things. When he was very little, America and Venusberg and a musician left me alone with him, and so we lived alone in a room high in the attic

204

of a thick brownstone house with windows that looked far, far down into a garden. The garden was filled with flowers for spring and summer and fall, and in each of its corners there was the statue of some goddess. In the winter, the garden was filled with snow—and the statues of goddesses. Every night after I put the little boy in his crib, one of three men would come to me and fuck me. When the man left, he would give me money so that I could pay for our room and buy the little boy things to eat. One day, this little boy wanted more than food, he wanted a white woolly dog with a red smile for a mouth. When I took it out of the store and gave it to him, he began to love the dog, passionately. He loved it as much as he loved me, passionately. One afternoon during the winter we played a game in the garden. He closed his eyes and put his head against a goddess's skirts to give me time to hide in the bushes with the little dog. When I called Ready! he began running in and out of the bushes, shivering and laughing, and then when he found us, the little dog and me, we jumped out at him and threw ourselves into his arms.

"After our game, late that night, a blizzard came, and then one of the men came, so drunk he was stupid, and left all the house doors half-open. And then, sometime while the man was still there, my little boy woke up. He must have watched us, but if he spoke or cried, I didn't hear him. He wanted his dog, but it was in the garden, where he had forgotten it.

"When I found him, in the morning, he was frozen against the same goddess he had hidden his eyes against during the afternoon. When I pulled him to me, the skin of his hands and face ripped away and stayed stuck there to the iced stone. . . ."

"I'm *glad* he's dead! I'm glad he's *dead!*" Margaret sang the words in her high soprano, to the tune of *"Voi che sapete."* In a low, reasonable voice, speaking as if she were giving practical advice, she said, "You shouldn't have done that anyway with that soldier anyway, you bad girl. You shouldn't have done that and had that ugly baby boy. You needed to take care of me, not some ugly baby boy; me. . . ."

"Shut up, you crazy shit! That story was a lie fit only for the likes of you and this place! Your craziness made me tell a lie. . . . In truth, he's home with May-Ellen and thinks V.B.'s his mama, in truth, you crazy . . ."

Ellen shoved the bear's thick paw in her mouth, silencing herself.

"I'm so sleepy," said Margaret. "You promised to sleep with me in the castle I made. Do it now."

"We're too big now, love."

"You promised."

Ellen blew the candle out and crawled into Margaret's shaky wooden dream. The room around the castle was so black the toys could see nothing of what they wanted from each other.

"Once," said Ellen, "—and this is the truth—I bought him a ten-cent harmonica. Some nights he would wake up and begin playing on it. He would suck and spit the tune. Sometimes I seemed to recognize the music. Occasionally, when I felt like it, I made words for his tune and changed it into a song."

The Southern Railway jolted, then simmered to a stop. Through the coach window, Ellen watched heat pile on heat in shimmering transparent layers. The glum redcaps wavered around the depot like fish through water; and the grimy thickness of the glass that Ellen saw through became the polluted surface of a pond.

It is only because I am so tired, she told herself, and because I want to scream out loud and have somebody hold me and tell me it will be all right. But she saw what she saw: a hybrid of night and day that seemed like water. And in the water were things and people that should have been set on solid dry land.

Inside the train, there was nothing wet. With every human shuffle and crunch, dust burst from the rough nap of the chairs, yellow-tinted dust from cloth the color of American Beauty roses. The passengers, if they had been talking, would have choked on their conversation. But conversation had stopped hours and miles back.

Margaret had caused the silence. A nice trip; I'm going to take you on a nice long trip and at the end of it you will be so happy, Ellen had told her. And Ellen had been forced to carry the bear and pack the dolls; had been made to drag a pasteboard carton of wooden blocks by a string that sliced her palms raw, so that Margaret would not go wanting on her journey home.

And there had been Margaret's screaming tantrum while Ellen skinned the salt and sand and knots from her hair; while Ellen ripped the green net from her back and forced her into a washed-out dress, pale clay-colored, that smelled, from its years of drifting in the house's only closet, of some woman's humble beginnings, and of sea water. It buttoned respectably; it was good enough for Margaret's journey home.

There was nothing wet inside the train but Margaret, though everything around her was as dead dry as dust; and Ellen was the driest of all. When they had been only a little way through Virginia, Margaret had made her real beginning toward home by wiggling, quick as a wink, out of her glossy underpants and then sighing with the satisfaction of a snake that has shed its old skin. Before Ellen could take her, hide her in the seat, Margaret had jacked her knees to her chin, had parted the folds of her genitals with her brown fingers, had whispered, in delight, "Somebody love me!" to a stout woman in widow black across the aisle.

At the sight of the rosy sex, Ellen expected the scent of roses to arise around her. Instead, the stale train air began to smell like a salted Atlantic wave, and she felt it break over her.

The train clanked, roared, shook. All through the night of traveling, the train's dim lights burned, letting everyone see everything. The conductor would not come. No passenger came to her when Ellen cried, "Help me, help me catch her!" But all of them muttered, laughed, discreetly screamed. And two soldier passengers smacked their gum and reached to touch when Margaret fell across their knees and ripped open her dress to show them breasts the size of two clenched fists. All the while, she called, "Somebody love me!" Nobody loved her; many touched her.

Nearly every passenger touched her. Each of them, because of Margaret and the journey through blacked-out landscape, was released from the people they had left, from the people they were going to. If they glanced through the windows they saw only their own jolting images; and they saw, behind them, the reflection of a dancing, naked Margaret. Margaret became the indulgence of as many secret dreams as there were passengers; at last the passengers could handle and kiss and violate their own dreams.

Or so it seemed.

Toward morning, when hedges and houses and fields began to show through the windows, everyone closed his eyes, even Ellen, and some fell asleep. Then the two soldiers took Margaret to the men's toilet. Before they came back, the other passengers had begun to smell again, in their sleep, the nutty chocolate, the dried sandwich bread, the slick pages of the magazines that had comforted them before Margaret had come. When they came back, the passengers did not seem to remember her or what she had done for them.

The two soldiers had been good enough, when they had finished with her, to get Margaret back into her dress.

It was the last stop, their town. Ellen pulled at the tangled hair that lay across her lap.

"Wake up now. We're here, we're home."

Instantly Margaret raised her head, looked up at Ellen. Her eyes had the huge, wide-awake stare of the successfully escaped lunatic.

Ellen, before her house, aching and bent, hiding behind the great green tree, let Margaret go and felt Margaret's collapse against her feet. Nailed to the sidewalk, she smelled the bacon's fry seeping into the thick wet of the grass. It was the first of June; the sight of home moved toward her through the heat. She closed her eyes and listened: the glider shrieked, scratched; a brush heavy with paint struck the clapboard; the coffee cups clattered; two voices moved, slowly, near each other and a redheaded laugh, suddenly, tangled them together. Above it all, pacing, glowing, was music. She opened her eyes to try to see what it was impossible to hear: she saw America's man on a ladder giving her house a new coat of white; Venusberg propped in the shrubbery, fatter, eating a Baby Ruth, reading *True Romance*. She saw, moving with the glider, a shaking old stick of a woman, her mouth glittering with drool and reading, seeing, nothing; beside her, Welch, sipping coffee, watching over the painting; beside him, Beloved, gleaming with black boots, black belt as wide as his hand. At their feet, stretched out in gorgeous Japanese silk, the nameless soldier, laughing up at the sky with a power to match the sun's. Above it, May-Ellen's voice, practicing scales, learning to sing; accompanying were the piano notes, dead sober, unremitting: she could see it: the Sanctissima touch.

Without warning, all the sounds ran together, reached silence, stopped, dissolved. Into the pause, the song and the piano soared, sped, broke against its notions of nobility, ecstasy, intrigue: *"Voi che sapete"* . . . "You ladies acquainted with love . . ."

Diggory comes speeding around her house, his shout like a bullet, his legs an engine. His hair leaps in the wind he causes and is as bright as fire. The tableau bursts into garlands of flame, and they all turn and see her:

She is bending, gathering the sleeping girl into her arms, trying to teach her, coax her to walk in her sleep. As they move to the house, their scalps burning with flame or sun, their legs trembling from the effort, it seems to Ellen that they are approaching the conditions of perfect love.